She'd known there would be danger, but she hadn't expected it quite so soon...

It all happened so quickly. The sound of movement was all around them and Aura was terrified. This was it. This was the moment they had been preparing for and hoping would never happen, though it felt all wrong. They were expecting any type of ambush to occur when they were either close to the portal or in the other world. Instead, they were only a half-day's ride from the center of the kingdom, in woods that were protected by her guards. There should not be bands of outlaws here. The only danger they should be facing should be from Winester, but there was no way he had caught up with them. Her eyes were trying, to no avail, to adjust to the low light. The sounds, though! The sounds kept continuing until she felt dizzy. They seemed to be coming from everywhere. An army, she thought. It sounded like an army trampling the ground around them.

"Resbuca," she said again in a panicked voice.

"Quiet."

She felt Resbuca move beside her and felt another body saddle to her other side. Kolas breathed heavily, his own panic making him lose his breath. She felt the other bodies close in on her as well in a reassuring protective manner. As much as she wanted them to run and save themselves, she was embarrassed to admit she needed this crush around her to keep her from screaming.

The sounds were now coming faster and closer. Aura took a deep breath and prepared herself for whatever onslaught was to come. She didn't even have time to react when the bag was placed over her head. A second later, she felt a sharp pain coupled with a loud crack and everything went to black.

Levi always knew he was different. The fact that he could smash a light bulb without touching it was only one clue, but he's about to find out how special he really is…

Sought after by those in a magical land, he meets Aura, Queen of Esotera. Her kingdom is in trouble and he's the only one who can help. But the powerful sorcerer who cursed Esotera will not give up easily. A collision of magic and fates, sealed long ago, will catapult the two into a race to save Aura's kingdom. Will they make it in time, or will they lose everything they love, and possibly both their lives?

KUDOS for *Four Corners*

In *Four Corners* by Kristin Durfee, Aura is a young
princess who discovers a dreadful secret on the day her
father dies—her kingdom is cursed. And the only way
she can break the curse is with the help of someone from
the other world—our world, Earth, an alternate world to
hers. So she journeys through the portal between the two
worlds to enlist the help of an unlikely hero—Levi, a
misfit who has magical powers he is unaware of. These
two set off on a mission any sane person would deem
impossible. And that's when the trouble starts. I found
the characters charming. The fact that they aren't super
heroes, hunks, or beauty queens only made them that
much more endearing. There's a good strong plot, in
which nothing seems to go as you expect. This is a book
YA and new adult should love. ~ *Taylor Jones, Reviewer*

Four Corners by Kristin Durfee is a coming-of-age story
about a young man, Levi, who is a misfit in his world
(Earth) because he has magical powers he not only
doesn't know he has, he couldn't control them even if he
knew what they were. And it is also about a young
woman who becomes the ruler of her world (Esotera)
when her father dies, only to discover that it is cursed and
our misfit Levi is the only one who can break the curse
and save her world. So she comes to Earth to find him,
but the evil wizard, who cursed her world to begin with,
gets there first. It's a story about growing up, accepting
responsibility for your actions, and sacrificing for a
cause. A lot of good moral lessons for young people.
Four Corners is intriguing. I liked the concept of the

alternate worlds, or alternate realities, or whatever, and the mix of fantasy with reality. Her characters are charming and, added to all the twists and turns in the plot, make Four Corners a fun and heartwarming read. ~ *Regan Murphy, Reviewer*

ACKNOWLEDGEMENTS

I would like to express my deepest and sincerest thanks to everyone who has helped make this book what it is today. It is an incredible journey bringing a work of fiction from an idea in the author's head to a piece that others (hopefully) will want to read. Each of these people helped in some way to make this book a reality, and I thank them for it.

Shannon, you took what was a pretty big mess and helped drag me from the self-doubt of my writing into having a confidence and love of my story and characters that I was previously lacking. You saw promise before anyone else did and helped make it a piece that someone actually wanted to publish. Your dedication to my work and characters means the world to me.

Jessie, Erin, Shary, Kristen, and Cierra, your early readings and suggestions all those years ago were invaluable in developing my story. You also became my cheering squad through bringing this book to the world. Cierra, whether you really knew this or not, something you said to me at Thanksgiving years ago was the catalyst in writing this story. You were truly the spark that started this all. I hope I created a world that you would want to live in.

My family and friends, the love and support you have given me has been truly humbling. You've all asked me with excitement to explain my book and rooted for me as each milestone in getting this toward publishing has occurred. I hope I've made it worth the wait.

Reyana, Faith, Lauri, and the Black Opal team, your suggestions have improved, not only this work, but my writing as a whole. I have learned so much from all of you and am grateful that you saw promise in a little story I wrote about a girl, a boy, and a dragon.

Matt C, thank you for giving me a cover that perfectly summarizes the whimsy and magic of my work. You endured endless back and forths with me with patience and kindness. Your work is amazing and I am proud to have it be the outer image of my inner work.

Amy, for your enthusiasm about my work, your company on countless hilly miles, and your photography prowess.

Newport, for keeping me company during endless hours at the computer and reminding me that sometimes you just have to take a break, go outside, and play.

And, finally, to You, you are holding in your hand a dream. A labor of love (and some pain and sometimes a little cursing), but just the fact that you are holding it in your hand, please let it be a reminder to you to never let go of your dreams. Hold them tight and when you see opportunities, go after them. It can be a scary process, but immensely fulfilling. Don't let rejection change your goals. Work harder. Seek those who want the same thing as you and will help you get it. Chase success. It may take many years, but the payoff will be sweeter than anything you could imagine. You got this.

Four Corners

Laura—
It's been so fun getting to
meet & hang out with you.
Happy reading, happy life! Enjoy!
★ Kristin Durfee

Kristin Durfee

A Black Opal Books Publication

Black Opal Books
BECAUSE SOME STORIES JUST HAVE TO BE TOLD

GENRE: FANTASY/PARANORMAL ROMANCE/SUSPENSE

FOUR CORNERS

First Publication: MAY 2015

Published by Black Opal Books **http://www.blackopalbooks.com**

To Matt

For making me braver
than I ever thought I could be

Si vis pacem para bellum
(If you want peace, prepare for war)

Chapter 1

Cursed

Aura had awakened with the first morning rays, just like she always did. She looked out the window and gazed upon Esotera—the rolling hills, flowers, and three waterfalls that made this one of the most beautiful places in the entire kingdom of Esotera, her father's kingdom.

She loved living here and getting to wake up to the warm sun upon her face and birds singing outside her window. She had little to want for in her life. Aura understood that she lived a privileged life, but she took her position very seriously and knew what her future held for her. At least, she thought she knew.

Her father was King Aldric, who'd inherited the throne from his father, who'd inherited it from his father, continuing back for hundreds of years. The powerful Lord Vertrous had decreed this place to her family, and it was to be handed down generation by generation—until there was a break in the chain.

Unbeknownst to her, Aura was that break.

This morning, though, she had better things with which to fill her thoughts. It was the "Day of Asking" and she'd promised her father her assistance in the daunting task. Each year, before spring harvest began, the people of Esotera came from all over to ask the king for blessings and assistance. While he held many appointments throughout the year, this was the one day that anyone could come and talk to him. Normally, the poor and the forest dwellers typically did not come to the main castle out of fear. In the old days, the Esoterans who lived close to the castle would ostracize those on the outskirts, thinking they were lesser people. To quell these feelings, King Aldric started hosting asking days so all the people of the kingdom could feel welcome and enjoy all that the castle and the grounds had to offer.

It had grown into a quasi-festival in years past and had quickly become an event that people looked forward to, immediately after the previous one had ended. However, it made for a long and exhausting day for the king as he listened to the most trite and trivial requests up to the most heartbreaking pleas. Before Aura was born, her mother had helped.

But following her death, shortly after Aura's birth, the king had performed this task alone. This year, however, he'd decided that Aura was finally old enough to join him during the proceedings.

She was excited and nervous at the same time. Aura had always looked forward to having more responsibility in the kingdom, but with that knowledge also came a reality that she was not quite ready to face. One day this kingdom would be hers, and all these responsibilities would fall squarely on her shoulders. She tried not to think about it as she headed to the great room in the middle of the castle.

"Aura, it is time that you start taking greater responsibility for the running of Esotera," King Aldric had told her several weeks prior.

"Anything I can do to help, Father," she'd said while straightening a flower arrangement on their eating table.

"The Day of Asking is coming up. Would you sit in on it with me?"

"For the whole thing?" She'd been slightly crestfallen. The day was always a festival for her as well.

"Yes, Aura. One day you will be taking over and you must learn what needs to happen to make this kingdom run smoothly."

"Of course, Father. Of course, I will help," she said, looking up at him.

Now, though, looking out the windows and seeing tents being set up with animals scattered all over the open land in front of the castle, she wished she did not have to sit in a stuffy room all day, listening to the problems of others.

Aura made her way quickly back to her dressing room to change. She had dressed in preparation to walk through the festival, but now felt as though she should be clad more formally. Once she changed her outfit, she also had to change her shoes, jewelry, and hair. By the time she was ready again, a jolt ran through her as she realized how long she'd taken to get ready. She flew out of the room, hoping she hadn't missed anything.

When she rushed into the great room, her father was already listening to a small woman quietly begging for something. Her father looked old and tired and Aura was suddenly struck by an image of him lying still in bed. He was strong and powerful, there was no doubt about that— even when sitting. But she could see the edges of him softening slightly as if, eventually, they would disappear and he would just melt away. She shook the thought from her head as she sat in a tall-backed chair next to him and began to listen.

After several hours, Aura's back and neck were starting to ache. Her father, however, appeared as interested in each person as the last. She was not sure how he did it. Some people asked for simple things, like blessings for their crops or permissions to graze their animals on the outskirts of certain lands, and her father quickly granted them his approval. Others had much more complicated problems or matters to discuss, and her father engaged them with equal time and attention.

"My blessed king," a man said, bowing so deeply Aura thought his lips might touch his knees.

"Please. Please stand," King Aldric said. "Please state your question. What can I help you with today?"

"I am starved, king, terribly, terribly hungry." The man did not look like he had missed a single meal in months, and Aura was sure her father would quickly send the vagabond away empty handed.

"Go to our kitchen, to the side door. Tell them I sent you and that you are to receive one loaf of bread, a slab of cheese, and bottle of wine."

Aura was flabbergasted.

"Thank you, thank you so much, dear king. May you live many more blessed years," the man said as he bowed continuously and backed out of the room. One of the king's aides went to tell the kitchen staff his wishes and to make sure they were properly carried out.

As soon as the man left the room, Aura turned to her father incredulously. "Father, that person was clearly not hungry. He looked perfectly healthy!"

Was her father's eye-sight failing? Could he not see the lies the man told?

"Aura, sometimes a man starves and it is not just from lack of food or a grumbling belly. Who are we to say that someone is hungry and someone else is not? We help when we can, where we can," he said firmly.

She stared at him, wanting to ask more questions, to ask him to explain what he really meant, but she could see his mind had transported him out of the room. His eyes were seeing memories that Aura could not. He looked wistful and...she wondered what that other expression was...nostalgic? She was about to open her mouth when another person walked in, snapping her father back to the present.

ℰℐℰℐ

It was incredibly late when they finally called the Day of Asking complete. King Aldric walked out onto his bedroom balcony and looked down on all his people. Faces turned toward him, people stopping in various stages of celebration to look up.

"Until next year, my dear Esoterans—" His voice carried and bounced back all around them. "Have a blessed and safe year!"

The crowd cheered and the king turned back into his chambers. Aura was sitting on a chair next to his bed, her muscles and bones aching from fatigue, wondering if she was even able to walk back to her bedroom. If this was what ruling a kingdom was about, she wasn't sure that she was the right person for the job.

"Father, I—" she began.

But he cut her off as if he had not heard her. "My dear Aura, thank you for your help today, but I am very tired and wish to sleep now."

"Of course, Father. Goodnight."

She bent to kiss him as he slowly lowered himself onto the bed. He seemed to wither away as the covers swallowed him up and, for the second time that day, she began to realize how old he was.

As she reached for the door to leave, she turned back to get one last look of him, but he had already turned off the light and disappeared into the darkness.

Chapter 2

Removed

"Mr. Roberts, Johnstown Prep simply cannot allow this behavior to continue."

No, not again, Levi moaned inwardly. What number would this be, six? Seven? More? Was it more terrible that he couldn't even remember?

"At this school," the woman…who was she again?…continued, "we pride ourselves not only on academic excellence, but also on personal conduct. A graduate of this school is held to a higher standard than most. Your parents are paying for that standard. I am meeting with them momentarily, but I simply do not see how we can keep you enrolled here. Do you understand? Do you have anything to say for yourself?"

Here it was. Here was the moment where he was supposed to get down on his knees and beg for forgiveness—swear he'd change and would never do it again. Levi was tired of the charade.

So forty-five minutes later, carrying a small box filled with his personal items, Levi followed his well-to-do parents out of the tenth—as his mother had just reminded him—school in the last four years.

Really though, what was he *supposed* to do? He couldn't help it, and he certainly wasn't doing it on purpose, at least most of the time. Sometimes when his mind wandered, as it had during the last incident at school, things happened that were out of his control. And people tended not to like uncontrolled things.

It had all started as soon as Levi was able to talk, think, and remember, probably when he was around three years old. He was constantly in trouble for breaking and moving objects, even if they were twice as large as he was or on the other side of the room.

Sometimes, he would have a bit of a warning—a strange tingling, like electricity running through his body—but just as soon as he was aware of it, it would explode out of him. Other times, without warning, it was just released, terrifying him and whoever was standing around him.

A specialist, who he was taken to, diagnosed him with various social disorders and made him see therapists, some of whom prescribed him pills. It didn't take long, however, for the medicines to stop working or for something to spook his doctors, and his parents were forced to start all over again.

Twice, they even took him to see different priests at opposite ends of the country for an exorcism and, both times, they were turned away because the power within him was deemed too strong.

The last remaining school in Montgomery County, Maryland, Johnstown Prep, had now kicked him out. Levi was 18 years old, completely lost, frustrated at his inability to control his life, and unsure of what to do about it.

"Levi, what are we going to do now?" his mother asked when they got back to their house.

"I don't know," he replied, looking at his hands.

"You're going to have to come up with something better than that," his father declared.

"There aren't any more schools for you to go to," his mother continued, "at least, not without you leaving the state."

"But you need to have your diploma," his father added.

"I can get my GED," Levi mumbled.

"What?" his father asked.

"My GED. I can get my GED," Levi repeated.

"That would be a good start, but—" His mother looked over at his father, who nodded. "You'll also have to get a job."

"All right." That seemed fair to him. He couldn't reasonably expect just to lounge around the house all day.

"And your own place," his father added.

"What?" Levi sputtered, shocked. "You want me to move out?"

His mother looked pained and his father moved to comfort her. Levi ached inside for all he was putting them through. He didn't feel like he was ready to move away from them, though. He wasn't ready to be a grown-up yet. How did one just suddenly get thrust into adulthood like this?

"We think it will be the best thing for you," his father said. "You need to start taking responsibility—not only for your actions, but also for your future. We really feel this will help give you direction and purpose."

"Fine. I'll look for places in the morning."

Levi stood then bypassed his mother's reaching arms to go upstairs to his room. He shook with such anger that he didn't snap out of it until the bulb in the lamp by his bed shattered.

Levi cleaned up the glass, taking deep breaths to steady himself. He felt like the pieces of himself and his life had imploded, creating rubble that he would have to sift through for weeks to come.

Chapter 3

Truth

Red hair flowing behind her, Aura laughed as her mare, Serenity, galloped along the lush riverbank. Riding bareback, she was able to feel every smooth muscle of the horse running beneath her. The mare came to a walk, snorting uneasily as they entered a small clearing.

"What is it, girl?" Aura asked, stroking the mare's golden coat.

Suddenly she heard the faint rustling that had spooked the horse. Serenity pranced in place, eyes wide and darting from one side of the meadow to the other. Without warning, a huge form broke out of the bush to her right. The horse bolted in the opposite direction, running away as fast as her legs would allow, throwing Aura off of her. Aura tried to catch her breath, after falling on the hard ground, directly in the path of a massive dragon. Heza sat on her back legs, cocking her scaled head to the side, assessing what was in front of her.

"Well," Aura said, slowly getting to her feet, "you

certainly gave Serenity a fright. I would imagine she is almost home by now."

The dragon hung her head in shame.

Aura laughed at the apologetic beast. Such misunderstood creatures.

Her father had thought it crazy when she asked for a dragon for her eighth birthday. He had gotten her Serenity—a beautiful, striking horse in her own right—and while Aura fell immediately and deeply in love with her, her want for a dragon continued. Finally, on her thirteenth birthday, after years of begging, the king finally determined that his daughter was responsible enough to own a dragon for herself.

While dragons existed in their world, they were not very commonplace. The kingdom had several, yet they were used mainly for protection and not as common pets. Aura and her father went into the southern region of the kingdom where the dragons were raised. She knew the wait was worth it the moment she saw Heza, and they promptly brought her home.

She was a smaller dragon—if such a thing truly existed—and, while impeccably trained, she did have a mischievous streak that made her handlers crazy at times, though Aura found it to be incredibly endearing.

"It's okay," she said now and took Heza's head into her hands. "You will just have to give me a ride home."

The dragon obediently lay on her soft, pink belly. When Aura was safely tucked behind her large purple and gold wings, Heza reared back and took to the skies.

Traveling this way never failed to take Aura's breath away. Esotera's lush forests, open fields, snaking rivers, and scattered houses made her heart swell with pride, especially when she was able to see it all together like this. She shut her eyes and leaned her face back toward the sun as Heza began her decent toward the king's stables.

Aura opened her eyes and, while the objects below were still specks, she could clearly make out the figures of Serenity and her stable hand.

Seconds later, after giving Heza a quick kiss goodbye, Aura walked toward the long building as Heza flew off. The horse and her groom, Theirra—a beautiful black-haired woman with skin darkened even further by the sun—turned in unison as Aura approached them.

Aura reached her hand out and patted the mare's neck. "Oh Netty, what shall I do with you?"

She embraced Theirra and thanked her profusely for catching and bringing back her mare. Aura had known Theirra almost her entire life. Theirra's mother had worked for the king for many years and would bring Theirra with her to the castle. Even though she was more than ten years older than Aura, the two had formed an instant and close bond.

"My dear Aura," Theirra said, pulling back from her embrace, "what trouble have you gotten yourself into today?"

The two friends smiled at each other and began walking, arm in arm, toward the stables, with Serenity obediently following.

೭ﻭ೭ﻭ

Aura returned to the castle later that evening, face flushed from talking and laughing for hours. The smile quickly vanished from her face as soon as she entered the residence.

Standing in a small circle, and talking in hushed tones, were about a half dozen men and women, five of whom she recognized as being part of her father's court. One woman was a complete stranger. She was almost six feet tall with the blackest skin Aura had ever seen. Wearing a perfectly tailored gray suit, she spoke with extreme animation to the other people in the foyer. Slowly, she turned her gaze toward Aura. Aura had to stifle a gasp. This woman was so beautiful, her sad onyx eyes brought Aura to her knees.

Soft hands pulled under her arms and wrapped themselves around her waist, slowly dragging her upright and over to a couch in the parlor. She felt like a rag doll, immediately crumpling as soon as the hands left her body.

"Tell me. Tell me what happened," she said in the softest of words.

The woman sat next to her, making no attempt to comfort Aura as she spoke. "The king is very ill. I have done everything in my power to heal him, but there is not much time left. He is resting comfortably, so you may see him if you wish, but I must warn you, he is very weak." And, without another word, the woman rose, nodded to the others, and walked out the door.

Aura slowly got to her feet and began walking up the huge staircase toward her father's quarters. She heard footsteps behind her, but shrugged off the heavy hand on her shoulder without turning around to see who it was.

The bedroom was dark, except for a single dim light. She walked to the side of her father's bed and looked down upon his sleeping frame. He looked so tiny, lying on the huge mattress. The image of him after the Day of Asking only a few weeks before, so tired and so frail, suddenly flashed into Aura's mind. She sat and took his hands in hers.

He slowly woke and lifted his eyes to lock them with hers.

"I did not mean to wake you, Father. Go back to sleep," she said apologetically as she brushed her fingers softly over his forehead.

"Do not be silly, my dear Aura. You are just who I wanted to see."

His voice sounded so dry it made her throat hurt. She moved to the bedside table and poured him a glass of cold water from a pitcher. He drank deeply, struggling to sit up more fully in bed.

Finally, he put the glass down and took Aura's hands back in his. "Aura, there is something I must tell you, something I should have told you years ago."

"Father, rest. Anything you need to tell me can wait until morning. You need your rest." She began to get up, but her father held on to her hands even tighter.

"No, no, it must be tonight, please sit back down," he said, suddenly stern.

Aura did as she was told, frowning at her father. They'd always had a very close relationship. What could her father possibly have to tell her that she didn't already know? What was so important that it could not wait until the next day?

"When I was younger," he began, "I was a foolish, selfish man."

"Oh, Father, we all make mistakes. Our youth is for learning what we need to do in our future."

"How right you are, Aura, but some mistakes—" He paused and swallowed. "Some things you cannot recover from. You cannot fix them, no matter how many lifetimes you have to try. I made a terrible mistake, one so deep it will spill over from my life to yours. One day you will inherit this kingdom, along with a terrible burden—one that I fear will doom you both."

Confusion washed over Aura and she gripped her father's hand tighter. He breathed as deeply as his tired old lungs allowed, not wanting to tell her the truth, but knowing that he had to.

"Soon after taking over rule from my father, I was traveling in the outskirts of the kingdom, when my guards and I came upon a wanderer on our path. This man begged for a scrap of bread and some wine and, even though we had an abundance of both, I refused the poor traveler and began to move on. After several steps, we found our way blocked by a powerful shield. I could not understand what was happening. I was so young and foolish," he said softly, rocking back and forth for several moments before finally being able to start again. "We tried to penetrate the enchantment, but were unable to. The vagabond now stood in front of me and pulled back his cloak, revealing to us the powerful sorcerer Winester.

"I was shocked and terrified and began offering the wizard not only the food and drink denied before, but also the finest meats and cheeses we had to offer. Winester refused these gifts and berated me for not sharing my bounty with the poor of the kingdom. As punishment, he placed a curse upon me so terrible that I dismounted my horse, fell to my knees, and begged the sorcerer to reconsider.

"Winester ignored my pleas. 'Your kingdom,' the wizard stated, 'will have unmatched bounty under your rule. Fields that have lain barren for centuries will flourish. The beasts that carry and protect you will be the best in the entire world. Your people will know happiness they have never experienced before, but soon your kingdom will be no more. Your kingdom can only survive if an Aldric rules this land. No rightful heir to your kingdom will exist. All sons will die at birth. A single daughter will be your only prodigy. Your death and her marriage will eliminate the Aldric name and break this spell of prosperity. Your kingdom will perish. Those you ask for charity from will deny you and thieves will ravage and steal your land. Your rule is ending. Esotera will soon be no more.'

"'Then my daughter will never marry. She alone will rule this kingdom,'" I said as I rose to my feet, pleased with myself for finding a loophole in the spell."

"'Ah, my dear king.' Winester smiled. 'Without children there will be no one to inherit the throne. And, must I remind you, that no rightful heir may be born out of wedlock. The descendants of Aldric's rule are numbered. Esotera's days are quickly dwindling.'"

Shock didn't even properly describe the feelings that Aura had coursing through her mind. How could this be? How could this have happened, and she none the wiser?

"But—" she started.

He promptly cut her off. "Then there was a puff of smoke and Winester was gone. Just gone. I loved my kingdom so much and I could not handle the thought that one man could take that all away from me. There had to be something I could do. I finally convinced myself that I would have many years ahead of me to figure out a solution to this problem. Surely, in the next ten or twenty years, I would be able to come up with something to fix it. I had intelligent people surrounding me in all aspects of my life. Together, they would come up with a solution. So I was satisfied for the time being, mounted my horse, and headed back to the castle."

Her father went on to tell her that, even with the most brilliant minds he could assemble, he was not able to overcome the curse.

"Your mother had three sons before you were born." The pain of the memory was as clear on his face as if it had just happened. Aura had never heard about these brothers of hers. "I never told her about the curse," he said. "I felt telling her would in some way make it true and I still did not want it to be. Childbirth is a dangerous matter and I reasoned that the losses were due to that. I was so frightened when she became pregnant with you, not only fear of losing another child, but what it would do to my loving wife."

He paused for a moment, having to catch his breath through the sorrow of it all. Aura felt the sting herself, as well, picturing what her father and mother went through, and tried to imagine their pain.

"When you were born and survived," he continued, "we were overjoyed, but your mother—" He paused again. "She was not able to recover and passed several days later. I knew the prophecy had been fulfilled. The throne would have a lone heir—you. My aides advised me to remarry, but I could not. I loved your mother too much and I did not want to put another person through that same pain. I knew I would have no more children. You were my one and only joy."

He apologized to Aura over and over again, pain cracking the edges of his already weak voice. She was too speechless to give him consolation. Throughout the story, she had wanted to ask him a million questions, but he kept gently shushing her each time she tried to interrupt him. He just looked so frail and she was so scared.

A half an hour later, a stunned Aura left the bedroom and started walking down the hall.

The king was dead.

The kingdom was hers.

Chapter 4

Meeting

The alarm went off, for probably the twentieth time, before Levi actually stirred and turned it off. It took a second for his brain to process what time it actually was before he sprang out of bed in sheer panic.

"No, no, no, no, no, no!" he cried as he flew around the room, getting dressed in a flash. He grabbed his keys from where he left them by the front door of his new apartment, ran down the stairs still buttoning his "24/7" shirt, and ran out to his car.

He pressed the accelerator to the floor mat as the car squealed in protest and silently thanked his parents, for the millionth time, for getting him the sporty—and very fast—BMW when he'd turned sixteen. Hopefully, it would get him to the store quickly enough that no one would notice he was an hour late.

Red light.

Another red light.

He drummed his fingers on the steering wheel as he checked the clock for the umpteenth time. Hour and fifteen minutes. He was still okay. He could still slip in. Hopefully, Becky was covering for him. Maybe the owner Mrs. Thomas would be running late too, for some reason, and he could beat her in, no one the wiser. At least, no one who mattered.

It had been three months since Levi had moved out of his parent's house and he was no closer to getting his life put together. Employers fired him almost as quickly as he was hired. Somehow nothing stuck. He was trying, really trying, but his brain seemed to be in a cloud all the time, almost as if it was preoccupied with some other task Levi wasn't privy to. His current employment at the 24/7 convenience store was his longest, at three weeks, though he felt it was in complete jeopardy.

He pulled into the parking lot and eased his car into the spot next to Mrs. Thomas's.

"Crap," he said under his breath.

One hour, twenty-two minutes late. Screwed again.

The little bell above the door rang loudly as he entered the store. It was vacant except for Becky and the surly old woman who owned the place. He cursed under his breath. Becky gave him a weak smile and he knew what was coming. He could see Mrs. Thomas's anger from across the room.

"Morning, ladies." Levi hoped what little charm he had might be enough to ease him out of this situation and save the paying job he so desperately needed. "Didn't realize I turned off my alarm this morning, and wouldn't you know it? Hit every darn red light on the way over here."

"I don't want to hear it, Levi," Mrs. Thomas said as she moved to the side of the counter and blocked his access to behind it.

She barely even said anything. In a matter of minutes, he was walking back to his car, wearing a plain white T-shirt. He could tell from the look on Becky's face that she had tried to stall as long as she possibly could.

His keys were in the lock of the car door when he heard footsteps behind him. Levi half smiled and turned around, expecting to meet Becky's gaze. The smile froze on his face.

Instead of the cute, petite brunette, a tall blond older man was slowly making his way across the parking lot. Levi fumbled with his keys and tried unsuccessfully to unlock his door more quickly. The man held his hand up, palm facing Levi's direction. A strange sensation coursed through Levi's body and he stood rooted in place.

"Mr. Roberts," the man said, "I have been waiting a long time to meet you."

He turned his hand and thrust it forward in Levi's direction. Levi hesitated for a split second before stretching his hand out as well and shaking the stranger's.

"May we take a walk?" the man asked while still gripping Levi's hand.

"S—sure."

They began walking, side by side, down the deserted street. Levi knew he shouldn't be alone with this strange man. Part of his brain was screaming at him— bombarding him with anecdotal information, after-school speeches, warnings from various adults—but a much larger part was too intrigued to listen. He wasn't exactly sure where they were going as the silence between them continued but, suddenly, they turned into a small park. The man motioned for Levi to sit on a bench a short way off the path.

Levi began twisting his hands as he waited for the man to start talking. Several minutes later, the stranger began.

"Mr. Roberts, I come from a place very far away and different than the one we are currently sitting in and—"

"Like California?"

Levi couldn't help interrupting him and the man let a slight smile cross his face. "Not quite. Where I come from, the impossible happens every day. The things deemed fantasies in your world are normal occurrences in mine."

Levi sat a little straighter. "What are you trying to say?"

"What can you tell me about your parents?"

"My parents?" Levi was terribly confused. Who *was* this man? "My mom is an insurance broker for some big company downtown. I don't really know all of the specifics, but I do know she is in a pretty powerful position at her company. My father is the head of cardiac surgery at Edmondton. But I don't understand what my parents have to do with this? Honestly, I don't really even see them that much. I've been living on my own for the past few months, and they both tend to work long hours." Levi stopped talking and the man smiled again.

"I mean your real parents."

Levi stared in shock. He had never told anyone before that he was adopted. Being adopted didn't shame him, far from it, actually. Anger quickly began to flare in him as he was able to sort through the words the man had just spoken. Levi had never considered the two people who raised him as anything other than his parents.

"If you mean my birth parents, I don't really know anything about them. I was abandoned as a newborn and they were never found. It was suggested that maybe they died or were just unable to keep me. Doesn't really matter though, my parents adopted me right away. They are my real parents," he said with as much conviction as he could muster.

A sign a few yards away from them began to sway even though there was no breeze passing through.

"Oh, my dear boy," the stranger said. He looked at the sign, shook his head, and chuckled. "It matters very much. Very much indeed."

"Look, I don't know who you are or what you are trying to do here, but I don't need this." Levi quickly stood up, shaking slightly, but trying to calm himself down. Where did this guy get off? Screw him. Hands in his pockets and head down, Levi began walking back along the path. As he turned the corner, he had to stifle a scream when he looked up just moments before almost walking into the stranger.

Levi looked around frantically for other people, but the small park was empty. He began backing up slowly as the man walked toward him with that same small smile on his face.

"Who are you?" Levi tried to hide the fear from his voice, but it still shook slightly.

"Levi, I am here to talk to you about your past and discuss the prospects of your future."

"Who are you?" Levi asked again.

"My name is Winester."

Chapter 5

Destiny

When the Earth was created, its parts were divided and given to two powerful people, Lord Vertrous and Lady Amadea," Winester continued. "While they were both as different as the worlds they ruled over, the two had great respect for each other and they ruled in harmony for hundreds of years. Over time, Lord Vertrous found himself deeply in love with Lady Amadea and tried on several occasions to join both kingdoms so they could rule together over one united world, but she would listen to none of it. He was heartbroken that she did not return his feelings, yet he put his hurt aside to be a good ruler for his people.

"Then one day Lord Vertrous met a very beautiful woman from Lady Amadea's part of the world. He fell madly in love with her, breaking Amadea's heart and greatly angering her for, while she thwarted his advances, she was truly in love with Lord Vertrous as well.

She banished the woman from her world and cut ties with Vertrous, ending the harmonious relationship the

Earth had for many years. Shamed, Vertrous hid his world and his people away. He refused to marry the woman he felt had wrongly seduced him, blaming her for the end of their peace, even though she was pregnant with his child.

"He split up the lands that had been given to him and gave them to four different families, whose descendants still rule to this day. King Theaus became ruler of the northern region and named the land after his beloved wife, Omaner. King Grustmiener named the eastern part after himself. The humble King Piester named the south region Vertronum, in appreciation for the gift bestowed upon him. And the great King Aldric reigned over the west, which he called Esotera.

"All his lands now in capable hands, Lord Vertrous decided his work on Earth was done and he left for the After, never being able to forgive himself for hurting Lady Amadea as he had and for leaving his son without a father. He hoped the men and women he left in charge of his lands would redeem his wrongs, somehow."

Levi was confused beyond belief. He had only agreed to follow Winester back to the park bench because the man had promised to explain everything to him. Ten minutes later, he was more mystified than before. "That's a nice story and all, but what does a fairytale have to do with me?"

"It is *not* a fairytale," Winester snapped, making Levi jump a little and his heart beat faster.

He quickly closed his mouth and waited for the man to continue speaking.

"The pregnant woman was heartbroken. She'd left her entire family, her world, for Vertrous, and what had she gotten in return? The man she loved had deserted her and left her alone to raise her child. She tried making a home for herself in the new land, but nothing felt right to her. In Omaner she was cold all the time, and the giant-haired beasts that roamed the land scared her. Grustmie-ner was not much better, with their terrible rainy seasons, followed by periods of intense drought. Vertronum's people welcomed her with open arms, but she felt their pity wherever she went, so she moved to Esotera. This land was beautiful. Lush forests, deep rivers, and lakes with waterfalls cut through the emerald green land, but King Aldric was not as hospitable as the people in his kingdom. He was Vertrous's favorite, as evidenced by the land given to him, and he could not forgive this woman for what she had done to his lord—"

"What *she* did?" Levi interjected, so immersed in the story that he forgot Winester had scolded him moments before. "But she loved him, too. She didn't make him leave. She probably didn't want him to leave."

Winester smiled, ignoring Levi's rudeness momen-tarily. He was glad the boy was interested and was play-ing right into his hands.

"She became a nomad," Winester told him. "Travel-ing from place to place, never staying long enough to put roots down or raise suspicions. Over time, people forgot about her and her story got lost, tangled up in myths, with only a very few having full knowledge of what had really happened. She gave birth to her son and, while she loved him very much, he reminded her of too much Vertrous. A family here in your world was left to raise him. She never told those people who she was, hoping to protect her son from Lady Amadea, and fled back to our world. She nev-er saw him again, dying shortly after of a heart broken one too many times. However, Lady Amadea did know of this child and, in one final act against Lord Vertrous, she made him and all his descendants prime rulers over the other land. Through him, she would be able to control both parts of the Earth."

The story had entranced Levi. "But why did she need him? Couldn't she have just taken over herself?"

"She needed his blood connection. He was the only one able to fight for the return of the power, since Vertrous was the one who divided the lands. Amadea suddenly died before he grew up and was told about the power he held. So the boy never knew. He later married and had children, grandchildren, and great grandchildren, none of them knowing the power held within their veins. Years and years later, the last living heir got pregnant. She was in love with the child's father, but he did not return her love. Very ill and, faced with raising the child alone, she gave him up for adoption and quickly withered away, dying shortly thereafter."

They sat in silence for several minutes while Levi thought about the story just told to him. He knew he should leave this crazy man, get back to his apartment, and start looking for a new job, but some invisible force was keeping him here.

"So you say this story is true? If this Amadea died without ever telling the dude's son, then how do you know about it?"

"I was the one Lady Amadea used to place the spell on the boy."

"Fine, then if you have all the answers, why didn't *you* tell the boy?" Levi asked.

"His new family moved before I was able to find him after Lady Amadea passed. Her successor…well let's just say he was not very pleased with my position during her rein. So I was forced to return to my world, but now there is a new ruler, and I was finally able to come back and start my quest to find the descendants, the last descendant as it turns out—the most powerful man in both our worlds."

"Well, that's a wonderful story. I hope you find your man." Levi got up and started walking away, finally hearing enough, but he stopped when Winester grabbed his arm.

"Oh, but I have found him."

Levi slowly turned around, staring at the face of the smiling man had who cemented Levi's fate hundreds of years ago.

Chapter 6

The Future

Aura awoke to sunshine as always but, for the first time in her life, she climbed out of her bed and immediately started getting ready, ignoring the view out of her window. She put on a long black dress and forced herself to brush her hair. She chose a short black veil, pulling it over her swollen face. She made her way down the long hall of the living quarters' wing of the palace, not pausing or even flicking a glance toward the door of her father's chamber as she passed it.

Throughout her walk to the front door and the waiting carriages, she passed numerous servants dressed in black, averting their eyes and lowering their heads as she strode by. One of her father's aides came to her side, handing her papers and asking her questions, but she heard and responded to nothing. The kingdom could wait one more day. There were more pressing matters. Today was the day she would bury her father.

She exited the castle. Standing before her was a small black carriage pulled by two huge black horses. Little Theirra stood between their massive bodies holding them still with the lightest touch. She immediately dropped their reins and walked toward Aura, collecting her in her arms. The aides gasped and looked at one another, frightened that the new queen would ruin her dress with whatever the groom may have on her. Not many outside of Aura's father knew of her close friendship with this *supposed* servant, and the thought made Aura cry even harder. Her father was the one person who knew her whole heart, and now he was gone. How did one continue living when so many parts of themselves suddenly went missing all at once?

Ignoring the glances of those around her, and not caring that her friend was in her uniform, Aura pulled Theirra into the carriage with her. She gripped Theirra's hand so tightly, almost fearing she'd float away if she let go. Turning around, Aura noticed that her father's beloved mare was tied to the back of the hearse.

Driving up to the royal cemetery, the caravan passed thousands of Esoterans who were lined along the road to pay their respects to their beloved king. Some threw flowers, while others waved or just simply stood there and cried. Aura saw them all with unfocused eyes. In the weeks following that procession, she would be able to fully appreciate what it meant to have all those mourning souls stand in remembrance for her father. But, right now, she could only look straight ahead and try not to fall apart.

The ceremony was beautiful. In attendance were the leaders from Omaner, Grustmiener, and Vertronum. Kings Grustmiener, Piester, and Theaus all gave their deepest sympathies, but all had a strange twinkle in their eyes, especially King Grustmiener and his wife. Aura couldn't quite put her finger on it. Was it that they feared suddenly being faced with their own mortality? Most of these men were around the same age as her father. Could it have touched a dark place of terror inside of them?

The rulers also each looked slightly out of place. King Piester had a strange, scaled outfit on. It almost looked as if there were gills or wings on it. King Theaus and his wife were dressed as if it was snowing out. Giant cloaks swallowed their large frames. The rulers of Grustmiener looked well-dressed, in tunics made of white feathers, but they appeared almost damp, as if they'd never had the chance to dry out. Aura felt slightly uncomfortable seeing strangers in her father's land, especially due to the way they looked at her.

"They keep staring like they might catch something from me," Aura confided in Theirra.

When the service was over and a flock of young hethronian birds were set free to symbolize her father's skyward journey, people flooded the streets and celebrated the king's life well into the night. There was loud music and so many people laughing, talking, and dancing that Aura could barely hear her own thoughts.

She never wanted to leave. These "life celebrations," as they called them, were supposed to honor the dead, but she had always felt like they were more for the people left behind, to comfort their own fears of death. Aura had never really understood them before, always assuming they belittled the dead, made light of pain and suffering. But in the midst of her own grief, she felt this loud throb of people pressing in on her as if it were life itself. She hoped it would give her the strength she needed to keep going, breathing, and living.

After she returned to the castle grounds, she went to the stables and met Theirra standing in the aisle.

"Are you ready?" Theirra asked.

Aura nodded, unable to find her voice.

The two women moved toward the stall reserved for the king's horse. The mare stood with her head out, surrounded by hundreds of black roses like a halo around her. The beautiful old mare nickered softly at them and followed them obediently out of the barn. They walked several hundred yards out of the city gates toward the heavily wooded area that surrounded the kingdom. Aura kissed the mare's velvet nose softly and removed her halter.

"Thank you for taking such good care of him for so many years. I know you loved him as much as he loved you. I hope you live the rest of your days in peace."

The mare turned and ran away, swallowed up by the night.

Aura and Theirra stared into the darkness a while before finally turning back to the castle. When Aura made it back to her room, she fell into such a deep sleep that not a single dream flashed across her brain. It would be the last peaceful slumber she would have for many months.

෴

The days and weeks following her father's death were a blur. Aura was thankful for the fast pace and she threw herself into all matters regarding the kingdom. She approved so many projects that inhabitants with the wildest of schemes started pouring in, hoping to capitalize. The aides around her rolled their eyes at one another, clearly not supporting the choices she was making, but they were terrified to speak up. To say she was a little on edge would have been an understatement. After one screaming match that Aura had with a member of the securities department, people tended to give her a wider berth, afraid to be the next one to take the brunt of her fury.

Even the few times she was able to sneak away to the stables and dragonry, both Serenity and Heza wanted little to do with her.

"Well, fine then!" Aura yelled at Heza's departing frame, trying to keep her voice from breaking.

"Aura?" a voice softly said from behind her.

She wheeled around in anger, which immediately vanished when the saw Theirra.

"Oh, Theirra!"

Aura rushed to embrace her friend. After they broke apart, Aura still clasped her hand, holding it as they walked the grounds around the castle.

After a few moments of hesitation, Aura pulled her friend down on a bench, deep in the secluded garden. Fragrant flowers, singing birds, and insects surrounded the two women. Her friend's expression turned to shock as Aura recounted the story her father had told her on his deathbed.

When she was finished, they sat silently for a long time before Theirra spoke. "Have you gotten the story verified at all?"

"Verified?"

"Not that your father would be anything less than truthful to you, but maybe he misunderstood. Maybe it was really something else that was said to him."

Aura looked so desperate and pained that Theirra said quietly, "Maybe it is worth trying to track down Winester and ask him?"

"I have tried," Aura said, burying her head in her hands. "No one knows where he is. It seems he has left the kingdom entirely."

Theirra sat thinking this over. She felt like there should be something she could do to help her friend. Suddenly, she brightened. "Resbuca."

"What?" Aura asked, obviously lost in thought.

"Resbuca. The sorceress. If anyone would know where Winester is, she would."

"Do you know where she is, how to locate her?"

"I think so. I think I know where to begin, at least."

"Then we must leave at once," Aura said, jumping to her feet.

"No!" Theirra covered her mouth as soon as the words left her lips. "I meant no disrespect, my queen."

"Theirra, this is no time for formalities. You are my closest friend. Please speak to me as such, but we are wasting precious time. We must leave right away."

"Aura, it is simply too dangerous. Especially knowing the information you just told me. If something happened to you—" Theirra broke off. "Esotera would cease to exist. It is simply too dangerous."

"If that is the case, then it is too dangerous for you to go alone," Aura said defiantly.

"It is not as dangerous for me as it is for you. I am a nobody. I can travel the countryside virtually unnoticed. I will be perfectly fine and will either bring Resbuca back here myself, or at least bring you the information you desire."

Aura looked deep into her eyes, searching them for any bit of fear or hesitation. Only calmness and loyalty stared back at her. "Fine, but you will ride Netty. And two of my guards will accompany you." She cut Theirra off before her protests could be voiced. "I do not know if I could handle losing you, too. I have to know you are safe."

Twenty minutes later, after a quick embrace, Aura waved at Theirra as the small entourage left through the palace gates. She said a silent prayer that, not only would they all return home safely, but they'd also have the information she so desperately needed.

Chapter 7

Decisions

Levi paced back and forth around his apartment. Bedroom, hallway, kitchen, living room. Repeat. Over and over.

"What do I do? What do I do? What do I *do*?"

Bedroom, hallway, kitchen, living room. The day turned black outside before he finally sat on his couch and lowered his face into his open palms. He looked down at the small piece of paper that held the strange man's hotel information. Winester would be here for three days. Levi would have three days to decide. He stood up and resumed his pacing.

How could an orphaned kid who was kicked out of schools his adoptive parents paid to keep him enrolled at—who couldn't even keep a job at a convenience store—be an heir to a magical kingdom? He felt like a fool to even consider the proposition.

There was no such thing as an alternate world filled with unicorns, wizards, and princesses. Why was he even wasting time thinking about this? This man was probably some crazy person—probably recently escaped from some mental institution—and here Levi was, actually considering what the man had said. Really, he should just call the cops and wash his hands of the situation. Levi stood, ripped the paper in half, and threw it in the trash on his way to bed.

∽∾∽

The next morning, Levi awoke without an alarm for the first time in months. He rolled over with a groan, finally peeling himself from bed around 11 o'clock. Half asleep and half dressed, he stumbled into the living room, catching the scream in his throat right before it left his lips. Slowly Winester turned from the window he was standing in front of—a magnificent multicolored bird on his shoulder—to face Levi.

"How, how the hell did you get in here?" Levi demanded, inching toward his cell phone on the hall table.

"I am a powerful sorcerer, Mr. Roberts," Winester said, looking into Levi's eyes with a hint of a smile on his face. "That and you left your front door unlocked."

"I thought I had three days," Levi said, keeping his eyes on the man as he groped for his phone, hopefully without any notice.

The bird made a terrible screeching noise right as the phone slipped into Levi's pocket. Levi jumped and looked up sheepishly at Winester.

"If you need to make a call, please do not let me stand in your way. And you will have to excuse Busu," Winester said while absently stroking the bird's blue and green head. "He is trained to alert me when someone is making plans against me or that may harm me. Though I have to say his talents are not 100% accurate—as in this situation, I am sure."

Levi nodded as the bird made a disgruntled noise. He let the phone go from his hand, feeling it drop into the bottom of his pocket. "Why are you here?"

"I was under the impression you were no longer taking my offer seriously."

The blood drained from Levi's face. Who was this person? Fear ran icy through his veins. "I don't know *how* to take it seriously. You find me walking to my car—moments after being fired from yet another job—give me this ridiculous story about me being the last surviving heir to a magical kingdom, show up in my living room when I've never told you where I live, holding a mind-reading bird, and expect me to gladly follow you. And to where, exactly?"

It was becoming increasingly difficult for Levi to keep his voice down and the sarcasm to a minimum.

"First off, for accuracy sake, Busu does not technically read minds, though he can transfer his thoughts to me, but that is beside the point. Secondly, you are not heir to a kingdom per se, but an entire world made up of four kingdoms. However, these are just nitty-gritty details, as I believe the phrase goes."

"Stop talking, just stop it." Levi's voice was rising again. "Look, whether your offer's real or not, I want no part of it. I want out. Heir, or whatever, give it to someone else. I don't want it. Now get out of my apartment."

At this point, Levi was shaking from fear and rage. Why wouldn't this man leave him alone? Levi needed to find a new job—or a new place to live if he couldn't find a new job—and he didn't have time for all of this. This person was making it all even more complicated.

"Mr. Roberts—" It seemed Winester was having just as much trouble keeping his voice even. "This is not a game. Millions of lives are at stake. The entire future for a whole world is in your hands. You do not need to worry about finding a new job." Levi looked up at these words, but Winester continued on. "You need to focus all your energy on this decision. On making the correct decision."

"Please," Levi begged. "Please leave here. Please."

This last word was spoken in a hushed whisper. Anything—anything—to get the man to leave. Levi looked down and, by the time he raised his eyes again, Winester was gone.

Levi promptly locked his door.

Chapter 8

Journey

For the next several days, Aura could think of little else, except for when Theirra would return with news for her. Once willing to hear and grant wishes to all those who asked, Aura became preoccupied and distant, saying no on a number of occasions before the petitioners could even ask. It did not take long before the villagers stopped asking altogether.

The waiting was becoming torturous. Finally, on the tenth day she heard Serenity's distinct whinny. Slowly, across the horizon, the form of her friend came into view riding the mare. Aura moved quickly and met the pair as they made their way toward the castle grounds.

"It was such a long trip," Theirra said, slowly dismounting from Serenity's back.

The guards, who had been traveling with her, nodded to Aura as they rode past her toward the stables. She quickly nodded her thanks back to them.

"What happened?" she demanded of Theirra. "Tell me absolutely everything. Speak!"

"I am so tired, I have been traveling for hours," Theirra said wearily. Both she and the mare were dragging their feet as they continued forward.

"Oh Theirra, please!" Aura begged. "Please tell me all you know. I have been dying for your return and the information. I will hold a feast in your honor and get you the softest bed to sleep in, but first you must talk to me!"

Theirra laughed at the impatience of her friend. "Yes, of course, Aura. But—" She stopped walking and looked seriously at her. "—we must not talk here," she said, looking around as if spies might be watching. "We must go somewhere safe. Somewhere no one can hear us talk."

"I know the exact place."

After Theirra handed Serenity off to a groom with a thankful pat, the pair moved deep within the palace. They ventured through the kitchen and to the deepest recesses of the building. To keep any trespassers away from them, Aura left a guard at a heavy door at the top of a long, dark staircase. Theirra was frightened as they descended into the abyss and was just about to ask where they were when the stairs abruptly ended, leaving them face to face with another solid door.

Aura pulled out a heavy iron key and opened the door, ignoring its loud, rusty protests. Theirra shuddered and goose bumps covered her arms in response to the sudden drop in temperature. Her eyes tried to adjust to the darkness but it was just too black. She felt Aura move in front of her and heard the tinkling of a chain a moment before a soft light illuminated the space. Moving behind Theirra, Aura shut the huge door, surrounding them in silence. Theirra looked around the dimly lit room. Multicolored bottles glinted back at her.

"Where are we?" she asked, running her hands lightly over the glass, dust clinging to her fingertips.

"In one of the liquid stores. There are many in the castle holding a wide variety of drinks, but this is one of the oldest and deepest. My father always told me that this was one of the few places in the entire kingdom where no one could hear you. All his secret and most important meetings were held down here."

She paused for a long moment, held deep in thought by old memories. She shook her head, trying to physically remove the thoughts from her mind.

She moved two stools from against the wall and motioned for Theirra to join her and sit. "Please, tell me everything," she said.

"Well, I did not know exactly where Resbuca was living. She travels a lot, though usually sticks to the Morski forest in the north. It took me two days just to find the group she normally travels with, then another day and a half to find her."

Aura perked up. "So you did find her?"

"Of course. Would I have returned here if I had not?" Aura smiled. Theirra sighed. "I found her. It was luck, actually, but at first she wanted nothing to do with me. I feared I was too bold. I came right out requesting the information from her. She regarded me fearfully, almost as if I were the witch and not her."

"So what did you do?" Aura asked.

"I just kept coming. Each day I would spend my mornings with her. At first, she just ignored me, but then slowly, she started giving me small tasks. Collecting water or herbs, crushing and mixing dry ingredients, things of that sort. Finally, I felt like I should ask her again."

Her eyes glossed over, almost as if she were seeing the events play out in front of her again…

❧❧❧

"Lady Resbuca."

The woman ignored Theirra and kept working on a complex potion.

"I need to talk to you. I need to talk to you about Winester," Theirra said. "Please, I need to find him."

She touched Resbuca lightly on the shoulder, freezing her in place.

The witch put her stirring spoon down and clutched the table in front of her with both hands, almost as if she needed its support to stay standing. "I loved him once you know, Winester that is."

She turned around and gave Theirra a look of such deep suffering, Theirra wondered when the last time was the woman had ever been happy.

"We were together for a time at The Beginning. Together we were very powerful. We helped people all over the world, but then he became more and more distant and became closer to Lord Vertrous."

"You knew Lord Vertrous?" Theirra's eyes widened, and she couldn't help but interrupt.

"You are too kind to think I am younger than I really am. Yes, Winester and I were alive then. He was a close confidant of the lord when the worlds split forever."

"What was it like back then?" Theirra was enthralled with the story. She had never met anyone who had been alive before their world and the other had been split.

"It was a scary time. No one knew what the future held for either world. Some were talking about all-out war. It was a very uncertain time. Winester left me for a short period during it all, traveling between both worlds and trying to mediate between Lord Vertrous and Lady Amadea. But it was hopeless. Winester returned to me, upset and defeated. He really thought he could help— help save us all."

"Does he know what caused the split?"

Resbuca smiled half-heartedly. "Is that not what you came here to ask me?"

"N—no," Theirra stammered, completely taken off guard. "I came on behalf of Lady Aura, Queen of Esotera. There is an important matter she needs to discuss with him about the future of—"

"Yes, yes," Resbuca interrupted. "I know what she needs to talk to him about. She wants to know if there is a way out of the curse—if she can do it and single-handedly save Esotera." She said the last part with a bite of sarcasm.

"Do *you* know the answer?" Theirra asked in little more than a hush.

"Of course. Of course I do…"

ᘓᘔᘓ

Aura was shocked, staring at her friend. The pause in the story brought her back to reality. She felt as though she were in those woods, listening to the actual conversation as it happened when Theirra was speaking.

"Did she tell you?" she whispered. "Did she tell you everything?"

"Eventually, though—" Theirra hesitated. "Lady Aura, I hope I did not over-step my bounds."

"What is it?"

"I promised her that she could return to the kingdom. It was the only thing that I could offer her that she really wanted. I am so sorry. I know how your father felt about those who dealt magic in Esotera." Theirra looked down at her hands, afraid to look up.

"Oh Theirra, Theirra, of course it is okay. We needed the information. You did well," Aura said, gripping her friend's hands. "Now, I beg you, tell me what she said."

"Winester became a trusted confidant of Lord Vertrous. The ruler shared everything with the sorcerer. Apparently, Winester tried to talk him out of separating from Lady Amadea and from splitting up his lands, but he would hear nothing of it. Winester could not understand his reasons for his resistance to reconcile. Finally, Vertrous broke down and told—his now closest friend—why he was doing this, why he had no choice, and what the cause of the split was."

Aura leaned forward in her chair in anticipation.

"It turns out," Theirra continued. "Well. It turns out Lord Vertrous had a child with someone from the other world."

"No!" Aura was shocked. How had this stayed a secret for so many years?

"Lady Amadea was furious. She threw the pregnant woman out of her world and told Vertrous the harmony that they had enjoyed for thousands of years was over. What happened to Lord Vertrous, The Division, you already know all that."

"So what does all that have to do with me, with Esotera?"

"The child, his child, lived. Lived, grew up, and had children of his own. The generations continued, but the story of their lineage got lost somewhere along the way. Resbuca was not sure exactly when, but somehow the truth of who their ancestor was disappeared. Apparently, though, there is still one heir left, one person who shares those original genes. That is where Resbuca thinks Winester went, to go find him."

Aura was not sure of what to make of this information. Whatever had caused the splitting of their worlds had been a point of debate for hundreds of years. Now she held some of the most powerful knowledge and secrets people had killed to find out. The more she thought about it though, the more confused she was on how this was relevant to her current dilemma. "What did she say that had to do with my father and kingdom?" she asked, trying to keep her voice calm and steady.

"This child not only has Vertrous's blood in his veins, but also his power. He has the ability to take back the worlds if he wants to. Resbuca believes it will not be as easy as saying it. He will probably have to fight to get these lands back, but he alone can declare war. But do you see what this power means? How it can be used for peace, too?"

Clarity washed the worry off Aura's face. "It means this person can overturn the curse! We can save Esotera!" Aura had a large smile on her face, which quickly faded. "But how will we find this person?"

"He is a boy, and I know exactly where to find him. Though, it will be a long, and potentially, dangerous trip."

"Where is he?" Aura demanded.

Theirra looked uncomfortable. "The other world," she said and Aura gasped.

Chapter 9

Travels

Aura was stunned. Unable to speak during the entire ten minutes it took for her and Theirra to climb up to Aura's chambers. Theirra looked worried and kept stealing glances at her, as if on the verge of speaking, but then promptly shutting her mouth.

"H—how will we g—get there?" Aura finally sputtered.

"Resbuca told me of several portals, passages really," Theirra said. "She said most are over-grown or blocked, but she knows of one not too far from here."

"How does she know such things?" Aura asked.

"Umm…" Theirra hesitated. "It is not exactly…well, she could get in trouble you see. It is not particularly legal, but she uses them to trade in goods and contact the other world."

Aura paused at the door of her room. "It is not exactly *il*legal."

"It is not?"

"Well, the rulers of the Four Corners feared what

would happen to them, what Lady Amadea could do to them if people from our world went to hers," Aura said. "To prevent them from traveling, the rulers created stories, bad omens, things that would happen to people if they went. Along the way, people began spreading rumors of great punishments, and they got it into their heads that it was breaking some law if they traveled across. The rulers decided this was easiest and never corrected them. You must tell this to no one. Chaos could ensue if people knew they could cross over. But do not fear. Tell me what Resbuca said. No punishment shall befall either of you."

And with that she stepped into her room, letting the information swarm in Theirra's head.

Back in her room, Aura quickly moved about, opening and closing drawers and cabinets, sometimes pulling out objects and placing them in a small bag, and other times turning away empty-handed after much deliberation.

Finally, she gave the room a last look and placed the satchel over her shoulder.

"We must get you packed and the horses ready. Is Resbuca meeting us somewhere?"

Theirra looked confused. "Packed?"

Aura stepped forward and grasped her hands. "Theirra, I *need* you."

Theirra was not particularly enjoying this position her friend kept putting her in. "Aura, you know I cannot. I am needed here. Plus—" She paused, hating to bring this up. "I am just a lowly stable hand. If you bring anyone with you, it should be a guard. Or some impressive looking adviser. I would only slow you down, and probably get one or both of us hurt or killed. This will not be a safe or easy journey."

"Exactly, which is why I need someone I can trust," Aura said firmly.

Theirra sighed. Aura, having always lived a life of privilege, never fully grasped the differences and expectations of class. Theirra was all too aware. The other servants and employees of the kingdom always viewed her in a way that let her know they didn't approve of her relationship with the queen. Even when they were young, she'd always had a feeling in the back of her mind that the way Aura treated her wasn't the norm and might actually cause them both problems one day. The trouble was, Theirra liked being seen that way. Aura never acted like they were anything less than equals, and their time together was the only time where Theirra felt a shred special. It was this feeling she kept coming back for and kept taking these stupid risks to keep it going. "Fine," she reluctantly said. "But we must bring a guard with us, just in case."

A smile broke out on Aura's face. She picked up another bag and threw in items identical to the ones she had just packed. It must have weighed 20 pounds by the time it she handed it to Theirra.

"Now, as I asked before, where is Resbuca meeting us?"

"I—I was not sure if you would want her to," Theirra stammered, "but I asked her to wait outside the castle limits, in case we needed her for anything."

"Of course, of course I do. We need not only her power, but also her wisdom and knowledge of the other world. Plus, if we end up meeting Winester…" Aura trailed off. "Frankly, she may be more necessary for our protection than a guard."

"I will go find her and inform her that the queen requests her accompaniment on our trip. In the meantime, get the strongest guard you can," Theirra said as she began to leave but suddenly she turned around. "I need you to do one more thing for me. I need you to personally promote Gustado to my position while we are gone. He is young, but the most qualified. I have a feeling the others will not listen to him if the word comes from me, but if you specifically demand it, they will obey."

"I will. Return quickly with Resbuca. Meet us at the stable and be prepared to depart upon your return," Aura said.

The two women exited the room and went their separate directions. Aura walked down the long side staircase and paused a moment at the bottom step, leaning against the banister. Everything was moving so quickly she felt like she couldn't breathe. Oh, how she wished her father was still here and she could ask his guidance. She knew going to the other world was the right move, but she still could not help but be scared.

She wasn't sure at first who she was going to ask to accompany them, but as soon as she saw him down the hall, she knew Milskar was the one.

"Milskar, a moment please."

He stopped mid-sentence, in a conversation with two aides Aura did not know by name, and excused himself. Milskar was an impressive-looking man. He was soft spoken in nature, but not many got close enough to figure that out. Her father had seen much promise in him and he'd moved up quickly through the ranks of the guards, even though he was on the younger side, only about twenty-six.

"What can I do for you, my lady?" he asked cheerfully.

"Something I need your utmost discretion on." Aura looked at him seriously and he nodded. "I need you to accompany me on a trip."

"Of course, miss, I mean, queen."

Aura waved away his formality. "It is a little more complicated than that." She moved them a little farther down the corridor and away from the others. "Theirra and Resbuca will be coming along with us as well."

Milskar looked at her with deep confusion and mild concern. "Theirra the groom? And Resbuca the sorceress?"

"Yes. I need you to not ask a lot of questions. The less you know the less you can tell others when they ask you, and they will probably ask you. I need you to prepare enough supplies for yourself for a seven-day journey. If anyone asks you where you are going, speak the truth, I asked you to accompany me on a journey."

"Yes, of course, my lady." He turned to leave.

"And, Milskar?" The man turned back toward her. "I need you to bring some forms of protection as well. Meet me at the stables in fifteen minutes."

He nodded at her and started back down the hall.

Aura found another one of her aides and informed her that she would be traveling throughout the kingdom for the next few days, taking with her a bodyguard and her head groom. She decided to leave Resbuca out of this. Too many questions would be raised and Aura was not in the mood to try to come up with answers to them. The aide went along with it, but more out of obligation than desire. Aura could tell the woman wanted to press her, but knowing her place and not wanting to disobey a direct order, she shut her mouth and simply nodded. Aura was starting to like this whole being in power thing and, while her heart was thundering in her chest and her hands were shaking slightly, she hadn't felt this in control in a very long time.

By the time she had all of her affairs in order—and loose ends tied just the way she wanted them—and made her way outside, Theirra, Resbuca, and Milskar were huddled together by the side of the barn, talking. They all looked up as she approached and she felt a swell in her heart for these three people who had stopped everything in their lives to help her. She was still getting used to the idea of being queen and, while they probably had no choice but to follow her orders, she appreciated them all the same. Their horses were saddled and waiting. The four swung up and were on their way.

Resbuca had the lead and the rest followed her in single file with Milskar bringing up the rear. Aura wasn't sure how the woman knew where she was going, but she didn't feel the need to protest, as she could offer no alternatives on the route.

No one spoke. The only sounds around them were the footfalls of the horses and the wildlife in the woods around them. The deeper they got into the forest, the darker it became and the more difficult it was to see. The animal sounds grew louder and more exotic, making the horse's fidget, ears flicking around at every noise.

"We will stop here and camp for the night," Resbuca said suddenly, coming to a stop. To use what little daylight was left, they stopped in a small clearing.

"How much farther do we have to go?" Aura asked. She found it difficult to get her bearings.

"About another day and a half's journey, but then the real trip begins. We need to be rested."

Theirra began unpacking and set the horses loose for the night, allowing them the freedom to find food and rest. Resbuca walked around the perimeter muttering things under her breath. *Protections*? Aura wondered.

Milskar also moved around the clearing, possibly securing it, but just as likely trying to find something to busy himself with, without getting in the way.

An hour or so later, under the cover of a million brilliant stars and planets from the far away recesses of
space, the four finally rested. Aura hadn't realized how
tired she was until she laid her head down, quickly falling
into a deep yet restless slumber.

Chapter 10

Lies

Levi paced in the kitchen at his parent's house. Where were they? Granted he hadn't spoken to them as often since his last attempt at school failed, but he still felt like they should have told him if they were going to be away somewhere.

Could they have left on a trip? It looked like all of their stuff was still in the closets, but his mother's car was gone. They never took his mother's car unless they were going on a long trip. The SUV his father drove got terrible gas mileage, so if they ever went farther than twenty miles they took hers. So where were they?

He was just about to pick up the phone to call them when he heard the garage door open. Levi froze. He hadn't really thought all this through. What the hell was he doing? What the hell was he going to say to them?

"Mom and Dad, I finally found out who my birth parents are! And it turns out I have the rights to rule a magical other world because of it, so you probably won't be seeing me around much because I am leaving tomorrow with this strange wizard dude I just met to go there! How great is that?"

Levi was fully panicking now. He thought about slipping out the back door but, all of a sudden, there they were, standing in the kitchen with arms loaded with bags.

"Levi!" his mother yelled out in almost a half scream.

He had startled her. All he could manage was a weak smile in return.

"Son?" His father recovered a little faster. "What brings you here? I wish you would have called us. We were out to lunch and shopping with the Michaelsons. We would have come back sooner if we'd known you were here."

His mother sat her bags down and began removing items from them.

"I…umm." *Oh hell*, Levi thought, *rip it off like a Band-Aid*. "I am going to be going away for a little while."

"Going away?" His mother looked confused. "Going where? With whom?"

"I am going out west." Technically, not a lie. "I feel like I need a change, and…and well, I have some leads that I might find some more information on my birth parents out there." This last part Levi said to the ground, unable to look his mother and father in the eyes.

Levi's parents never kept hidden the fact that he was adopted. They had always been quite open about it, but he never had any desire to know anything about his biological parents. He'd never had any interest in knowing more. Standing in the kitchen now, watching his parents—these incredible people who had raised him—exchange glances, he doubted himself and what he was doing. It looked as though they had been expecting this, as if they knew that someday this would happen. It broke his heart to see this. Still, he knew it was the only way. They would freely let him go without too many questions, but he saw the pain on their faces. Levi wished he could just take it back and tell them the truth, but he knew deep down it had to be this way.

"Is there anything you need, anything we can do?" his father asked in a shaky voice.

Levi's heart sank. How could they be so loving and understanding when it was clearly crushing them? It was a love so beyond his comprehension.

He finally looked up at them. "No, Dad. No I have everything I need. I love you both so much, but this is something I feel like I really need to do on my own."

"We know, sweetheart," his mother said, stepping up to embrace him. "We love you too."

Levi stayed a little longer talking, hugging, and crying. They asked again if they could help in any way, but didn't fight him on it when he said no. Finally, he agreed to take a little money and then he was off, not sure when—or if—he would see them again.

He still had so many doubts about what he was doing. Who just up and left their life because some stranger told them information that might or might not be true?

Levi made his way back to his apartment to pack. Winester said he had a few things to take care of before they could begin their journey, giving him about two days to prepare before they left. Levi paced around his small apartment, debating on what to bring.

There really wasn't a checklist of "things to bring when you are about to embark on a journey to a magical kingdom," and he had no idea how long he would be gone. Would the weather be warmer or colder, dryer or wetter? Did he want to take books or pictures with him?

The feelings of panic had started boiling back up in him when a knock at the door startled him out of his trance.

Chapter 11

Kolas

Aura woke up groggily as the first rays of the sun glittered on her eyelids. She hadn't slept very well, waking at every noise the forest made. She'd had no idea how loud it really was outside, always envisioning nature as a quiet, calming place. After just one night of sleeping under the stars she would have given anything for the silence of the castle she had always taken for granted.

She looked around and was startled to find she was all alone. A thick fog lay upon the clearing. For a moment, she wondered if she was dreaming, if the noises and everything else were just a figment of her imagination.

Through the mist, a huge figure appeared. It looked like equal parts man and…what? Lion? But it also had…what was that? Wings? Aura tried to scream, but lost her voice amidst her fears. Instead, her fight-or-flight instincts took over and she began fleeing backward as quickly as her hands and feet would take her.

"Stop," a booming voice said.

Aura froze, terror pumping through her veins. She looked up just in time to see the figure separate from its lower half. It took her a second to realize that the creature was actually two separate beings. A man and a griffin— part lion, part eagle—and probably the largest of both— man and griffin—she had ever seen. Intrigue momentarily replaced her trepidation.

"Kolas." Another voice, much softer, came out of the fog, followed moments later by Resbuca. Aura watched as the two stepped toward each other and quickly embraced.

"My dear Resbuca. It has been entirely too long," Kolas said warmly.

The fog was slowly moving away from all of them, allowing Aura to finally make out Theirra and Milskar close to the road. They were clearly trying to convince the startled horses that the griffin would not hurt them. Aura understood their apprehension. She had only seen these creatures from far away, as they typically did not travel from their native lands in the north.

The beast was huge, nearly as tall as the horses, but weighing at least twice as much. Folded against its side were shimmering gold wings which lightly brushed the ground. Coupled with the massive man called Kolas, they made a menacing-looking team. Milskar always seemed so large and strong to Aura, but now she saw how quickly this person could overtake him. For the first time since they had left, she had a grasp of how dangerous this journey could truly be. She was so used to a constant level of protection, that now she felt very vulnerable without it.

On shaky legs, she stood up straight, trying to draw herself to her full height in a vain attempt at bravery. She stood in silence, though, knowing her cracking voice would give her away in an instant.

Resbuca led Kolas to a fallen tree and asked him to sit with her. "I appreciate so much you meeting us here. It has been so long since I have traveled to the other world. I am afraid I would become terribly lost without guidance."

"I owe you much more than guidance for all you have done for me. It is the least I can do. So what exactly do you need my services for?" Kolas asked.

"We need to find the heir of Vertrous." Her words sat there on the tree with them for a long time.

Kolas's mouth froze in a slight O. "Everyone knows that is a tall tale," he finally said. "There is no heir. Do you honestly think it could stay a secret for this long?"

"With the right person, a secret can be kept forever." She proceeded to re-tell the story again of Winester's involvement and eventual discovery of the boy.

"Do you know what this means?" Kolas asked.

Resbuca stayed silent, but the smile on her face coupled with the twinkle in her eyes said they were thinking the same thing. Aura looked from one to the other, unsure of what the exchange meant, but she was pretty sure it was going to spell trouble at some point for them all.

About twenty minutes later, with their camp broken down and all traces of their presence removed, the five set off down the trail. Aura stayed back a little and rode in a line with Milskar and Theirra, allowing Resbuca and Kolas to take the lead about a quarter mile ahead of them. The two had been quietly talking non-stop to each other since his arrival, though Aura was still unsure of what his involvement meant.

"So who is this person?" Aura asked the others.

"Obviously someone Resbuca knows," Milskar said, "but I have never seen him before in my life. I am assuming he is some kind of outlaw or something. I mean, do you see what he is riding?" All three looked up ahead as if they needed a reminder.

"What is wrong with that?" Aura asked, confused.

Theirra cut in before Milskar had a chance to answer. "They are illegal in most of the world."

"Illegal?"

"The Winged Beast Protection Act. A person cannot take them out of their natural habitat, which would be the Snow Mountains in Northern Omaner. Until it was discovered that captivity made them sterile, they were hunted and captured for riding animals. Almost the entire population died out. Now it is illegal to do anything with them. That man could be killed if he was caught with that griffin. Crimes in that part of the world are not taken lightly."

They rode on in silence for the rest of their journey, each coming up with their own ideas about the outlaw stranger in their minds.

Resbuca finally announced they had gone far enough that day and would break camp for the night. Aura used the opportunity to have a moment alone with her.

"Resbuca?" The woman did not look up from what she was doing. "Resbuca, who is this man? If he is going to be traveling with us, as I expect he will, I have a right to know who he is."

Aura stood up straight and met Resbuca's eyes as the woman looked up. Since they'd left on this journey, Aura felt what little power she had slipping away more and more and moving into the fingers of the sorceress.

"All right." Resbuca smiled. "He is here to ensure our safe passage and journey through the other world."

"I thought that is why you were here." Aura's anger suddenly flared up. "How many more people are you going to let in, to tell this 'secret' to? Before I know it, there's going to be an army going after this guy."

"No one else." Resbuca stopped what she was doing and proceeded to give her queen the answers she desired about the strange man.

Aura walked toward Theirra and Milskar, who were making food and setting up camp, respectively. Kolas had muttered something about hunting with Gilbert, his strangely named companion, and hadn't been seen for some time. The other two soon joined Aura as she sat on a large rock.

"What did you find out?" Milskar asked, rolling a reed in his hands.

"Well, you were right about him being an outlaw. His main source of income is dealing in stolen goods, but here is the kicker. He does not just trade between the Four Corners. He travels to the other world as well." Their stunned reactions mirrored hers from moments before. "Resbuca said it has been many years since she has traveled there and wants someone she can trust."

Theirra chuckled to herself. "And she decided on a criminal?"

"He knows his way around there better than anyone she knows. She said if we want to find someone, he is the person we want looking."

"And you trust her to be telling you the truth?" Theirra asked.

"Do we have any choice? Plus, why would she lie to me?"

They all looked at each other, wondering.

☙☙☙

The next morning, Resbuca informed them that they would reach the passage after a few hours' travel. Kolas would meet them there, having left camp before dawn, with clothes for them to change into.

"Clothes?" Aura asked confused, gesturing to her bag filled with them.

"They wear less…" Resbuca searched for the words. "…ornate items than you do. We need items that will help us blend in."

This thought had never crossed Aura's mind. For a moment, hundreds of other thoughts poured in. What else had she not prepared for? It was becoming too numerous to count the amount of times she felt this journey swell into an even more daunting task than the one she had originally thought it was going to be. She wondered if she should just turn her group around, tails between their legs, and head back to the safety of home, allowing fate to decide what to make of them all. It was in these moments of intense doubt where she felt the weight of her responsibilities crushing down upon her. Sometimes, it was all she could do to keep standing up, much less standing up for something.

Then she would think of Esotera.

Not only was she entrusted with a kingdom, but also with the care of its people. Some who had lived their whole lives on her father's and, now her, lands. Some who fled their own regions for the promise of safety and a better life in her kingdom. She could not let them down.

"Okay," she said, shaking some of the fear off of her. "Clothes. What else? What else must we do to blend into this world?"

"The animals must be left behind. The griffin, for obvious reasons, but also the horses. We would possibly be putting them and ourselves in danger if we got caught. Their presence alone would add a level of scrutiny that we do not need."

"How will we travel without them?" Theirra asked with mild panic in her eyes.

"Kolas said we do not have to travel far. I know you do not trust him," Resbuca said, turning to Aura. "But he is our only hope in getting in and out of there alive, and with what we need."

"You talk of all this danger, but who would the culprit be? Who would want to hurt us?" Aura asked.

"Not us," Milskar said. "You."

They all looked away from her, as if just locking eyes would transfer something to them. She forced the fearful thoughts down with a heavy hand.

"You are royalty, my queen, and there will be those out there who will want to hurt you simply for that fact," Milskar said. "There are evil people out there who will commit heinous acts for the simple reasons of wealth and notoriety. I do not want terrible things to happen to you, so that is why we must stick together and do what those who know more than us tell us to do. Understand?"

"Yes."

"Good, then we should get moving," Resbuca said, "Kolas will be waiting for us."

Chapter 12

Crossing Over

They fell in line, once again, in tense silence. Aura was now fully aware that the mission was out of her control and how much danger she was putting them all in. She had never had regrets before in her life, but this made up for it. Part of her wished she had stayed behind, listened to Theirra, but now that she was here she had better make the most of it. Or, at the least, not hold the rest of them back.

Sooner than she had expected, Kolas became visible in the distance. As they got closer she saw that he had already changed into what she assumed was the clothes meant for them to blend in. He looked strange, wearing blue pants and a white shirt, replacing the black dragon skins he was previously wearing. They all dismounted and walked toward him.

"My friends," he said with open arms. "Come, come. Let me show you the things I have brought for you."

He led them toward a pile of items and began handing them out among the four. They looked at the clothes in their hands, then at each other, with perplexed expressions on their faces. Aura wasn't even completely sure how to put hers on but, after a few minutes of fumbling and some instructions from Kolas, they were all wearing the new items. Even if they didn't feel like it, at least they would look like they belonged in the other world. Aura helped Theirra untack the horses and turn them loose while Milskar spoke with Kolas and Resbuca.

"Are you still sure about this?" Theirra whispered to Aura, after releasing the last horse and watching it chase after the others.

"We cannot turn back now," Aura said in a matter-of-fact tone.

"We can always turn back. *You* can always turn back." Theirra grabbed her arm, stopping Aura in her tracks. "We can go on without you. It is just too dangerous. Esotera cannot lose another ruler."

"I know, and I have thought a lot about this. But I stand by my decision. I need to do this. For Esotera, my father, and myself. I know what I am doing." Aura figured the more she said it, the better her chances of believing it. She smiled weakly and moved back toward the other three. "All right," she announced. "I am ready. Kolas, tell us everything we need to know so we can get going."

"You may not talk to anyone, I mean a single person. Even to each other while we are there. I will do all the communicating if we run into any people. Do not make eye contact with others. Just keep your heads down and your mouths shut. We do not need any added attention drawn to you. We will hide under the pretense that you are all foreigners who do not speak the language, which is basically true. You must trust me and cannot second-guess me. It will compromise not only our mission but also, potentially, our safety. No one will be expecting you, queen, and we do not want to give anyone any reason to think otherwise. I hope that we do not come across anyone, but if we do and you do not think you can abide by these parameters, speak up now and stay behind. There is no room for negotiation. Is this understood?"

He looked at each person individually, not moving his gaze until they each told him yes.

"How do we get through exactly?" Milskar asked, eyes scanning the horizon.

"There are portals scattered throughout both our worlds, but only certain ones are open at particular times. This one here is the closest to your kingdom and opens twice a day for five minutes, right after sunrise and right before sunset."

They all looked toward the sky, the sun moving closer to the horizon.

"Now," Kolas continued, "we must move quickly. We need to not spend too much time there so we can make it back in time for the morning opening."

Milskar went first, followed by Theirra, then Resbuca. Aura was about to move after them when Kolas's hand firmly gripped the back of her arm. It was a trap! She momentarily panicked, cursing herself for being so foolish, for being so trusting of this stranger, but then his grip softened and she realized he pulled her back simply to tell her something. She cursed herself for letting fear be her default response to everything.

"My queen. You more than anyone else are my priority. Your safe return is my mission above all else. Do you understand?" She nodded. "You must always do as I say and heed my warnings, even if it puts others in danger. You may have to sacrifice your friends in order to save your own life. I will do all I can to ensure we all make it back, but you *must* make it back. Do you fully understand?"

"Yes," she said, her voice steadier than it had been in her entire life.

He took her hand and they moved forward together, the sun slipping into darkness seconds after they passed through.

Chapter 13

Visitor

Levi looked through the peephole. Standing there was a woman about his age and height with dark, short hair. While she was too far away to tell, he knew that freckles splattered her face. He groaned and opened the door.

"Hey, cuz." She maneuvered past him, somehow ducking under his arm placed on the doorjamb in a wasted attempt to keep her out.

"Em, look, now is really not a good time," he said as he tried to usher her back out the door.

Emily Roberts was his uncle's youngest of four daughters, and because of his disappointment in not having any boys, he decided to raise her as one. Emily and Levi, separated in age by mere months, grew up together and managed—unlike so many families tend to do—to stay incredibly close. She was the closest thing to a sister—or brother depending on how you wanted to look at it—that Levi ever had. He loved her dearly.

"So," she said, flopping down on the couch and putting her feet on the coffee table with a loud thud. "What's this I hear about you running away? A little late for rebellion, don't you think?"

"How did you know I was leaving? I just decided myself." He closed the door, determining it was futile trying to herd her out.

"Oh, come off it. You know our dads are like fourteen-year-old girls when it comes to gossip. Your parents called after you left and I overheard enough of the conversation to know to get myself right over here. So come on, spill. I need details."

"There are no details. I decided to follow a lead on my birth parents, end of story."

"Bull."

She stared at him hard and he had to look away. He always hated how easily she could see through him. The worst part, though, was how desperately he really wanted to tell her. When Winester first visited him and gave him all that crazy information and stories, she was the person he really wanted to discuss it with, but what would she say? Okay, he knew. She would call him insane. Probably use a choice selection of her favorite curse words. She would forbid him from going and, maybe even worse, tell his parents.

It wasn't exactly that Emily would want to get him in trouble—far from it, actually. She would just be worried about him and would not want to see him hurt or in danger.

"Oh, cut out the crap, Levi. I can see your little internal struggle going on. I know you don't want to tell me the truth, which probably means it's bad. Am I right?" He didn't meet her gaze. "Okay, so it's bad. I doubt in the legal sense because you don't strike me as the bank-robbing type. Plus, if you were going to rob a bank I would hope you would know better than to leave me be-hind."

Levi couldn't help but laugh a little as he sat down on the couch next to her. "No banks," he said.

"No, of course not. What then? A baby mama?" They both burst into laughter at the same time. "Okay, okay, no love child. Are you in some kind of other trouble? Money trouble?"

She looked at him with such tender seriousness in her eyes, it almost brought him to tears. "Nothing like that," he said in a small voice.

"Because, well, I don't have a lot of money, but if you need it, I swear I won't tell anyone."

He hugged her close, breaking off any more words she might have spoken. She hugged him back tightly.

"Thank you, Emily, really," he said. "But this whole—this whole thing is me and just something I need to do. I hope you can understand."

"I do." They sat in silence, staring at the wall for some time before she spoke again. "So when do we leave?"

The words were pushing against his teeth so fiercely it made his mouth hurt, but he fought against the pain. He had to figure out a way to get her to leave, and quickly. He was positive moments before that the knock on the door was Winester coming back to take him away. It was only a matter of time before the man returned.

"Look—" Levi started but she cut him off.

"Don't give me any of that 'I need to do this on my own' crap. You've never done anything on your own."

She had a point there. He began to speak again, some other lame attempt to convince her, but another knock at the door interrupted him. His heart stopped and then flew into double time. Levi looked in terror toward the door then at Emily. He saw the reflection of his fear in her eyes and he wished he could have undone everything.

His hand was suddenly on the knob, though he didn't even remember standing and walking toward it. Even though she didn't make a sound, he could tell Emily had gotten up and was right behind him. He opened the door and was immediately confused.

The strangest hodge-podge of people stood in front of him. There were two huge men, one dressed in denim jeans and a cowboy-like button up shirt, the other in pants—a terrible green color—paired with a shirt in such a shocking blue Levi's eyes kept drifting to it. The three women didn't look much better. The oldest woman had a patchwork dress on and the two who looked around his age were in bright, patterned smock-like shirts and neon green leggings. They each looked equal parts homeless and cult recruiters.

"Mr. Roberts? Heir of Lord Vertrous?" the one man said in a husky accent.

The other members of the group looked shifty and nervous, constantly looking over their shoulders.

"Um, yes?"

It sounded more like a question back than the answer the man was looking for. Levi shifted slightly and the group took the gesture as an invitation to come inside. He momentarily tried to stop them but, seeing the two men up close, moved farther away.

Emily came and stood slightly in front of him, confrontation written all over her face. At the root of it all, Levi was glad she was there with him. He could always count on her to be in his corner, helping to fight his battles, even if she had no idea what the conflict was about.

"Whatever problem you have with my cousin here," she said fiercely, "you have with me too."

The strangers looked at one another as if they were

unsure of what to make of her. The redheaded girl stepped forward, eyes locked with Levi's. The others made a grab for her, but she shook them off. It wasn't until that moment that he realized they had formed a kind of protective circle around her.

"Mr. Roberts?" Her tentative voice sounded like silver. "We do not have much time, but it is imperative that you come with us. We will answer your questions as best we can when we get to our destination."

"I've become a very popular person these last few days it seems. First this crazy man named Winester—"

He broke off at the reaction the name had on the group.

Shock and panic touched their faces in equal measures. The redhead turned to the man in green pants.

He nodded solemnly back at her. "We have no time," the man said.

"What about the girl?" the other man asked.

They all turned their attention back to Emily. Levi placed himself protectively between her and the group.

"Wherever you take him, I'm going too," Emily insisted.

Levi wished he could have grabbed the words out of the air and forced her to put them back in her mouth.

"Fine," the old woman said, "but I suggest we go a slightly different route than the one we took to come to here, to avoid certain—" She paused. "—obstacles."

"Agreed," the redheaded girl said.

He and Emily were dragged out of his apartment by the group before he even knew what was happening. Levi was barely able to shut and lock the door behind them before they made their way out of his building.

The two men held the cousins' arms firmly but without violence. Still, Emily's scared eyes kept trying to meet Levi's.

She wanted to know what was going on, but was too frightened to ask him. What if it was some information these people wanted? She wasn't sure yet if these people were good or not, but she certainly had a bad feeling about them.

They ran as a huddled group down sidewalks and alleys for what seemed like miles. Levi's lung ached, but they never slowed. They seemed to double back slightly and then headed toward a vast parking lot behind an abandoned grocery store blocks from Levi's apartment. In the months he'd lived in this area, he had never gone back here—some tug in his chest telling him to turn back each time, almost like a warning. Now he felt it even stronger, as if there was an invisible force keeping him away.

He wanted to speak up, to tell them all he thought it was a bad idea. One look at Emily's face told him she felt it as well. The words were about to leave his lips when a huge, brightly colored bird began making circles around them before landing on an old shopping cart.

"Busu," the older woman whispered. "That is Winester's bird." Her voice rose in panic. "He must be close. We have to hurry."

They all began to run toward the woods behind the crumbling building as the grips on Levi and Emily were tightened.

"My name is Queen Aura of Esotera," the redhead gasped as they ran.

Her words knocked the wind out of Levi and he came to a sudden stop, breaking free of the hand that was holding him. The rest came to a stop as well.

"Queen? I—I thought it was a king?" He thought for a moment. "King Aldric."

"My father. He died," she said solemnly. "My kingdom is in danger and you are the only one who can save it."

"I know, because of my great-great to the hundredth degree grandfather," Levi said sarcastically.

Emily's eyes flew back and forth between him and Aura.

"Yes, well, there are those that want to see my kingdom fail. Winester is one of them. He wants to use you to get in power."

"And why should I believe you over him?"

"You will just have to trust me," she said firmly.

He wanted to, but so much information was strumming in his head. He wasn't sure what the truth was anymore.

"Please. We only have a precious few minutes to get you back to our world before the portal closes behind us. We must get there before Winester finds us."

In the distance, they heard a bird call. The sound snapped Levi out of his trance and he grabbed Emily's hand. "Let's go," he said.

She tightened her hand and he squeezed it back as they started sprinting through the trees again.

They reached a clearing and the group stopped, causing Levi and Emily to almost crash into them.

The older woman explained that this was the portal area. "You first, my queen," one of the men said to Aura.

Levi could tell she wanted to protest, but some look passed between them, so she stepped forward and disappeared without another word. Next, the man reached for Levi. He was still holding Emily's hand and they were both thrust forward. They stumbled and fell on the ground, landing at Aura's feet. The others quickly followed and gazed over at a formation of light just cresting the tip of the horizon.

"Where is Kolas?" Aura asked.

Levi realized that they were, in fact, missing one of the men from the group.

"He thought he heard someone coming and wanted to make sure Winester did not get in," the other man said.

"He better hurry! We need him through and the portal to close right after—somehow," Aura said, exasperated.

Just at that moment, the man called Kolas burst through, panting.

"What happened?" They all asked.

"It was Winester. I tried fighting him off and was doing a good job, but then I noticed the portal glowing, like it does before it closes. I shoved him and ran for it. Apparently, just in time, too. The thing must have closed the second I got through or he would have been able to follow me. I was not able to push him far and he was on his feet chasing after me seconds later."

"But the sun has not even completely risen yet. How could it have closed?" Aura asked.

"That might have been my fault," Levi said tentatively. "I sort of...well, things sometimes happen when I think of something. I was just hoping for the portal to close when he came through it."

He looked sheepishly at their expressions, not quite able to place them. Suddenly, Aura threw her arms around him and kissed his cheek. He instantly turned bright red.

"You better watch yourself, my queen," the older woman said. "He may keep trying to save the day so that happens again."

Chapter 14

Return

"We must keep moving," Kolas said. "I think we are safe, but I would feel better putting a little more distance behind us."

The group nodded and began walking in the opposite direction they had just come from. Emily and Levi were able to catch up to one another again, once the hold on them was released.

"Levi, what the hell is going on?" Emily whispered.

Even with her voice as low as it was, he could still hear the fear laced in it. He was about to say something when a scream cut through the air. It took him a moment to realize the sound came from Emily. He looked over his shoulder and muffled his own scream. Before them stood a huge golden beast with scaled tree-trunk legs, wings, and a gigantic lion-shaped head. Its huge claws dug deep fissures in the dirt.

"Gilbert!"

The beast turned and practically ran to Kolas, who stroked its massive head. Several horses came out of the same area moments later and joined the group. Emily was shaking now next to him. She'd had enough.

"What's going on?" she yelled.

Everyone, animals included, turned to look at her.

Aura finally stepped forward. "I am sorry if we frightened you. We were in such a hurry to leave, I did not have the time to properly explain to you why we are here. As I said before, my name is Aura, queen of this land called Esotera," she said with her arms outstretched, gesturing at everything around them. "This here is Theirra, Resbuca, Milskar, and Kolas," she said pointing to each person as she said his or her corresponding name.

"And what does this have to do with us?"

"Well, it has to do with Mr. Roberts here, actually. No disrespect, but we were only coming for him. We brought you out of necessity. Frankly, you put us in a difficult position."

"Difficult position," Emily practically screeched. Levi took a step toward her, knowing how intense her explosions could be. "I put *you* in a difficult position?"

"Yes," Aura said, not backing down from her, "and if you would like, I can finish telling you exactly why we are all here."

Emily crossed her arms, but didn't say another word.

Aura proceeded to tell her a similar story to the one Winester had told Levi only days before. Mouth wide open as she listened, Emily was in complete rapture by the story and stole occasional glances at Levi. He tried to make his face as vacant and expressionless as possible to be strong for her. He had thought that the more times he heard the story, the easier it would get, but the opposite was true. If anything, being here—wherever here actually was—and with these people was making his anxieties increase.

The truth of what this all meant was surrounding him and beginning to settle in.

They sat in silence for a long time before Emily spoke.

"I—" was all she managed to say.

"We have a long way to travel," Milskar informed them. "We should start moving to put as much distance between us and the portal by nightfall."

"Levi, you shall ride with me," Aura said, "and you…I am sorry, what is your name?"

"Emily."

"Emily." Aura brightened as if this information had solidified the fact they were going to become great friends. "You shall ride with Milskar. He will take good care of you," she quickly added, after seeing the look on Emily's face.

Levi knew her apprehension didn't stem from the fact that Milskar looked about seven feet tall, but that his massive black horse looked about ten.

When they were younger, maybe around nine years old, Levi and Emily's parents decided to go to a dude ranch for a week with the entire family. The two of them were so excited, convinced it would be like the Wild West movies they had seen, but in all reality they just rode around hoping to glimpse one of the two cows housed on the "ranch." The boredom made the two bicker the entire time until, finally, on the last day after a particularly brilliant shouting match, Levi wished something bad, like Emily's horse running away, would happen. Sure enough, it spooked at something, bolted, and ran back to the barn. He felt terrible and knew to this day that it was his fault she was still terrified of horses. He never had the guts to admit to her what he had done. It was one of his secrets, one that he knew he would take with him to the grave.

"We can walk," Levi suggested, wanting to do this small bit of penance.

"Don't be silly." Aura shrugged his comment off. "It will be much faster this way."

Before he was able to protest, Aura had grabbed Emily's arm and, with Milskar's help, pushed her on top of his horse. Aura then mounted her own horse and reached her hand out for Levi's. He was barely able to wrap his arms around her waist before they were galloping after the others. Emily's screams became a muffled noise when mixed with the wind swooshing around his ears.

The forest around them had turned into an inky black by the time they stopped. The group dismounted and left Levi and Emily just outside the clearing as the others began working to quickly set up camp. It took him a second to get his bearings, with how dark it was.

"You okay?" he asked Emily, feeling her stiffen slightly as he brushed against her arm.

"Not particularly," she responded tersely.

"Come on, Em, I tried to get you to stay."

"Don't even go there, Levi. Or should I call you *Mr. Roberts*?" Her tone was sharp and, even though he couldn't see her eyes, he knew anger boiled in them.

"I'm really sorry, Emily. I really am. I wanted to tell you the second I found out. You have no idea how much I wanted to tell you, but I was scared. I thought I was going crazy."

Emily harrumphed at him.

"I just didn't know what all this would mean, and I didn't want to put you in any danger by telling you."

"Levi, you are my best friend." Her voice softened and she touched his arm. "You know you can tell me anything."

"I'm terrified," he confessed, "and really glad you are here."

"What are we going to do? How are we going to get out of here?" She looked around wearily as if someone might over-hear the conversation.

"Do?"

"Levi, we can't stay here. Our parents are going to start worrying when they don't hear from us for a few days. Not to mention the fact that we don't belong here, wherever this freak show—"

A branch close to them snapped, stopping her mid-sentence. Theirra stepped out between two trees, a small, lit torch in her hands. Both Levi and Emily looked away, embarrassed and hoping she hadn't heard any of their conversation.

"Camp is ready," she told them, motioning for them to follow her. "Oh, and I think in the future," she added, turning back, "addressing us as the queen and her court would be a bit more respectful than *freak show*."

She smiled weakly. Levi was glad the darkness was able to hide the deep blush forming on his chest and face. Emily groaned softly and moved to follow her.

The camp glowed and danced in front of them. The fire was so bright but in such an odd way, almost like it sparkled at the edges. There was no smoke rising from it, but Levi could feel its warmth, even though he knew he was too far away from it to actually feel anything.

The fire became the center that the group loosely arranged themselves around. Theirra had sat down next to Kolas, already engaged in deep conversation, when Emily and Levi stepped into the circle.

Aura looked up and smiled at them. "Emily, Levi, are you hungry? Kolas was kind enough to catch and cook us some food. Please help yourselves." She gestured to a smaller fire Levi hadn't noticed before with something large straddling it. He got up and walked toward the appetizing smell.

"What is it?" Emily asked softly beside him.

"Some kind of animal I think."

"No animal I've ever seen."

Levi reached forward and pulled a small bit of meat from what he figured was the middle of it.

Emily snatched his hand. "What are you doing?"

"What?"

"Who knows what that is or what it will do to you? Do you really trust them? What if...I don't know...it does something to you?" Emily's voice was steadily rising into a mild panic.

"From what I've gathered so far," Levi said, "they seem to want to keep me around. I kinda doubt they would poison me," he said and popped the piece into his mouth.

"What does it taste like?"

"Chicken," he said.

She punched him lightly on the arm. He ate several more bites, but Emily was still too wary to try it. Her stomach had other ideas, though. It growled painfully. It had been almost a full day since she had eaten and the food smelled too good. She stood closer, began pulling large clumps of meat off, and placing the hot flesh in her mouth. She hadn't realized Levi had stopped and was staring at her until a burp paused her bingeing.

"Well, at least we will know who will croak first if the food really is tainted," Levi said, smiling at her.

"Oh shut up." She turned and made her way back to the circle, ignoring the faint laughter behind her.

With his belly now full, Levi realized how physically and emotionally drained he was. Between the stresses of the last few days and the miles they ran and rode, he was exhausted. He looked over at Emily, who was trying to pay attention to a conversation Milskar was having with her, but her eyes kept drooping then snapping open again.

Finally, what little adrenaline the group had left, after escaping Winester, had dissipated, and they all became silent. After a few moments, Kolas started snoring with the rest of them falling asleep soon thereafter.

Levi briefly stirred when Resbuca sat up, said something quietly, and lay back down. He swore it looked like the fire became dimmer, yet somehow warmer. The thought quickly passed through his mind as he fell back asleep.

ᘓᘓᘓ

Levi groaned and peeled his eyes open as the sunlight tugged at him. He rolled over and accidentally kicked Emily, who responded with a protesting grunt. He tapped her again, on purpose this time, and she suddenly sat straight up, her gaze flying in all directions. Once she realized it was him who woke her, she lay back down with a grumble and went back to sleep. Levi smiled, stood up, and began making his way to the edge of camp.

Aura was standing there, looking off into the distance, arms wrapped loosely over her waist. There was a silent chill to the air, the ground still damp with dew. She glanced sideways when Levi reached her but made no further movement.

"How much farther do we have to go?" he asked her.

"About another two days' journey. More, if this rain keeps up."

"Rain?" Levi looked up, but didn't see a single cloud, much less any heavy black ones. She turned away without speaking, went back to the campsite, and began to wake the others.

It was all really starting to annoy him. He was getting just enough information to keep him interested and willing to follow, but without really telling him anything. Each time he started to bring it up, something more important, like running for their lives, got in the way.

About ten minutes after their ride started, there was a large crack of lightning and the rain began dumping out of the sky. Resbuca shouted out some things over the downpour and suddenly the rain seemed to be drizzling on them, instead of the volumes that were hitting them moments before.

"I can only hold off so much for so long," Resbuca yelled over the noise.

It sounded almost as if the rain was hitting a tarp above their heads before bouncing off.

"Over here," Milskar called back, turning his horse off the path, and began taking them deeper into the woods.

Levi could see how tightly Emily was gripping him as they rode ahead. They finally came upon a cave with a giant mouth set into the side of a rocky mountain base. There was room for all of them, including the horses, and they soon settled in to wait out the storm, Gilbert happily lying out in the rain.

Emily, who could get a chill on a warm summer day, was shivering violently from being cold and wet. Milskar had thrown a huge arm around her trying to warm her up. Her desire for the heat had removed all the previous fear she had and she moved even closer against him.

Aura was trying hard to fight the chill that was on the verge of sending her into convulsions. She turned to Resbuca and asked her, through clattering teeth, to light a fire. Slowly its warmth began to fill the space and Aura was able to relax. She started going through her bag, pulling out clothing, and handing it to the members of the group.

"I think it is safe now for us to change," she said, giving one final look of disdain at the things she was wearing. "Emily, Levi, I do not have an extra change of clothes for you both, but I assure you once we get back to the kingdom I will have items for you there."

The group quickly changed back to their normal garb and Levi was momentarily rendered awestruck by how beautiful Aura looked in her royal dress. They looked almost medieval in their clothing, but there was an expensiveness to her dress that made it just enough different that he could not really describe it fully. Kolas's outfit was the strangest of all, almost looking like dyed alligator skin from head to toe, but no one else seemed to pay his clothing any attention.

"The rain is coming from the north," Kolas said, standing at the mouth of the giant cave, "which means it will be a cold rain, but should not last more than a few hours. It is safer for us to stay here. We are still far enough ahead of Winester that there is no point in risking freezing to death just to put a little more distance between us."

"In that case," Levi said, "I have some questions I need answers to. This seems the perfect time. How did you find me?"

Several members of the group shifted their weight and stole glances at each other. Milskar stood so suddenly that Emily almost fell into the spot he left.

Aura cleared her throat and began. "Well, it certainly was not easy," she said, looking briefly at Milskar, who nodded back at her. "Luckily, Winester left a pretty good trail we were able to follow. Everything was progressing smoothly. We had crossed over and had made it almost all the way to your building, but then we hit a—a snag."

"What kind of snag?" Levi asked.

"Well you see, normally our worlds do not mix. More of our inhabitants are aware you all exist than the other way around, but there are a few in your world who know about us. Luckily, the skepticism spell keeps most of you from believing."

"Skepticism spell?" Emily asked.

"When The Division happened, the split between your world and ours, your ruler, Lady Amadea, was so upset she had a spell placed on all her people that would make them not only forget about the other world, but also to not believe anyone who said otherwise. I believe you have clinical terms for such people and they are typically disregarded, but really they are genetic descendants of those who, for some reason, were immune to the spell."

"I felt something when we were running to the trees," Levi interrupted. "Was that part of the spell?"

"Powerful protections were placed by various witches and wizards," Resbuca interjected, "but not because of some order, mainly to keep traders from dealing in areas that were off limits to them. Spells were cast to keep most people away so those who controlled those areas could deal without harassment or worry from competition."

"These people became sort of liaisons between both worlds," Aura continued. "Trading goods and information desired by both sides. We came across one such person here as soon as we passed through,"

"He somehow recognized Queen Aura, or at least was alerted to something amiss with such a large party traveling through," Milskar said. "This obviously created considerable trouble for us."

"So what did you do?" Levi asked.

"Measures had to be taken to protect her," Kolas said.

"You killed him?" Emily asked with eyes wide in horror.

"She had to be protected," was all he said.

Silence fell over them. Levi remembered when the group arrived at his door, eyes shifting, looking as if they were expecting someone to run up on them. The protective way they stood in a circle around Aura. A slight sickening feeling began spreading in his stomach.

Chapter 15

Forces

Several days before when Winester left Levi's apartment, he was finding it hard not to get impatient with the boy. He had waited many years for the opportunity to present itself and he didn't want to wait any longer. Pretty soon he was just going to have to kidnap Levi and take him to Esotera himself. Obviously having the boy decide to go on his own would be easier for all parties, but any way necessary Winester would get Levi there.

Walking away, he pinched the bridge of his nose. He felt like he was getting a little too old for all this. Technically, he had lost track of how old he actually was, but he knew he was too long in his life to have to be fighting for his placement in it all the time.

Levi could change all of that. The kid was impressionable. The fact that he so readily believed the things Winester had said solidified that, and Winester was hoping to use this naiveté to his advantage. He needed to somehow convince the boy to turn his authority over to him. Then Winester would finally have the rightful place of power he'd deserved to have so many years ago.

He'd enjoyed many years of splendor when he was Lord Vertrous's confidant. He had all the material possessions he wanted and was able to get his way in most situations. His rise was swift, but completely justified in his eyes. Winester's powers had come in handy for the lord and had helped keep peace for many years. While Vertrous was an all-powerful ruler, there was still a dark underground of those who tried to oppose him. These people needed to be taken care of swiftly so none of their movements could progress, and that was where Winester stepped in. However, while he was off doing the lord's bidding, he was not around to protect Vertrous from himself.

It was on one of these trips when someone from the other world caught the attention of Vertrous. By the time Winester returned, the previous threat successfully extinguished, the unraveling of the worlds had already been set in motion. He tried desperately to mediate the situation, but was quickly pushed aside and driven away. He returned, hurt and dejected, to Resbuca, yet still held on to a small hope that he could take his place back on the top if he could somehow restore peace.

After The Division occurred, Lord Vertrous, completely ruined and demoralized by the hateful words Lady Amadea had said to him, sought Winester out one last time.

"My dear friend," Vertrous said in his deep, soft voice.

Somehow, his sad tone made Winester know that the end was near. He took a deep breath to prepare himself. "Yes, my lord."

"I want to thank you for all you have done for me throughout the years but, sadly, no amount of outside protection could keep me safe from myself. I have failed you, my people, and myself."

"No, my lord. This is something you can recover from. This is something that we can rebuild from. Let me help you. Let me help make our world whole again," Winester begged.

"As much as I like that idea, it is much too late for such grand dreams. The damage has been done and thus my time here is complete."

"No. No, my lord. There is still so much more for you to do, to accomplish. So many more things." Winester was trying to keep the pain out of his voice, but he had a feeling the attempts were unsuccessful.

"Winester, I need you to listen now. I have divided my lands up into four regions. Four great new leaders will rule the Four Corners. I have picked these men my-self and I trust in them the continued prosperity of my lands."

Hope boiled in Winester's chest. He knew the time he'd spent cultivating his relationship with Lord Vertrous would pay off. He wondered what area would be given to him. He preferred the lands in the west, but the north would be just as good.

His lord then proceeded to tell him how the lands would be divided up and who each new ruler would be. Winester was crestfallen. After all the things he had done for Vertrous and, in this moment of great change, Winester had been overlooked. He had stood by his lord for more years than he could remember and, in the mo-ment of truth, was passed over.

The rest of the conversation had become a blur to him. He found it difficult to hear Vertrous over the loud noises in his own head and the sound of blood pumping in his ears. Winester paid little attention to the thanks and promises of key roles in the future that were made to him. Soon the great lord walked away and was never heard from or seen again.

Winester was momentarily frozen by the vivid memory which floated through his head. It had been a very long time since he had thought of Vertrous, actively trying to forget him for so many years. After his departure, Winester tried to return to Resbuca and his old life, but he was not the same man anymore and did not fit into his old roles as snugly as he had in the past. Soon he left her for good, breaking both their hearts, and set out on his own. He had wandered for years and constantly stirred up trouble wherever he went. Finally, he settled for a time in Grustmiener and performed similar tasks for the king as he had done for Lord Vertrous. He found this gave him a level of power, having this great man owe him for the security Winester was able to give him.

This gave Winester an idea. Soon he moved on to the other three Corners and began performing similar tasks for those rulers as well. It did not take long, though, for him to create enemies, and soon two of the four worlds had banned him.

Decades after The Division happened, he found himself traveling on a wide road toward the center of Esotera. Dejected and still resentful of the position he was now in, Winester seriously considered ending it all and joining his lord in the After. Hope, however, began walking toward him over the horizon.

Winester had only seen King Aldric from afar, but even from his current distance, he recognized the man coming toward him. Anticipation fluttered in his stomach and promise rose up. Winester saw this as his opportunity, maybe not to regain his past glory, but to at least dispatch some of his pain and aggression. Any damage he could do to the king would be a bonus.

He slipped among the trees on the side of the road, hid his horse and pack, and transformed himself into a frail old man. The king acted just the way Winester envisioned and soon the curse was placed upon the doomed land surrounding him. It felt good to see this powerful man on his knees begging. Pleading with Winester for mercy. It felt even better to deny him.

Leaving the broken man behind him, Winester had again traveled to Grustmiener. There he found a place with the new king and, more importantly, the queen. For years, he lived there, feeling a sense of home for the first time since leaving Resbuca all those years ago. Though he was eventually forced to leave that place, as well, and was disappointed that the feelings could not last.

Winester moved deep into the forest outside of Omire and into the shadows that would hide him for the next twenty years. He would make appearances between the different kingdoms and the other world, but mainly he kept to himself, licking his wounds, and preparing for the future. He would need something, some catalyst to move him back on top. He thought of the curse he had placed and knew it alone would not fulfill his wishes. Of course, it would make him feel better to be there the moment Esotera fell but, even more than that, he wanted to be in a position to pick up the pieces when that happened. That was when his obsession began.

He began researching and tracking down the descendants of Lord Vertrous. It was a painful process, as it brought up many of his old memories and feelings of failure, but he knew he had to do this to regain his rightful place in history.

After years of searching and numerous dead-ends, he finally found a viable lead. He came across a man who remembered meeting a young couple who'd given their son up for adoption and then died in a car crash shortly after. There was something about the man's tale that interested Winester. The man found the couple strange, the husband especially. He spoke about how uneasy the man had made him, like the man's skin was made of electricity. Winester's hope glimmered on the surface of the story.

It had been many years since the boy had left the adoption system, but with Winester's powers of persuasion, he was able to gain access to the files and track him down. He studied Levi from afar for several weeks to learn about his patterns, in the hopes of it would help him to connect with the boy more quickly when he finally made contact. What he found, however, surprised him.

The boy was a loner. Kicked out of various prep and public schools, he'd moved out of his parent's house into an apartment several months prior and had a new job every few weeks. Winester was fairly confident he could have kidnapped the boy outright and gotten him away without anyone coming after them for some time. It was the perfect fallback plan, but first he would try to get the boy to come with him willingly.

After that first contact, Winester knew if he only pressed the boy a little harder, Levi would be at least curious enough to follow him, even if he did not believe the information outright. Winester reluctantly left him that last time to make sure they would have clear passage to the portal. He fought his desire to force the boy to follow him. He knew he would be able to coax the child with fanciful tails and promises of truths he could see the boy wanted. He was just about to return to him when Busu alerted him that something was amiss.

He ran as fast as he could to the apartment, quickly bypassing the lock, and found it completely empty. He took a picture off the wall and threw it, feeling a bit of his anger dissipate as the glass shattered on the floor. Again, he heard the great bird cry out and began running toward the sound. He chased Busu's calls down streets and through alleyways for what seemed like an eternity. He tried to ignore his aged legs and pounding heart. In the distance, lit by dim streetlights, he saw a large group of people running and knew it was them.

Winester did not recognize everyone in the group, but his heart was pained to see Resbuca with them. He was able to pick out Levi and, though he did not think it could be true, that it couldn't be him, as he got closer he saw Kolas was indeed with them.

The two had met about ten years prior. Kolas was a young man, maybe twenty-one at the time. For a reason never given to Winester, he had been banished from his home in Omaner, but the two began traveling together. Kolas was unbelievably skilled in stealth, and Winester often used him to travel between the two worlds, looking for, and in some cases stealing, goods. The two had made a considerable amount of money together, but just as quickly as Kolas appeared, he left. No explanation was given. One day Kolas simply never came back. The boy's change in heart had confused Winester.

Years later he found out the real reason Kolas had been on the run. Winester's only regret was that he wasn't able to catch the fugitive. King Theaus would have been indebted to him.

Seeing him suddenly standing right there threw Winester so off guard that he was unprepared for the clash that sprang up between them. The rest of the group had gone through the portal, but Kolas stayed behind, presumably to fight.

"I see what side you are now taking," Winester said with a sharp bite to his voice.

"Things are not always black and white," Kolas said.

"Apparently. I did not know this was an issue worth debating. I assumed the facts were pretty clear." Winester did not want to fight this man in front of him. "So we are done then it seems."

"It seems that is the issue in front of us."

Winester had removed his wand and Kolas his sword. The old allies had, in a matter of moments and the consequences of a lifetime of choices, become enemies. Strangely though, as soon as the fight broke out both men paused and looked at the glowing portal. They both glanced up at the sky—at the sun that was still very much in its place.

"Impossible," Winester said seconds before Kolas pushed him and ran for the portal, disappearing before Winester even knew what had happened.

Anger coursed through him. He paced in front of the portal, cursing softly under his breath. Busu came close to him, but feeling his terrible and potentially dangerous mood, swooped by him and landed on a light post, instead. He looked up at the sky and what he saw confused him. How could the portal have closed when the moon was still out?

The fact that he was going to have to spend another day in this terrible place angered him even more. He hated the other world and tried to travel here as little as possible. Winester had enough connections here that he could often get those people to gather any goods he needed and, typically, he could enter and leave from the same portal in a matter of minutes without having to spend much time here, passing well within the time frame in which the portal stayed open.

He moved slowly toward the area he had been staying in for the last few days. It wasn't supposed to happen this way. Levi was supposed to come back with him.

Through their travels to Esotera, Winester was going to tell him of all the injustices that kingdom had committed against the people of his world and, by the time they arrived, Levi would have been chomping at the bit to do Winester's bidding.

He had been looking forward to gaining Levi's trust and hoping that, by the end of the week at the latest, he would be the new ruler of Esotera. His dreams of ruining the kingdom of King Aldric, who had been handed down a kingdom that never belonged to him in the first place—the dream Winester had dedicated his life to—had almost come to fruition.

Now everything had changed. Queen Aura and her group of renegades had somehow gotten Levi to turn on everything Winester had been working for. He had to come up with a new plan and quickly. He ruled out trying to enter at one of the other portals. The journey would be long enough that he might as well just stay put and wait until morning. He also knew that with the half-day head start the group had, there was little chance in him catching up with them. He chided himself for not setting up a quicker form of transportation to get himself back to the kingdom, figuring he would have Levi with him and could use the several days' journey to convince the lad to do whatever he asked.

Winester wondered if he could possibly get in touch with those who owed him favors. If maybe they could circumvent the group and, somehow, get their hands on the boy. That way he could, at least, buy himself a little more time. That was what he would do. While the portals were closed to him, there were other methods of communication he could go through, hubs that connected the two worlds through hand-held devices. He found one such hub, thought for a second, and spoke the name and location of the person he needed. Crossing his fingers, he hoped the person would respond.

"Hello?"

"It is Winester."

On the other end, his voice was met with silence.

"Winester," she said at last.

"Lady Grustmiener, I am calling in my favor."

Chapter 16

Obstacles

Levi was exhausted. They had left the cave hours before and it was well into the night before they stopped to sleep. The rain lasted a little longer than expected and they had tried to make up some of the time they'd lost by riding a little longer. By the time Kolas felt they had gone far enough to warrant a bit of rest, Levi was barely able to keep his eyes open.

The group had been fairly quiet since leaving the cave. They all seemed deep in thought about the conversations that had occurred earlier in the day. Levi could tell Emily was a little on edge and she regretted her insistence on being included in this journey.

Several times, she turned around and looked back at the path they had just come from, almost as if she was debating if they had gone too far for her to turn around. There were a few moments where he feared she might take the reins out of Milskar's hands and gallop back to where they had come from in order to return home. Levi would have followed her in a heartbeat.

Now, though, all he could think about was sleep. He stumbled through the camp area like a zombie, followed closely by the rest of the group, who were just as groggy. Aura had sat down as soon as she got off her horse and had not moved in the ten minutes since. It took them almost twice as long to get camp set up with how slow everyone was moving, but finally they were all settled for the night, the eerie campfire twinkling in the middle of the group.

A snapping sound woke Levi with a jolt. He bolted upright and strained to listen. He wasn't able to see his surroundings clearly, as only the slightest amount of light was given off by the softly burning embers of the dying fire. The snap happened again and he felt the hairs on the back of his neck stand.

"Did anyone else hear that?" he whispered.

"Yes, shh," someone responded.

Levi began trembling. Here he was in a dark place in the middle of the night with a group of strangers, and now it sounded as though they were being hunted. As if they were being surrounded, snapping noises seemed to be coming from all around the clearing.

"Resbuca," someone said in an urgent tone.

"I am doing all I can," she responded in a strained voice.

It all happened so quickly. The sound of movement was all around them and Aura was terrified. This was it. This was the moment they had been preparing for and hoping would never happen, though it felt all wrong. They were expecting any type of ambush to occur when they were either close to the portal or in the other world. Instead, they were only a half-day's ride from the center of the kingdom, in woods that were protected by her guards. There should not be bands of outlaws here. The only danger they should be facing should be from

Winester, but there was no way he had caught up with them.

Aura's eyes were trying, to no avail, to adjust to the low light. The sounds, though! The sounds kept continuing until she felt dizzy. They seemed to be coming from everywhere. An army, she thought. It sounded like an army trampling the ground around them.

"Resbuca," she said again in a panicked voice.

"Quiet."

She felt Resbuca move beside her and felt another body saddle to her other side. Kolas breathed heavily, his own panic making him lose his breath. She felt the other bodies close in on her as well in a reassuring protective manner. As much as she wanted them to run and save themselves, she was embarrassed to admit she needed this crush around her to keep her from screaming.

The sounds were now coming faster and closer. Aura took a deep breath and prepared herself for whatever onslaught was to come. She didn't even have time to react when the bag was placed over her head. A second later, she felt a sharp pain coupled with a loud crack and everything went to black.

⌒⌒⌒

"Ugh," Aura groaned.

Her head hurt terribly. She opened her eyes but, for some reason, could not see anything. Had she gone blind? She thought her eyes were open, but why did darkness still surround her? Aura tried to shift but felt a strong restraint on her wrists and chest. She fought hard against the rising panic and tried to replay the last moments she remembered. She was confused even further when she realized that they were all jumbled together.

"Hello?" she was finally able to croak out.

"My queen? Oh, thank goodness," Theirra responded. She sounded so far away, though. Where were they?

"I think I may have been blinded," Aura confessed.

"Do not worry," Resbuca said. "I will get us free in a moment."

Aura felt the ropes. Yes, she could now tell there were ropes binding her. They tightened for a split second and then released. She blinked hard against the light as, just as suddenly, the darkness was ripped off of her. She felt foolish once she realized it was just a dark cloth that had been over her face the whole time.

"Oh my God," Emily yelled. "Where is Levi?"

Aura stood quickly and almost fell back down when the rush of blood hit her head. Little black speckles came into view, but were quickly extinguished. Her gaze flew around the group, taking a headcount. Resbuca, Theirra, Kolas, Milskar, and Emily. No Levi anywhere. "Where is he?" she asked Resbuca.

"I am not sure, but someone must have been following us and waiting until we had all fallen asleep before trying to take him."

"Could it have been Winester?" Theirra asked.

"I do not think he could have caught up to us that fast," Kolas said, "but I do believe that he had a strong hand in this."

"We will find him," Milskar said to Emily, trying to reassure her.

She shook him off. "You better," she said coldly.

Aura started absently, rubbing her head. She felt a large lump on the back of it starting to swell. The hope she had been feeling the last few days was slowly deflating, leaving her with a hollowness in the pit of her stomach. She had gotten too close to making everything right, to correcting the wrongs surrounding her father and king-

dom for so many years, to lose it all to a band of renegades.

"What do we do now?" she asked the group.

"Go back to the kingdom," Milskar said. "Regroup.
Send out search parties and teams to figure out who took
Mr. Roberts and where they took him. Then we get a
group, the whole army if we need to, and go after him.
We get him back."

The plan seemed too easy and she feared its failure
would lay in its simplicity, but it was the best anyone
could come up with and, thus, had to be followed until
something better could be thought of. She was so angry
that someone could just swoop into their midst and steal
something that was so important to her, to their future.

In the moments after gaining their freedom, the
group walked around the parametcr of the clearing, trying
to find some sort of trail the kidnappers had left. There
was barely a stick out of place. Resbuca was quiet the
whole time and Aura knew she was blaming herself for
what had happened. It was her job to secure the area
where they were staying with various spells and incantations to protect them from intruders—and also to alert
them of their enemy's arrival. She had failed on both
fronts. They all gave Resbuca her distance, knowing that
nothing they could say could actually help, and also secretly believing it was her fault.

Emily hung back, deep in thought and worry, kicking
rocks in her path. At least when Levi was around, she
didn't feel so alone in this strange place. Now, she felt
tears pressing against the back of her eyes all the time.
She desperately wanted to just call her father and have
him pick her up. Why did she always rush into things
without thinking? Why did she always have to be so hot-
headed that she would foolishly stand up and refuse to let

Levi go with these people alone when she had no idea about the situation? Emily made a silent promise to herself to never let her emotions guide her actions again. She just hoped she would be able to keep it.

They walked most of the way back on foot, instead of riding the horses. Emily knew none of them wanted to say it, but they all figured if they went on foot it would be much slower and, if somehow Levi were able to get away, he could then find them all. Milskar hung back from the pace with her and, while they did not speak, she was very glad for the company.

"I think this is where I shall leave you all," Kolas announced suddenly. "My queen, it has been an honor to assist you. I am terribly sorry that my presence did not lead to a better outcome for you."

"Please do not feel like you need to leave us prematurely," Aura said, grasping his hands.

"Yes, please do stay," Theirra said and then instantly reddened and turned her face away. It seemed she had become quite smitten with the strange traveler.

"The kingdom is not really a welcoming place for people in my… position," he said guardedly.

"What you have done for us over the last several days far outweighs any grievances Esotera may have had against you. I ask you to come as a guest and be treated as such for as long as you wish to stay in our company."

Kolas smiled and nodded. Resbuca moved closer to him and squeezed his hand, obviously happy with how the events of the last few weeks had played out. Theirra looked pleased as well but took great care to hide any further expression of emotions from the rest of the group.

The woods began to thin out and the road became a little more packed down. They went around two more bends and suddenly the whole kingdom seemed to spring up all around them. High walls now flanked their left and

Emily began to hear the noises that accompanied a bustling city. Her eyes widened when the castle appeared high on a hill in the distance. She exhaled. "Wow."

"It still does that to me each and every time," Theirra said with a smile.

Emily could tell the group was anxious to get home, no matter how poorly the expedition had ended up. As they passed through what she assumed was the outer gates, a group of small children—barefoot and hair flying behind them—came running up to greet them. They bowed to Aura and she returned the gesture with a smile before rumpling one of the boy's hair.

"How are you doing today, Matty?" she asked him.

"Fine, my queen. We are very glad to have you back."

"And I am very glad to be back. Can you all do me a favor?"

The group nodded. Being tasked by the queen clearly overjoyed them.

"Can you run ahead and inform the guards that we are back?"

Without a single word, the group turned, ran up the path ahead of them, and were soon out of sight.

Aura turned and smiled at Emily. "The guards saw us coming about a mile out, but the children love to be included in matters of the kingdom. Plus, if they can be taught at a young age that they matter in the day-to-day running of this place, they are more willing as adults to help out when it is required of them."

It made sense to Emily. Soon the group began moving again in the direction in which the children had disappeared. When they crested the next hill, the huge castle loomed above them. A group, of what she assumed were the queen's guards, was heading toward them. The hair

on the back of Emily's neck bristled and she had an uneasy feeling.

"What is going to happen to me?" she whispered to
Milskar.

"Honestly, I do not know, but I would not worry.
Until this matter can be sorted out, we will take care of
you. Until then, you will be treated as a guest of the
queen, in other words, better than any place you have
probably ever stayed." Milskar tried to smile reassuringly
at her, but she could read the doubt in his eyes and felt
little comfort.

The guards spoke quietly to Aura and soon they
moved forward again. A young man met them with several other people. They collected and led away the horses.
Theirra began to follow but Aura grabbed her wrist lightly. The two exchanged a knowing look and Theirra nodded, though she didn't look too happy about whatever
was decided between them.

Emily hung back a few steps, but followed the group
dutifully. She noticed all the wide-eyed glances being
thrown in Resbuca and Kolas's directions. It didn't take a
genius or a native of this land to figure out that the two of
them were outcasts. Emily had been able to tell their at-
tire was different from the rest of the group when they all
changed in the cave. She was sure the residents of this
place noticed their clothes as well. The way Resbuca and
Kolas carried themselves, with almost a sort of jumpi-
ness, made her think they were normally in a constant
state of having to protect themselves. Even here in the
supposed safety of the queen's presence, they seemed
unable to relax inside the castle's inner walls. They
looked like caged animals. Emily sympathized.

Before they entered through the large doors in the
middle of the castle, Milskar motioned to Resbuca and
Kolas to follow him elsewhere in the grounds. Aura and

Theirra nodded their goodbyes and entered the huge stone structure. Emily was left standing, unsure of which group she was supposed to follow. She wished for the hundredth time that Levi were there with her.

"Are you coming?" Aura said sweetly over her shoulder and Emily jogged to catch up.

Chapter 17

Omire

"Ugh," Levi moaned loudly.

His head hurt badly. He touched the side of it and instantly winced as a deeper pain shot through him. Where was he? He looked around—well, tried to look around—but found it difficult to move his head from side to side. His eyes didn't seem to be focusing properly, either, and he found it hard to get his bearings.

He tried to think back to the last thing he remembered but it was all so fuzzy. He remembered walking through the woods, being so tired, and falling asleep by the strange fire, but after that—just nothing. The concentration hurt his brain even more. Was Emily here, too? Levi had just remembered about Emily. More memories came flooding back to him. Aura, Theirra, Resbuca, Kolas, and Milskar. Winester. Running from his apartment and the portal. Then nothing.

He heard something behind him and all his muscles stiffened in response. The sound was quiet at first and then became louder and louder. It sounded like a group of people coming up on him and he braced himself for whatever may come.

"Please don't hurt me," he managed to croak out of his dry throat.

A male voice chuckled. "Hurt you? Oh, no."

Levi tried to look up at the man but was unable to raise his head high enough. As if the man could read his mind, he bent down until the two were eye to eye.

"Please," Levi begged again.

"Told you he would take this the wrong way, Omire," a woman to the left of him said.

"Hush, Amaline. There is no way to take this because we have not done anything to him. We will explain our situation and let Mr. Roberts decide for himself how to take that information."

"How do you know my name?" Levi whispered, terrified.

"Oh, we know a lot about you, Mr. Roberts. It is our job to know about you," Omire said.

Amaline looked at him questioningly, but Omire just shook his head slightly at her confused expression.

"Who are you?" Levi asked.

"My manners! Here I am, knowing you and you do not even know what to call me! How rude. My name is Omire," the man said, smiling at Levi who was finally able to focus a little better.

"What am I doing here?" Levi tried looking around again but still found he could not move his head. It took him a second to realize that his head was actually strapped to something. Again he tried to move and found the rest of his body equally immobilized. He began to panic and thrashed against the restraints.

"Quiet, quiet," Omire hushed. "Amaline, I think we are ready to begin."

For a second, Levi thought something had been placed over his head as everything went momentarily dark, but then several lights flashed in front of him. He was in a room of some sort and there were things like TVs along the walls. They flashed with hundreds of images, causing the pain in his head to flare again.

"Just watch." The voice started to fade away along with the footfalls. "Just watch."

Lights and sounds flashed in front of Levi's eyes, bombarding him with visions. At first, there were pictures of forests, animals, and bodies of water. The music was friendly and upbeat. Then images of people began appearing. Young and old couples, children, people playing in the outdoors. They all appeared happy and loving. Then the music changed.

The pictures became darker and more desolate. The meadows with lush flowers were replaced with barren lands. The people were sad and thin. The music became more melancholy. Words began appearing.

Depression.
Despair.
Disillusionment.
Destruction.
All caused by King Aldric.

෴

"How long should we leave him in there?" Amaline asked.

"As long as Abaddon feels it should take."

The two turned to the thin older man standing in front of a control box. He was pressing buttons and pulling levers, all the while staring straight ahead through a small window into the room. The man secretly loved his job, though he pretended to others it was a task he would rather not do. One was not supposed to like the torture of others but Abaddon felt a strange pleasure in it. The shaping of a mind using sounds and images intrigued him and he was always happy to try out his experiments on anyone he could get his hands on.

For hours, he stood there pressing, pulling, and watching. Omire and Amaline came and went after quickly becoming uninterested in the process. Abaddon loved it. He looked through the portal and saw that Levi was slumped in the chair. The initial phase was over and Abaddon shut everything down.

"Move him to some place comfortable where he can recover. Preferably a place where he cannot injure himself if he has some sort of spell while waking up. For a few hours he will be disoriented, but I need you to come get me as soon as he wakes up. It is important that we talk to him and question him to make sure he absorbed what we wanted him to."

Levi was very heavy and required the help of two additional men to move him. Omire could tell Amaline was upset by the whole process, having never actually seen it before. She wouldn't make eye contact with him and quickly walked out of the room once they had the boy settled.

"Amaline," he said, after catching up with her down the hall.

She whirled on him. "Why are we doing this?"

"I told you, the lady requested it."

"Why? Who is this kid? Why did you say that you knew about him?"

"It sounded ominous, might make him more cooperative if he thinks we already know everything. It does not really matter though. She asked and we obliged.

There really is nothing more you need to know about it."

Amaline didn't like the formal tone of his voice but she knew she was in no place to argue. Instead, she left him and walked to the cafeteria where the guards and staff ate their meals. There were a few people scattered throughout the tables but, for the most part, it was quiet. She grabbed a dessert and sat down to poke at it several times with a fork before pushing it away.

"It is not our place to question," Omire said, startling her.

"Why not," she demanded, making him chuckle.

"Your curiosity and defiance only benefits you so far. Pretty soon it will become a chain that will hold you to the past. You must be able to let go and trust that the future will happen. Just do what is asked of you and let those who make the decisions figure out if they are for the best or not."

"And you can just follow blindly like that, without a single care for what any of it means?"

"It is not a matter of not caring, but these people know much more than us. They hold worlds more information than we can ever hope to gather in an entire lifetime. We are only seeing a small part of it and, while our small part may seem like the incorrect thing to do, once the whole is looked at, it may be the only thing to do. Trust that they know the big picture."

"We destroyed him," Amaline said with a hint of regret in her voice.

"And now it is time to rebuild." Omire looked up at one of the guards motioning for them to come meet Abaddon outside the room Levi was being held in.

Even with the door shut, muffling the noises inside, they could still hear the screams from within. Amaline looked uncomfortably from Abaddon to Omire. Her feelings of misgivings were flaring up again.

"Do not worry," Abaddon said, without making eye contact with her. "This is all completely normal, but this is why I asked to be fetched when he awoke so I could make sure of his stability. Nothing appears out of order."

This did little to ease her wariness. They moved closer to the door and all jumped a little when a particularly loud yell escaped from behind it. Abaddon recovered quickly and opened the door. Amaline was shocked by what she saw.

The boy had seemed nice enough when they had first picked him up. Sure, he was scared but never raised his voice or yelled at them, which was not typical for those she often came across in the same situation. Now, however, he looked like a wild animal in a cage as he cautiously paced the room.

"Can he see?" she asked nervously.

"Not yet, but it will come back to him quickly."

At the sound of their voices, Levi froze. He looked right at them, but his pupils were huge and unfocused. He kept gripping the walls with both hands to help him stand, but his palms and fingers sank into the soft material of the padding that covered the walls.

"Hello?" he croaked. His voice sounded raw and painful.

"Mr. Roberts, welcome back." Abaddon moved toward Levi with palms up in a surrendering posture. "I am coming toward you slowly and will not hurt you."

Levi still jumped at the sound of the man's voice, but he also tilted his head as he tried to figure where the person was. He lifted his arm out in front of him and grabbed at the air with his hands. "Where are you?" he demanded, his voice laced with panic.

"I have some questions for you, Levi. May I call you Levi?" Abaddon didn't wait for an answer. "I have some questions about you and what you are doing here. Do you know why you are here?"

"I can't remember. I can't remember how I got here. Is Emily here?"

The group looked back and forth at each other.

"Emily? Who is Emily?" Omire asked.

Abaddon gave him a stern look to keep him quiet. "What else do you remember?"

"I—um—I remember the forest? I remember the fire, the strange fire."

"What do you remember before the forest? What do you remember about what brought you to this world?"

"Aura. Queen Aura."

Amaline froze. The men turned and locked eyes with each other. Amaline grabbed Omire's hand and tried to get his attention. Why was Queen Aura involved in this? It was all becoming deeper and more complicated than she was comfortable knowing about.

"What do you remember about Queen Aura?" Abaddon asked.

"She—" Levi paused and his posture and expression suddenly became violent. Omire took a step forward but the doctor quickly blocked his way. "Her father," Levi spat out.

"What about her father?"

"All those terrible, terrible things. All that destruction and death. All his fault. She inherited a kingdom of lies."

"And who will correct those lies? Who will make sure such terrible things never happen again?" Abaddon asked with excitement brimming in his voice.

"Me. I will," Levi said defiantly, eyes slowly beginning to focus on the forms in front of him.

Chapter 18

Plans

Emily awoke, stretched to her full length in the bed, and felt the relief of her joints cracking and popping. She relaxed back into the soft mattress and sighed. It felt strange to no longer have an agenda for the day. Normally, she would have already been up for an hour or two to go to work, but now she just spent her days in a lazy stumble to get from one end of it to the other.

At first, small search parties were sent out to try and find any trace of Levi and his captors, but it had become more and more infrequent as nothing was ever found. More than two days had passed since Emily heard of any search parties going out for him. That made it almost three weeks that he'd been missing. For a while, she'd held on to the hope that he would make the same curve around the castle they had and would come upon them out of the blue, but even that fantasy had begun to fade.

Of course, she was worried about her life back home, but she'd stopped asking questions about when or if she would ever return there. At first, her inquiries were brushed off then ignored outright. Finally, Emily got the hint and stopped bringing it up. It wasn't so much that she felt like a prisoner, just that she wasn't really in a position to return to her old life. She tried not to think about it too much or it would make her panic and want to run around screaming for someone to help her. She was trying not to appear crazy.

Emily dressed in the fancy clothes Aura had loaned her and made her way down to the dining hall where she started out most of her mornings. As always, Milskar was waiting down there for her with two plates of food in front of him. He smiled up at her with one side of his mouth and pushed a heaping plate in front of her as she sat down.

"Morning," he said gruffly.

It was all he ever said to her. They spent the rest of the time in silence. When finished, she picked up the plates and said goodbye to him as they went their separate ways. She wasn't quite sure what their relationship was but she always looked forward to seeing him in the morning. It was one of the only things she really had going for her during the day.

Next, she went over to the stables. Theirra wasn't there much anymore, taking more of an administrative role with Aura. Since spending all those hours riding, Emily's fears seemed to have dwindled a little. She liked sitting and talking to Serenity for hours until her stomach's growling finally made her go back to get dinner. Emily was surprised when she walked into the mare's stall today and found Aura sitting in the straw, absently stroking the mare's ears.

"Aura!" Emily exclaimed.

Aura smiled at her. "Emily."

"I haven't seen you much lately," Emily said while

taking a seat next to her. Serenity moved over to munch some hay and let the girls catch up.

"I am terribly sorry that I have not checked up on you recently."

"I know you're busy."

"There is still no excuse. You are a guest in my house and I have not been treating you as such. How are you holding up, all things considered?"

"Fine," Emily lied. It was easier than getting into all the complications.

"That is good to hear. It may not seem like it, but we are still actively searching for your cousin. It is important for us to find him. I know he means so much to you, but he also means a great deal to my kingdom and me. We take his safe recovery very seriously."

"I appreciate that."

"I sent a long-term search party out several days ago but, unfortunately, have not heard any word back from them as of yet. I will inform you the second I hear otherwise," Aura said.

"Please do."

"How are your accommodations? We can move you to a different area of the castle if you wish. Or perhaps you would like to stay in the town?"

"No!" Emily realized too late that it came out as a half shout. Strangely, Milskar's head had suddenly popped into her mind and she couldn't help the gut reaction, no matter how confusing it was. "No, no thank you. I am perfectly comfortable where I am. I appreciate all you have done for me."

"Appreciate?" Aura chuckled. "After all I have put you through, the last thing you should be doing is thanking me. I am keeping you from your home, from your family, for my own personal gain. I should be thanking you."

"I don't think I understand," Emily said, a little confused.

"Do you really think we can risk sending you back to where you came from?"

"I won't tell anyone. I promise." Emily shifted to her knees in a half begging position. Now the shred of hope that she could go home was consuming her and it was suddenly all she wanted.

"Emily, of course, you would have to tell someone. How could you explain your return without Levi's?"

"I would make something up, I would tell them I ran away from home, looking for him, but I wasn't able to find him. I would make something up," she repeated. "I can be trusted. Please just let me go home." Fat, hot tears were now streaming down her face, erasing any image of Milskar from her mind's eye.

Aura looked away from her. Emily tried to stop crying but now that she had unplugged the tears, she was unable to control them. She dug her fingernails into her palms but it was still several moments later before she was able to calm down. "I am sorry," she said, after wiping the last remnants of wetness from her cheeks. "I'm just scared, that's all."

"Please stop apologizing," Aura said with her back to Emily. "I will try to figure out a way to get you out of here, but I am not able to promise you anything."

Emily nodded to Aura as the queen brushed passed her and left the stall. Emily walked over to Serenity, buried her head in the horse's neck, and let go of a fresh round of sobs.

Emily made it back to the dining hall well after dark. Milskar had a worried look on his face but brightened slightly when he caught sight of her. The plate of food looked cold and unappetizing but she pushed the food around on her plate to spare his feelings.

"Is everything all right?" His voice startled her and she looked up at him.

"It will be, thank you."

"Queen Aura means well. She just has a lot on her plate that she is trying to work through. She is young and still at a point in her rule where she thinks she can fix everything and help everyone."

"I just need her to fix one thing. To help one person," Emily stood up from the table and left the hall.

Milskar sat with his mouth slack and half open.

Emily wasn't even halfway back to her room before she began to feel terrible about herself. She knew it was not Milskar's fault, no one's fault really but hers, but she was still unable to keep her anger inside any longer. She was in a constant state of cursing everything, these people, herself, and Levi. She absurdly cursed the fact that he had this gift and that she followed him in the pursuit of understanding it. If he were standing in front of her right now, she would slap him first then hug him.

Emily lay down on her bed and sighed loudly, then jumped up just as suddenly. She couldn't stay in place any longer. She quickly left her room and headed down the hall. It took two rounds of knocking before Milskar came to his door. He looked startled to see her and reflexively pulled at his shirt to shut it.

It took him a moment to realize he had no shirt on. "Emily."

"I'm sorry to just spring up on you like this." She averted her eyes, just as embarrassed as he about barging in on him. "I just wanted to apologize for my behavior tonight and for taking my bad mood out on you. Sorry."

She glanced up at him for a second before turning around to leave.

He grabbed her wrist and turned her back toward him. "Wait."

They stood there for almost a minute straight, just staring back at each other. Emily finally smiled and turned to go. Milskar let her hand drop. She didn't look back when she heard the door click shut behind her.

She felt her smile quickly fall off her face when she rounded the corner and saw Theirra standing in front of her door. The woman didn't look particularly happy. Emily smiled dryly. She tried to run through the events of the last twenty-four hours to pinpoint why, exactly, Theirra could possibly be here.

Emily decided to play dumb. "Theirra! So good to see you!" she said with fake brightness.

"Emily," Theirra responded curtly.

Emily motioned for her come into the room. "Please, come in."

"I cannot stay long, but I wanted to speak with you in private."

"Is there something I can help you with?" Emily felt the sweetness in her voice and wondered if Theirra could pick up on its artificial nature.

"There are several things. Seems you have had a pretty busy day here at the castle," Theirra said and Emily was not able to place the tone of her voice. Was she angry or amused?

"I lost my temper and I'm really sorry. I don't mean to cause trouble for any of you here, or to seem ungrateful for everything you have all done for me. I won't be a problem anymore, I promise." Emily felt trapped in the room and, for some reason, experienced a chill on the back of her neck, as if some harm were about to come to her.

"I wish it were that simple."

Silence hung between them and Emily felt a panic rise within her to fill the space with some kind of words. Words that might fix whatever it was that she broke. Instead, she just stood there, trying not to make eye contact with Theirra.

Emily respected the former horse groomer. She'd heard about how Theirra had worked her way up through the kingdom and now held a position of power as the right-hand woman to the queen. From what little she was able to gather, as the other stable people did not often like to talk about it, Aura and Theirra always had a special relationship, but after the death of the king, they had become increasingly close.

Emily could tell Theirra was intelligent but she also felt a kind of pity toward her. It was clear that Aura abused their friendship, even from the little time Emily had spent close to the two.

The second Aura would wish for something to happen, Theirra was doing everything in her power to see it to fruition. Emily wondered on whose behalf Theirra was standing in front of her now.

"I can take you back to your home. We will leave first thing in the morning and follow a similar route to the one we previously took. You will be home in about three days. It may go a little quicker as we will be a smaller party and without the added danger of having the queen with us."

"What? No!" The words fell from Emily's mouth before she even knew what her feelings were. Wasn't it just hours ago that she was pleading to go home?

Theirra looked startled by her outburst. "I thought this is what you wished, what you implored the queen to grant you."

"I did. I did think that was what I wanted, but now—now, I'm not sure. I just can't leave Levi behind."

Was that the only reason for her newfound resistance? Was the real reason down the hall?

Theirra was now pacing the room. "Queen Aura had to use a lot of favors to secure safe passage for you. It is a rarity that someone from your world comes to ours and even more rare for us to allow that person to return. You could potentially put us all at great risk but the queen feels that she can trust you."

"She can, she can trust me. I just don't know if I can actually go. If I can actually leave here. Can I have some time to think about it?"

"This may be your only chance to leave here. You need to understand that. Even if—" Theirra paused and corrected herself. "—when we find Levi, you may not be able to go back to your homes. It may be too dangerous at that point to allow you to leave."

"I need to think about it." A million thoughts were buzzing around Emily's head and she needed to be able to sit down and sort them all out.

"I can give you until dawn. We are scheduled to leave soon after, but I will await your word before beginning to pack. Think long and hard about this opportunity Aura has given you, and about what you would like to do with it. We cannot force you to leave, but we can force you to stay for longer than you wish in the future."

Emily nodded. Theirra smiled, a sad smile, and left the room. What was that sorrowful look?

Did Theirra think she was making a mistake by leaving or by staying?

Emily wished she had someone she could talk to, someone she could work the problem out with, so she could be sure.

The pangs of Levi's absence prickled in her again.

She thought she knew what her answer was, but just needed to check one more source of advice before she made her final decision.

Chapter 19

Old Friends

Winester felt like he'd been traveling forever. His feet ached and not having the luxury of a horse had taken its toll on his whole body. He slept little, feeling equal parts vulnerable about being out in the open and excited about finally arriving at his destination. He had not spoken to anyone since leaving the other world, but assumed everything was in order or at least beginning to fall into place.

Busu had left his side almost a full day ago and he had not heard anything from the bird since. Winester assumed he had gone hunting, but when he hadn't returned after the morning, Winester began to get a little irritated with him. They had spent time apart, but Winester felt like this was not the time for wandering. They would have to have a talk upon Busu's return.

The forest began to thicken and block out the sun. Winester knew he was close. It had been many years since he had been to these parts, but the memories flooded back to him, as if it were just yesterday that he had traveled these trails. The flowers and trees began to feel familiar and the second he wondered where a particular building or marker had gone, it appeared right where he thought it should be. Of course, there were things that were different. Some things larger or smaller than the last time he had seen them, but the feel of the place was the same. He knew he had arrived.

The steel door jumped out on the left of him, just as it had done all those years ago. There was a time when he had needed refuge and had found it hidden deep within that place and the people who resided there. He'd paid back what he owed to them ten-fold and was now looking forward to having them indebted to him. It would be a nice change.

He knocked five times. Twice fast, once slow, and two more times in rapid succession. The door opened and he came face to face with a beautiful woman. She was tall and pale, almost blending into the soft background, with ink black hair that fell all around her like moving water. Her eyes looked past him and into the surrounding area. It was clear she was not sure about this stranger who knew the access code and clearly did not really want to let him inside.

"Can I help you?" she asked, staring at him.

"No. I am the reason why all of you are here. If anything, I should be asking you if there is anything more you could do for me," he said briskly, brushing against her as he entered.

"Hey!" she hollered after him. She grabbed on to his shoulder but he quickly shrugged her off. In the next second, he was bewildered to find himself staring at the ceiling, not quite sure what was going on. "I did not invite you in."

She was standing above him. Winester was quite impressed not only by her speed, but also her stealth. She glared down at him but he could not help but smile back. She swiftly kicked him in the side.

"Amaline!"

The voice boomed out behind both of them. Winester saw the woman jump. Her fingers were clenched and he saw the darkness brooding in her eyes, but she took a miniscule step back.

"Winester!" Suddenly a hand came down and grasped his, pulling him upright, and straight into a crushing hug.

Winester exhaled. "Omire."

"You *know* this trespasser?" Amaline spat.

"He is the reason we are all here," Omire said, taking a step back and admiring Winester.

"Omire," Winester said. "It has been many years, and many years too long."

The two embraced again, laughing and slapping each other's back as only men will do.

"Someone explain," Amaline said curtly, while tapping one foot on the marble floor.

"He," Omire said, "is the one who requested that we talk to that boy in there."

"Ah, so it is you that requested such terrible things."

"Impressed?" Winester said with a half-smile and a wink.

"Hardly," she said, unamused.

"You will have to excuse Amaline here. She has a bit of a conscience problem we are trying to work through."

"Pity," Winester said. "With the kind of back kick she has, it would be a shame to waste it for good."

The two chuckled and walked away, arm in arm, leaving a fuming Amaline to follow in their wake.

Abaddon intercepted them before they were able to reach the holding cell. The doctor greeted the sorcerer with fake over-excitement. Amaline couldn't watch the charade any longer and left the group for the serenity of her private quarters.

"What have you accomplished so far?" Winester asked, peering into the room's window.

"Go and see for yourself," Abaddon said with a smile, turning the knob of the door and motioning him to enter.

Sitting in the corner was Levi, but he looked much different from the last time Winester had seen him. The boy was paler than before and had lost about ten pounds. His eyes were red-rimmed and looked painfully dry. Everything about him looked wild. His stance was hunched over like he was ready to spring at the slightest provocation. Even Levi's fingers were curled into claws. Winester was about to speak when a soft knock on the door cut him off.

He noticed both Omire and Abaddon bowing beside him before his brain could process what it meant. He turned and first noticed the blood red fingernails on the doorjamb.

Looking up, his eyes met Lady Grustmiener's and he quickly glanced away.

"Oh, Winester." She chuckled softly. "This is hardly the time for formality, especially from you. Can we talk somewhere more—" She wrinkled her nose at Levi. "—pleasant?"

Winester could tell Abaddon was clearly disappointed. He had been looking forward to showing off what he'd done to the boy.

It would just have to wait.

They all followed her out of the room, but she had stopped Abaddon and Omire before they made it farther down the hall.

After they separated, it wasn't until they turned left that Winester realized they were heading a direction he didn't think he'd ever been to before. The walls, floors, and lighting all appeared to get slowly darker the farther they went.

"Where are we going?" Winester asked her.

"To my private quarters. We can speak more freely there."

Something about her request didn't feel particularly right, but he was not able to defy her and obediently followed. They passed a set of extremely large guards who let them go by while keeping stern eyes on Winester. He was a very powerful man but, in that moment, he felt very vulnerable.

He thought he'd visited every part of this section of the half-buried castle, but this was all new and unfamiliar to him.

He tried to remember each bit he was seeing, in case he either needed to make a quick escape or to one day return to this same place, but it was almost too dark to actually be able to make anything out. Winester followed dutifully until they reached a fork in the hallway. It was only then that Lady Grustmiener turned to look at him again.

"These are my and the king's private quarters," she explained and Winester stiffened at the mention of the ruler. "Do not worry. He is in other parts of the kingdom on business and will not be returning for about four weeks. We have plenty of time to get everything in order."

"And what is in order so far?" He had held off questioning long enough. He was bursting with anticipation to see how far along they were.

"Abaddon is happy with the progress Mr. Roberts has made and believes after only a few more treatments he will be ready. It is only a matter of time. After that we will be ready to leave."

"This pleases me very much."

"You have done much for my kingdom, Winester, and for me, but after this is completed, I want you to consider us even. I owe you nothing more."

"That seems perfectly fair to me."

She nodded and turned to open the door on the left. Winester followed and found a lushly decorated bedroom with light as soft as in the hallway. It took him a second to adjust to the new objects and figure out their placement in the room. He did not have much time to gain his bearings before she was on him, kissing him hungrily.

Chapter 20

Answers

Who was that man?" Amaline asked Omire when he joined her in the dining hall that evening. She'd been pacing her room for hours before she felt calm enough to join the rest of civilization again.

"That man is Winester, the great sorcerer."

"Winester, like Lord Vertrous's Winester?" she said, astonished.

"One and the same."

"What is he doing here?"

"All these questions, always questions," he admonished. "I am not sure completely but I do know it has something to do with that boy. Honestly, I am trying to figure out the specifics myself as well."

"How do you know who he is? I have never seen him around the kingdom before."

"Oh, he has not been in these parts for many years, probably not since before you were born. He has been alive for many years, even before the original King Grustmiener was given this land. Rumor had it that once the lands were divided, Winester tried to form alliances between all the rulers of the Four Corners. A sort of insurance for himself, I believe, a way that if, he ever needed anything, he would have those who would readily provide for him. To get in their good graces, he performed tasks, almost like favors, for all the rulers, but these were not simple things. He would find the deepest and darkest secrets of each and figure out how to exploit them. Some were to just fix a problem, or to threaten exposure, but whatever it was, each of the four rulers quickly became indebted to him."

"What kinds of things?" she asked eagerly.

"Not many specifics are known, as gossip is told and retold so often it is difficult to separate what was once truth and what are now dramatizations. I do know that many years after becoming ruler of Vertronum, King Piester was caught in a rather precarious situation. His purity was something he was always known for and whatever information Winester knew could have led to his downfall. Instead of exposing him, however, Winester helped the king rid himself of the problem, though now the king owed his renewed lease on life to Winester. It is a powerful thing when someone is indebted to you for something. I do not know if that favor has been cashed in yet, though, with Winester being a sorcerer, it is quite possible some spell was placed on each king that makes it impossible for them to defy him. Again, there is a lot of speculation, but for him to stay in a position of power for so many years, it can only be assumed he is using outside forces to keep himself there."

Amaline was riveted. "What do you think he did for King Grustmiener?"

"I could not even imagine, though I have heard that the first king was a ruthless ruler in his time. He would not hesitate to kill or imprison anyone who got in his way. For a while he felt that he should be the supreme ruler, the next Lord Vertrous, and wanted to stage war against the other kingdoms."

"Why didn't he?"

"It is not allowed. Lord Vertrous was luckily smart enough to make it impossible for each king to wage war on another's land. Exchanges could only be peaceful and with the full support of the remaining rulers, though, the king devoted a lot of his time and energy in trying to fig-ure out a way around this. All I can imagine is that possi-bly, with Winester's help, he did find a way."

"And how do you personally know him?" Amaline asked.

"He used to help the current king and queen. He left suddenly, though. I always wondered what caused the departure, but I never found out," Omire said with a shrug.

The two sat in silence for several minutes while Amaline digested everything she had heard. She had only been in the guard-ship for eighteen months and, in that time, she felt like she had learned a lifetime of secrets. There were moments when she wished she could go back to being ignorant, but now she knew she was in too deep and there was no way she could return to her previous life or naiveté.

Amaline had always been the best, brightest, and fastest in pretty much everything for her age group, boys or girls. Omire, one of the king's aides at the time, had actually approached her family when she was twelve years old about her becoming a royal guard. They were ecstatic, but Amaline was heartbroken. She had never re-ally thought much about her future, but when they pre-sented it to her one night during dinner, it was all she could do not to break out into sobs. She had always

vaguely pictured herself in some sort of art profession—
dancer, sculptor, singer, but certainly not one that inflicted, or was at least meant to appear to be able to inflict
harm on another being.

She was strong and good at sports, but did not particularly like the confrontation they always implied.
There was no room for gray areas there and she was not
one to live in the black and white. It took her a long time
to get accustomed to the idea, but really there was no way
around it. One could not simply tell the king "No, I don't
think that is particularly something I would like to do."

His asking permission was more of a formality than
an actual question.

So on her eighteenth birthday, just as it had been decided so many years before, a man came to her parent's
house, deep in the outskirts of the kingdom, and took her
away. At first, she was terrified of Omire and there were
times she still was, but mostly she clung to him mentally
and physically. He was the one bridge between her two
worlds. She probably could have just as easily blamed
him for dragging her away but she didn't see it as that.
He was sent to do a job and her job was now to follow
him. It didn't always occur so smoothly, but she did the
best she could to obey and stay relatively out of his way.

The training was intense and mostly one-on-one. It
was a full six months before she actually met another
guard and, even then, for some reason, she felt that she
should keep most of her experiences a secret. It seemed
that while she was training for the same purpose, what
she actually did was a little different from the other re-
cruits, who'd been taken out of their homes at young ag-
es, as well.

While they spoke of late-night running drills, shoot-
ing, mounted patrol practices, and other skills one would

assume necessary for someone protecting a person of high power, it seemed Amaline was having a much different course taught to her. Sure, there were still the physical things she needed to learn how to do, but most of it all was psychological. She would have day-long intensive sessions where she was only permitted to stare at one spot on the wall and not allowed to speak. Or where she had assignments to track other guards, almost as a spy. She found it grueling and she was often exhausted by the end of their sessions.

Amaline was not quite sure what it was all adding up to, but Omire seemed exceedingly pleased with whatever progress he deemed she was making. Even if she did not understand it, she was determined to make him proud.

This was the first time they'd had an outside person in their midst. Normally, she would train on other guards or townspeople. This Levi person was obviously not from around here. She could tell the first moment she caught a glimpse of him and was not sure what tipped her off. But he seemed to scream "stranger" to her. His strange clothes were just a part of that.

The whole vibe of him being there felt odd to her and she made a silent promise to herself to somehow figure out what he was doing here and what it meant for her.

Chapter 21

Knowledge

I need more time," Abaddon said loudly, pounding his fist on the table.

"We do not have such luxuries," Lady Grustmiener told him flatly.

"Well then, you cannot reasonably expect everything to go smoothly. I cannot guarantee anything if the program is not completed."

"That is a risk we are going to have to take. Now, I am going to need you to wean him off all you are doing to him so that he is ready to begin the journey in four days' time."

She said it with finality then turned to leave the small office they were in. Winester nodded to the scientist and followed her.

"What does he mean that it may not have fully worked?" Winester asked when he'd caught up to her.

"He means nothing. He is a crazy old man with crazy old ideas. Abaddon likes to push his subjects farther and farther past the brink. He has actually made some go insane, instead of actually training them for the purposes we need them for."

"Purposes?"

"Oh, Winester." She chuckled. "Did you really think you are the first person who has requested our special services?" She chuckled again.

"Do you think Levi is ready?"

"I think he is as ready as we need him to be. I also do not want to delay the journey any longer. The king will not be away forever and I would prefer to return before he does."

Winester nodded absentmindedly at her. He wished he did not have to rely on others for this mission. The more people involved, the more he felt removed from the actual decision making process. He knew that Lady Grustmiener was doing everything she could and she was the proper person to go to with this request, but he had a strange suspicion that she might feel as if he now might owe her a small part of something for all her help.

When he came into power, he knew that she would expect something in return for all she had done. How silly she was being, he contemplated, assuming that he would give her a second thought when he was ruler of not only Esotera, but of all the other lands as well. Pity is all he would be willing to give her.

They met her generals in a secure conference room he'd been to before. Several people were huddled over maps scattered on a table. They froze when he entered the room and all turned to look at Lady Grustmiener.

"He is why we are all here," she said, without looking up.

They all quickly went back to work.

"What is going on here?" Winester asked her quietly.

"We are coming up with our attack plan."

"Attack plan?" He'd assumed it would be a much

simpler process. Basically, they would just have to get Levi close enough to Esotera and simply have him declare war. Winester figured that fighting would not be necessary, since they would be taking them pretty much off guard.

"Of course. What, do you think, they will allow us to just come and take their lands and power?" She was looking at him as if he were a foolish child. "That is what you thought, is it not?"

"I thought the shock of the declaration would be enough to prove our seriousness."

"They know we are going to attack. We stole him from them. They are probably stationed all over the forests, just waiting for us to come for them. Obviously, if you know what kinds of power he has, they do, too."

"Power?" Amaline whispered to Omire.

They were standing in the back of the room watching all the chaos around them.

"I do not know what they are talking about," he replied out of the corner of his mouth without taking his eyes off the conversation happening in the middle of the room.

"Everyone, out," Lady Grustmiener said.

The room quickly cleared, leaving her and Winester behind.

Omire pulled Amaline into a side corridor, opposite from where the rest of the guards were headed. He waited until they were completely alone to start speaking, but still spoke in a hushed tone. "Something big is obviously going on."

"What does she mean by declaring war? I thought that was not possible," Amaline said.

"No one can. Fighting a war is not something we are prepared for. The guards of the kingdom are to protect the citizens from each other and from attacking the government, not to fight with the other lands."

The two stood in silence for several moments, thousands of possibilities running through each of their heads. Suddenly Amaline brightened. "We should go ask him."

"Ask him? Him who? Winester?"

"No, Levi," she said, grabbing Omire's hand and running them both down the hall.

"How are we going to ask him?" he replied, huffing beside her.

"Abaddon."

The pair flew into the small office of the scientist. Abaddon jumped and looked up with wide eyes as they burst through. "I prefer a knock first if it is all the same to you," he said when he regained his composure.

"We are sorry, but we're in a terrible rush," Amaline said. "We need to speak to Mr. Roberts. Now. It is very important."

"That is just not possible. He is recovering from his last treatment. I need him well rested for his next. I only have so much time left with him," Abaddon said, standing up from his desk. "How can they expect me to work within these conditions?" he mumbled to himself.

"Abaddon—" Omire started with a stern voice, but Amaline cut his off with a soft touch to his arm.

"Abaddon," she said in a much sweeter voice. "I know your work is very important and we would not bother you if we did not think that it was crucial. Lady Grustmiener requests more information from him. I just thought that we would be able to get that information quicker, delaying your very important studies as little as possible."

"She does tend to delay me," Abaddon said to himself.

"Which is why we offered to come on her behalf," Amaline picked up the lie where she had left off. "I would hate to have to send her back here because you were uncooperative."

Omire held his breath. He had never seen Amaline in this role and it greatly intrigued him. He watched the two curiously and saw the moment the air shifted in their favor. He could see the options weighing in the doctor's brain.

"All right, but make it as quick as promised. I can give you five minutes, but not a moment longer."

Amaline nodded and brushed past Omire to enter Levi's room. They found the boy sitting straight in a chair with his eyes wide open and dazed. She approached him with palms up and walked with slow, purposeful steps.

"Levi?" His gaze shot in her direction when he heard his name. It seemed as though he was not really registering anything above the sounds itself. "Levi, I need to ask you some questions," she said, using the same sweet voice. "Why are you here?"

"To take my rightful place," he said in a robotic tone.

She looked up at Omire. "Your rightful place?"

"As ruler of your world."

"Ruler? What would give you the right to be ruler?" Omire interjected over her shoulder.

"As the rightful heir," Levi stated flatly.

"Rightful air?" Amaline was so confused. "Air as in breathing?"

"Heir as the descendent of Lord Vertrous."

An instantaneous shock ran through her like electricity. Her mouth was dry and, for a moment, she forgot how to breathe.

"Time has expired," Abaddon said behind them.

Amaline had to stifle a scream, he had startled her so.

Omire grabbed her from behind and dragged her out of the room. He thanked Abaddon and pulled Amaline down the hall back toward their living quarters. She was breathing heavily as if they had run a hundred miles. He looked up and down the hall, to make sure no one had seen them, then opened his door and shoved her into his room.

"What are we going to do?" she asked in a shocked voice.

"I have no idea," he said as he paced back and forth.

She collapsed into a chair and began playing with the silver ring on her thumb. "What did he mean?"

"I have no idea."

"Omire, we have to do something."

"I know," he snapped at her. "Sorry."

She nodded. "They are going to start a war. An actual war. If he was telling the truth, that is. If that is the truth—" She paused, unable to go on.

"I know. We have to do something, but I am not sure what. Or if we should be for or against it."

"For or against? What do you mean? You want to be a part of this? You actually want to support this?"

"I am not sure what I want to do, but it is our kingdom and we have sworn to protect it," Omire said.

"We are sworn to protect our people as well. What do you think this will do to them, if they are involved in a war? Do you really think that only the guards will have to fight? People are going to die if this happens. Do you really think Esotera will give up without fighting back?" Her voice was beginning to raise several octaves.

"So what do you want to do?'

"I have no idea," she said.

Omire came and sat next to her. A knock on the door

made both of them jump. Amaline's eyes quickly turned to meet his.

"What do we do?" she asked in a shaky voice.

"Nothing, for right now. Nothing. We will figure it out, but for right now, we must act as if we know nothing. Act perfectly normal," he instructed her as he rose to answer the door. "Sauture."

"Omire."

The large guard stood behind the door. Omire held it open as little as possible so the man would not be able to see a shell-shocked Amaline sitting in his living room area.

"Lady Grustmiener is requesting your presence. She wants to know where you went after you left." He turned to leave but not before calling over his shoulder. "She would like to see you too, Amaline."

Chapter 22

Schedules

A few more days had gone by and the information was less than it had been the week before. Aura was becoming frustrated with her guards and felt like she was taking it out on those around her. Earlier that day, she had snapped at Theirra and was not really surprised when her friend had given her a wide berth the rest of the day. So she was even happier to see one of her aides who had been sent out the week prior on a reconnaissance mission.

"My queen," the woman said, bowing deeply.

"Please." Aura impatiently brushed her off formality. "What information do you have for me?"

"It seems as if they are putting together some sort of army."

"Army?" Aura immediately perked up. "What kind of army?"

"Not sure exactly, but it seems as though their guards are in training."

"That does not mean anything. Our guards train from time to time."

"Battle training. Hand-to-hand combat. With weapons I have never seen before, and while wearing some kind of armor or protection," the woman said.

"Protection?" Aura asked.

"Like I said, it seems like they are planning for some type of battle. A battle like I have never seen before."

"Thank you," Aura said. "Thank you for all of your hard work. Go get a hot meal and some rest."

The woman looked as if she was about to protest, to offer something else, but weariness took over and she turned to leave the room with a simple nod.

"Wait." Aura remembered something. "Was there a boy there about my age with brown hair and strange clothing?"

"No, my queen, no one fitting that description that I can recall."

Aura nodded and the aide left.

What did this information mean? She was still waiting to hear back from those she had sent to the centers of Omaner and Vertronum, but she figured that if Levi were anywhere, it would have been in Grustmiener. It was no secret the country had a brutal past. She was trying not to let things that had happened long before she was born affect her decisions, but there was only so much that she could ignore.

Though she knew that just because the aide hadn't seen Levi, it didn't mean he was not hidden away some place in the castle. She was not sure, if there would be time to try to find and extract him, or if they should prepare their own army. She didn't even know where to begin.

Her guards were trained, but just for the protection in

fights between the citizens, just as all the guards in the Four Corners were. Aura didn't even know who to go to about training her men and women for combat. Suddenly, an idea flashed in her head. It was so perfect, almost as if it had been sitting in her brain her whole life.

She ran across the grounds, ignoring several people who yelled questions after her. There were more pressing matters. She would deal with the problems of her court later. Looking up across the manicured courtyard, she saw who she was seeking.

He was sitting at a bench deep in conversation. Normally, she would have stood there, quietly waiting for them to finish before speaking, but there were pressing matters. Manners would have to wait.

"Kolas," she said breathlessly, "it is imperative that I speak with you. Immediately." She nodded toward the other man in a rushed apology.

Kolas stood and gruffly excused himself. Aura led him several paces away before turning to speak with him. He did not look particularly pleased with her.

"I appreciate you coming with me."

"Not that I had much choice," he snapped, obviously in some sort of foul mood himself.

She ignored this. "Kolas, I need to tell you some very delicate information, and I need you to keep it with the utmost secrecy, at least for now."

"I do not believe I need to prove anything to you. You know where my loyalties are."

"Yes, yes, of course. But I need to use a particular piece of your expertise." She spoke slowly, not really sure how to address her request. It was not every day one needed to ask someone else to potentially kill for them.

He looked at her with a deeply furrowed brow. "Expertise?"

"I need you to train my guards. I need to create an

army. We need to be prepared for war." It all just fell out. The words were coming faster than her brain could process them.

"War." It was more of a statement than a question.

"Yes. I have it on good authority that the kingdom of Grustmiener is preparing for battle. And I believe Esotera is the target. We need to not only be ready, but also to prepare for victory. My only starting point, our only shred of hope to come out of this alive, rests in you, Kolas. I know you have done so much for me and my people, but I must ask you for this one more thing."

"And what is in it for me?"

"For you?" She was shocked at his boldness. "The knowledge that you helped save a people."

He laughed. "I am not sure what impression you had of me, but I am not one who typically performs acts for the warm and fuzzy feeling they give me. I did not become an outlaw because I helped people."

"I—I—" she stammered. "What do you want?"

"Pardon."

"I do not understand."

"As I said, I did not become an outlaw by being a law-abiding citizen. This fact has kept me from having a permanent home for the last ten years. I would like that to change. But with my current—" He hesitated. "—situation I am not able to live in a populated area. You can change that. Pardon all my crimes. Give me a home to defend and I will defend it. Do this and I will not only train, but also lead your army."

"Fine." Her brain was whirling. Had she just done the right thing? She didn't even know what crimes he had committed to warrant his banishment and, with one word she had forgiven all. She hoped this would not come back to haunt her in the future.

"I will begin first thing in the morning," he said. "Tell your guards to get a good meal and a good night's sleep. This will be the most difficult thing they have ever done in their lives. I need them well rested." And with that, he turned away from her and walked back toward the castle.

Aura was out of breath from the stress of it all. She knew deep down Grustmiener had to have Levi, but she still didn't want to believe it. There was no other way, though, that they could declare war on Esotera. She knew of the word war, though little of what it actually meant. Her father had told her stories about the violence in the other world, but she had little ability to wrap her brain around what it actually was. All she knew was that it tore the other world apart. The notion of that terrified her.

She slowly walked the high-walled perimeter around the castle grounds. In this courtyard area, children ran and played, adults talked and traded stories and goods, and animals grazed with tails swooshing in the late afternoon air. Aura breathed in deeply and staved off the tears that were pressing against the back of her eyes. She needed to fight for all these creatures. She needed to do whatever was in her power to protect them all.

⌇⌇⌇

Aura tossed and turned that night, restless in her bed. This was the moment. Her place in history would be sealed by this moment.

Would she be the one who let her kingdom fail? Who let death and destruction into the lives of all inhabitants in this world, or would she be the one who was able to rise up and defeat evil? The one who defeated those who tried to take everything away from her people? She was determined to be the latter.

After an hour of staring at the ceiling, she decided to go for a walk. The halls were quiet and deserted. It felt eerie to be in this normally busy place all by herself. She momentarily lost track of where she was and was surprised to find herself in the great hall. Her footsteps echoed loudly off the walls of the huge room. She often met with townspeople and held government meetings in this place but now silence reverberated all around her. Suddenly, she heard a noise in the distance and froze, her eyes unable to adjust fully to the darkness and see what was in front of her.

"Hello?" she called out with trepidation.

"Aura?" a sweet voice answered.

Aura breathed out a sigh of relief. "Theirra?"

Out of the darkness, her friend stepped. Aura's wide smile immediately died when she saw Theirra's tear streaked face.

Aura rushed toward her friend. "What? What is wrong?"

Theirra waved her concern away. "Nothing."

"This is a large number of tears for nothing."

Theirra laughed weakly and wiped the tears away. She let Aura hold her for several moments before pulling away. "I am keeping you up," she said.

"You are doing nothing of the sort. Now, speak. What is all this for?"

"Did you pardon Kolas?"

The boldness of the question took Aura by surprise. "What?"

"Did you pardon Kolas?" Theirra asked again.

"Yes. It was necessary—" Aura started but Theirra abruptly cut her off by throwing herself at the queen.

"Thank you," Theirra said through a new bout of tears.

"Theirra. Theirra," Aura said, laughing. "Speak to me. What is all this about."

"I think. I think I may be in love with him," Theirra sobbed.

Aura could not help but laugh. She patted Theirra's back and cooed to her softly, trying to calm her. Suddenly, she was completely exhausted and, while she wanted to hear everything her friend had to say about the matter, she felt it could wait until morning.

"Theirra, I think it is time for bed. We shall speak about this over breakfast in the morning. Would that be all right with you?"

Again, Theirra pulled away. "Yes. Yes of course," she responded in a shaky voice.

Aura held her hand as they exited the hall. She kissed her lightly on the forehead before turning to head to her chambers.

"Aura?"

She turned.

"Thank you."

Aura smiled and nodded. Once in her room, she collapsed into the bed and was asleep before her eyes had even fully closed.

Chapter 23

Preparations

Agian," Kolas groaned.

The men and women stood in a line, doing jumping jacks then dropping down into a pushup, just to stand and do it over again. Kolas was admittedly frustrated. For a group of people who were supposed to be protectors, he seriously doubted they had any ability other than the fact they looked possibly menacing.

"Ugh! Again!" He'd had enough for one morning. "All right, stop. Just stop."

Several dozen pairs of eyes were staring up at him in obvious pain. "Go shower, eat, and rest up. Be back here by dusk."

Kolas walked the opposite direction of the group toward Aura who was sitting on the side of the hill where they had been training. She didn't look particularly happy and he couldn't blame her. He was not sure how much time they had left to prepare, but he felt like, no matter what it was, it would not be enough. Armies trained for years. They had days.

"My queen," he said, bowing when he reached her.

"Kolas," she said sternly. "I am not seeing much improvement."

"Neither am I."

"I thought you said having multiple sessions a day would help them."

"I thought it would."

"What is our next plan then?" she asked.

"I am not really sure. They just have no concept of what I am trying to train them for. They do not understand what war is. What it can do to them, to their families, to their lives."

"How do we make them understand?"

"I need permission to take them off the grounds. I need to be able to make it real for them."

"That is out of the question. What if the attack happens while you are away? It is a risk I simply cannot undertake. There must be some other way."

"There are no other options," Kolas said, beginning to pace in a circle. "It has to be shown to them. They need to experience it. Without that, without that real fear, they will be useless in battle. They will not know what to expect and how to handle it when it happens. We do not have to travel far."

Aura stood and crossed her arms. She did not want the vulnerability they would risk with all her guards gone. However, this had to be weighed against the need for her army to be well trained. She didn't like the decision she had to make, but she did it anyway.

"You may keep them away for three days. And you must have a runner that can be in constant communication with us here. I need you to be able to come back at a moment's notice if the need arises," Aura said, relenting.

"We can have townspeople be lookouts. Make it seem like some important assignment. It should come from you, for they will take it much more seriously. They will be instructed to report directly to you or the runner and then the information can come to us and we can come back."

"Take care of them. And us," Aura said and he nodded.

"We will leave tonight. I must get several things in order first. I shall be back." Kolas turned on his heels and walked away from her.

逆∽逆

Emily had decided not to go home without Levi and was wandering the halls when she almost literally ran into Aura.

"Oh, Aura!" she said, startled.

Aura smiled warmly back at her. "Emily."

"I've noticed a lot of stuff going on around here. Kolas seemed to be moving a large group out the castle walls late last night."

"I am sorry he woke you." Aura looked a little guilty, almost as if she had gotten caught doing something wrong.

"I was having a little trouble sleeping and just happened to be sitting by my window. They actually didn't make a lot of noise. Don't worry, though, I won't tell anyone what I saw," she added as an afterthought.

"I appreciate that. I would not want anyone to panic at the guards leaving the grounds. Hopefully they will be back before it is known they are missing."

"I thought they looked like an army."

"Army? Yes, of course!" Aura's eyes brightened. "You know of war!"

"Huh?"

Aura pulled at Emily's arm and dragged her into a small empty office. Its impressive desk and small, yet regal-looking conference table hinted that it had once been occupied by some official, but the amount of dust indicated that had been some time ago. They sat at the table and Emily wrote her name in the dust.

"Tell me all that you know. Everything."

"I don't understand. Everything about what?"

"About war. What happens during it? Have you even fought in a war?" Aura asked with an edge of excitement.

"Fought?" Emily asked, confused. "Oh no, no. I am not in the military. I was too young to enlist, and now, well…" She paused, searching her brain for a reason. "Well, now I am not really sure what I am doing with my future, to be quite honest."

"Interesting. Interesting," Aura repeated. "Tell me more."

"Well, honestly I don't know a lot about it. There hasn't been a war in America in like, forever. We fight overseas, but I don't know a whole lot about that either. I just know every day on the news they show a list of people who have been killed."

"There are multiple?"

"Hundreds."

Aura looked pained and shocked. Her head was spinning. Why hadn't she thought to ask Emily before? Of course, she would know about war. The stories Aura had heard made it sound as if Emily's world was always at war.

"How long does it last?"

"I dunno. A year? Sometimes they can last for years. The one right now has been going on for…um…seven or eight years." Emily felt foolish for not being able to answer these questions better. War had never actually touched her family or people she knew, so she'd paid it very little attention to it. An embarrassingly little amount of attention.

When—if—she got home, she swore to herself she'd brush up on current events.

Aura's face turned pale. "Years?"

"Sometimes, though I don't think it always lasts that long." They sat there for several more minutes before Emily became brave enough to ask. "Aura, what is this about? Are you going to war?"

"I am so sorry not to have informed you sooner, but I wanted to have all the information before I approached you. We think we found Levi."

"What?" Emily stood involuntarily then quickly sat back down. "What, where? When? How is he? When is he getting back?"

Aura raised a hand to quiet her. "No one has actually seen him, but where we think he is being held, it appears that the residents there are preparing for some type of battle. They need Levi to do this, thus, we think they must have him."

"I don't understand. What do you mean they need Levi?" Emily asked.

"I think they have figured out who he is and the powers that he has. I think they know that using him, they can declare war on us."

"Who are they? Why would they want to go to war with you?"

"They are to the east of us, the land known as Grustmiener. I believe they may be working with Winester, though that is just a feeling that I have. I have not shared this with my guards as I do not know how accurate it is."

"How long until they get here?" Emily asked, concerned.

"A week, hopefully more."

"Don't worry, Levi won't give in to them. He wouldn't do that to you, to me." Emily smiled at Aura, who did not return the gesture.

"It may not be up to him. They are a powerful people. They have ways of making one do their bidding."

"Anything I can do, anything at all? I know I don't know a lot about war, but if I can help at all, I'll do anything I can," Emily said.

"I appreciate that greatly, Emily. I cannot think of anything as of yet, but if I do, I shall come to you directly."

Aura got up and left the room, leaving Emily alone at the table. Her brain was buzzing, the noise filling her ears. What did Aura mean that Levi might have to obey? Emily was suddenly frightened of what it meant for all their futures.

She left the small space and made her way to Milskar's room. She knocked several times and then realized he must have left with Kolas and the rest of the guards. Her stomach fell again at the thought of him getting hurt. Or any of them. She had really grown to love this group of people. She had even befriended several members of the town.

She would be sickened if any were lost, not even to mention Levi and what might happen to him. Suddenly inspired, Emily walked out of the castle in search of Resbuca.

The sorceress had not been around much. Emily could not think of the last time she had seen her. With Kolas taking more responsibility within the castle, Resbuca seemed to have faded into the background a little. Emily felt a bit guilty that this was the first time she had thought to seek out the woman.

She found her sitting on a bench at the edge of the

woods. "Resbuca?" Emily said softly. The woman did not look up at her. "Resbuca? May I join you?" She sat without waiting for an answer.

"What do you want?" Resbuca asked in a huff.

"I don't want anything. I just haven't seen you for a while," Emily said as the sorceress turned away from her. "Where have you been these last few days?"

"Here. I am always here. Now, though, it seems that there is little care for me. I helped so much at the beginning, was so needed at the beginning, and now it is only Kolas anyone cares about. And who was the one who brought him here? It was Resbuca."

"I don't think anyone has forgotten that. There's just a lot going on around here."

Again, Resbuca made a noise under her breath. "All right." She turned to Emily. "What are you really here for?"

"I told you," Emily said.

"I know what you told me. Now tell me the truth."

"Well." Emily took a deep breath. "I just spoke to Aura about some things, and I don't really understand them. I was hoping that maybe you could help me."

"What kind of things?" Resbuca asked.

"Levi was taken to a place called…um…Grus something?"

Resbuca sat up. "Grustmiener?"

"Yes. Do you know of this place?" Emily asked, trying to hide the excitement in her voice.

"Oh yes," Resbuca said.

"Aura said something about them being able to force him to do things that he may not want to do. Do you know anything about this? Do you know if they can really do that?"

"If any people can, it is probably them. I have not

had many dealings with these people, but I know
Winester has."

"Yes, Aura thinks he may be behind having Levi
there," Emily said.

"He probably is. The lady there owes Winester greatly."

"For what?" Emily asked.

"It is not important. A story for another day."

"What can they make him do?"

"Anything, really. I remember Winester telling me
stories about a doctor, if you can call him that, who can
bend minds. Mold them, I guess you could call it, to
make them do whatever he wishes," Resbuca said.

"How?"

"Winester was never sure, but it enabled them to extract information from those who tried to deceive them.
The only thing that he could figure out was that it had to
do with changing their brain somehow. They were able to
distort whatever the person thought was real. It was dangerous, though. I can only imagine what testing had to be
done to perfect the method. Whatever they wanted your
cousin to think or do, I am sure they were successful in
that mission," Resbuca said softly.

Emily was shocked and devastated. Only hours before, she had been looking forward to the prospect of seeing Levi again. Even though it meant an army was coming, she was sure that as soon as he saw them all, he
would break away from the other side and they could go
home. Leave this war—leave all this for the people it actually concerned. *Or else*, she thought, *as soon as he
leaves the other side, the spell will be broken and no war
will happen.* Now, though, she wasn't sure how she felt
about seeing Levi again. What would he be like? Would
he be the same person she had seen weeks ago? Or would
a stranger be there, standing in his skin?

Chapter 24

Practice

They walked slowly through the woods, quick shallow breaths mixing with the sounds of leaves and branches crunching and snapping. They were scared. They were terrified. Each sound made them all jump. Abruptly, they stopped—someone in the front signaling them all to halt—and held their breath. Then, suddenly, chaos everywhere.

Men and women were running all around them. Some screaming, some mirroring their terrified looks. Combat began. People began falling and staying down. Some were stopped as they tried to run away. It was hard to tell who was on what side. Several people just sat down, too traumatized to do anything.

"Stop, stop!" Kolas yelled over the noise. "Everyone put your weapons down and listen."

He had to wait several minutes for it all to settle. Those who ran came back slowly, obviously ashamed with themselves. No matter what side they were on, the people who had been split into teams were now helping each other up.

Kolas was fuming. "Listen!" Silence quickly fell. "This is not even a small sample of what you will experience with the Grustmienerian army. There will be more of them. They will be better trained and hungry for a win. They are a people who feel that they have a lot to prove. They will try to prove that against all of you. Those who fell around you will not get up again during the actual battle. They will be dead. You will be on your own. You must think this way. You must get fear out of your head. It is going to be loud. You are going to want to run, but you must fight that urge and then fight your enemy, because they will not be running. When you turn to flee, they will stab you in the back. They will use your fear to their advantage. They will defeat you. You must protect your people. You must protect yourselves so you can protect your people, for if the Grustmieners get through you, if they are able to pass your ranks and go into the kingdom, they will slaughter everyone."

Wide eyes stared back at him. There were some younger people in the crowd and he felt somewhat bad for frightening them, but he needed them all to understand. He needed them to get the concept of this unimaginable thing. To somehow prepare them for it so, when it happened, when it was worse than any nightmare they could ever dream, they wouldn't just shut down. They would be able to fight.

"Now. We will try this drill again. You must learn how to listen to the warning sounds. Hundreds of people rushing toward you do not do it quietly. Though the other team must learn how to do it as quietly as possible. We do not want them to hear us coming. You all must take this seriously. If you get hit, drop down. You must get a feel of what it will be like to continue fighting when people are dropping all around you. Start again."

After three more run-throughs, it finally seemed like they were getting it. Not as many were falling and not nearly as quickly. Each side seemed to be sensing the other better. Though there was one person who was clearly doing worlds better than the others.

Each time when Kolas had them stop and restart, there was always one person left fighting. Milskar. He did the work of three men, successfully weaving in and out of his own side and focusing solely on the attacking side. Several times he saved those who were about to be "killed." Kolas was encouraged. Though he knew that Milskar couldn't fight an entire army, he hoped between the two of them they would be able to take a large chunk of fighters out of the mix.

They went back to their campsite—a large clearing in the middle of the woods—for a hearty meal and a good rest. Kolas worked them hard, but he knew just how much they could be pushed, and he let them rest and recover right before they reached the point of being so frustrated they would quit. He enjoyed the work of training the army. He was not used to being the person folks turned to for help and information, and he took a deep pride in being able to do this for his new kingdom.

Kolas had once lived in Omaner and lived a relatively happy life there as well. He was close to getting married and was an important guard for Queen Theaus. It only took one wrong decision to make it all come crashing down around him.

He was a young man but already staking his claim as someone important in the kingdom. Kolas had fallen in love with a merchant's beautiful daughter and the two were planning an extravagant wedding. The night before it was to take place, he went out with some of his friends to celebrate the impending nuptials.

Several hours and drinks later, Kolas found himself walking on the dark road back to his house alone. In the distance, he heard a commotion and decided to investigate. Two men had cornered a young woman and looked to have impure intentions toward her. She spotted Kolas out of the corner of her eye and silently begged him to help her.

Luckily, he carried his knife on him at all times and snuck up on the men. Pressing his knife to one of their backs, he ordered the two to stop and leave the poor girl alone.

Suddenly, one of the men turned on him, producing a knife of his own. They were no match for Kolas though, and he soon killed both attackers. Panting, he turned to the woman and asked if she was all right.

"What did you do?" she asked in a shaky voice.

"Do?" he asked, confused. "Those men were hurting you."

"Yes but—" Somehow she looked even more terrified now. "Do you know who those men were?"

Kolas looked down at the two men and matched the girl's horrified expression. He did not recognize them at first, it had all happened so fast and it was so dark out. He was just trying to protect this woman, this person who screamed and needed help—his help. Staring back up at him were the king's son and personal guard.

"I—I—" he stammered.

"You need to get out of here. We both need to get out of here," she said, eyes scanning their surroundings.

"No, we must explain."

"Explain what? Explain how these two important people attacked a prostitute? And some drunken man came and killed them? Who do you think will believe us?"

"They must believe us," he said with conviction. "It is the truth."

She laughed under her breath. "Fine, then you stay. But I am leaving. I will not be caught with blood on my hands."

Kolas stood rooted in place for several more seconds before making a decision. Quickly he turned and ran the opposite way he'd come and into the arms of his fiancée. He was covered in blood and bruises.

She listened in horror as he recounted his story. He suggested going to the king and queen, going to his parents, her parents, anyone to clear his name. She would hear none of it. Like the prostitute, she knew that there was little hope of clearing Kolas's name. There was no way the rulers would allow their son to be called a rapist and killed by a man in the queen's own court. With tears in her eyes, she told Kolas that he would have to leave. When the truth about what had happened came out, she would never be allowed to marry him and, in all probability, he would be jailed or put to death.

Heartbroken, and in fear for his own life, he left Omaner and became an outlaw. Teaming up for a number of years with Winester, Kolas lived a life of prosperity but sorrow. He thought of his fiancée and family often and longed to see them again. Through his travels and dealings, he was able to put together what happened in the days and weeks after he left his home.

The girl he saved was found and named Kolas as the murderer, neglecting to tell her true side of the story. Unsuccessful searches were made to find him. It was also rumored that King Theaus had petitioned the other rulers to return Kolas to him if he was ever found in their lands, making him a wanted man the world over. His reputation as a killer seemed to be his saving grace in his business dealings, and no one ever challenged him or spoke to any one of his whereabouts.

Soon though, he was tired of working with Winester, who carried his own demons on their travels. Once when the two had first met, Winester briefly told him about a woman he used to love. Kolas met this Resbuca on occasion in his work and the two became quite friendly with one another, yet Kolas never spoke of this to Winester.

After years of traveling together, Kolas simply decided to stop his life of crime. He tried returning to Omaner, hoping that the years he was away had eased some of his sins, but he still found wanted posters with his face plastered all around the kingdom. Before leaving for good, he purchased a griffin from a vagabond in the city outskirts. Kolas had a feeling that the man recognized him but sold him the animal anyway, or maybe because of who he was.

He had been running from his past ever since.

Chapter 25

Justice

Winester awoke and felt excited, the moment his eyes opened, at the prospects of the day. It had taken him so many years to get to this point. To finally be in a place to obtain what was owed to him. The world, which had turned so crazy since Lord Vertrous had split it up, now had hope. This was his chance to right it all, to place it back in order. He would finally be in power and bring the Four Corners under the control of one supreme ruler again. All would be right with the world when he was done. Maybe he would even be able to go into the other world. He shuddered at the possibilities of ruling it all.

The Grustmienerian army appeared strong and well prepared. Winester had watched several of their training exercises and was impressed with their continued improvement. He felt confident they would be able to take over quickly. He knew there would be casualties from the other side, but thought that those who fought against him *should* die. He wanted those people removed from Esotera so that only those who would easily bow down to him would remain—those who would gladly follow him if it meant an end to the death and destruction that would be occurring.

Now there was just the matter of gaining that control. Levi was clearly a tool they could use, but Winester had to figure out how to make that tool solely his. He needed to convince the boy to turn the power over to him once the battle was over and Esotera was theirs. He was not very concerned about the matter. Lady Grustmiener just wanted to see Esotera fall. She didn't really seem to care who picked up those pieces.

Winester walked up the long staircase to the first floor of the castle and out a side door onto the grounds. He was barefoot and the soft grass felt refreshing in the already warm morning air. Even though it was still dark, it was growing hot. The temperature had been steadily rising the last few days, reminding him why he did not care much for this part of the world.

He heard movement off in the distance and quietly walked around one of the side walls of the castle. In the distance, he saw a man and a woman who looked vaguely familiar tacking up two horses. They were placing sup-plies on the horses' backs in a rushed manner. They looked like they wanted to move quickly without getting caught. Winester moved upon them quietly.

"Need help?" he said in a normal speaking voice.

The woman screamed and almost dropped the heavy bag in her hands.

"No, we are in a bit of a rush," the man said gruffly, giving the woman a stern look.

"I do not know if we have been formally introduced. My name is Winester."

"We know what your name is. We do not have time for this. The lady requires us to leave immediately for a special mission we have been tasked with. We can sit and chat upon our return."

"I do not recall Lady Grustmiener mentioning any special tasks. Especially nothing leaving so early in the morning. Under the cloak of darkness. Shall I call her?"

"I do not believe she wishes to be questioned in such matters that regard her kingdom," the woman said. "You may call on her if you want, but I would not want to be on the receiving end of waking her for such unnecessary matters."

Amaline held her breath as she held her ground. She was terrified, her heart beating so loudly she was afraid it would wake the birds sleeping in the surrounding trees. She tried not to make any eye contact with Omire but desperately wanted to look at him, to have him reassure her that their disguises would hold as he'd promised they would.

"Fine," Winester said reluctantly. "You better start moving so you can get back before we move out. You only have a few hours. If you are found missing from the front line—"

"We will not be missing," Omire said. "We will be fighting."

The two mounted up, turned their horses, and galloped off, leaving Winester to blend into the darkness as they moved farther and farther away. Once they crested a large hill, Omire pulled his horse down into a walk, the animal huffing with its sudden excursion.

"Omire," Amaline said when she pulled up beside him.

"I know. We must keep moving. We must not stop for anything. We will not have the head start we thought we were going to have. I have a feeling if we are not back within the hour, Winester is going to start asking questions. Our absence will be mentioned soon to the lady and the truth will come out. Pretty soon we will have the army chasing us as well."

"Do you think he recognized us?"

"No," he answered. "Winester never would have let us leave if he had."

"What do we do?" Amaline asked, terrified. Her eyes were wide, trying to take in whatever bits of light she could grab on to, trying to make out her surroundings. She could only match the hoof beats of Omire's horse and hope she didn't run into anything solid.

"We have to move, if we can make it to the country line we should be safe at least for a little bit. Hopefully, the army there will be in position and can protect our entrance."

"What if they mistake us for the enemy?" she asked in a strained whisper.

"It is a risk we are going to have to take. One that we will hopefully be able to alert them to before they make any critical moves."

Amaline didn't like the answer, but had little choice in the matter. She moved her horse on faster as Omire's moved away, light starting to peak through the trees on the horizon.

∽∂∽

Her lungs were burning and their horse's breaths labored when they finally stopped that evening for a rest by a stream. It felt like they had been riding hard for hours and she was not sure how much more of this she could take before something, or someone, collapsed.

"How much farther?" she gasped.

"Hopefully not too much." He looked up at the sky and their surroundings. Then he motioned to their mounts. "I am not sure how much farther these two will go."

"I am not sure how much farther *I* can go," she muttered under her breath.

They stopped only for a few moments before moving on again at a recovering walk. With greatly heightened senses, Amaline found it difficult not to jump at the sound of every branch breaking or animal scurrying out from in front of their path.

"Shh," Omire said.

Amaline held her breath. The only sound she could hear was the thrumming of her own heartbeat pumping in her ears.

Then, in the clearing in front of her, she heard hushed movements. She had to listen very carefully to even pick that up. Her horse's ears were swiveling back and forth. Amaline tried to pick up any other noises, but was unable to. Suddenly, both horses startled, sending her heart racing again, and a figure appeared in front of them. They instinctively put their hands up.

"We mean no harm here," Omire said.

The man in front of them didn't move.

"We have information for you," Amaline squeaked, her voice unable to rise above a whisper. Still the figure did not move. "What should we do?" she asked Omire.

He just shook his head. "I have no idea. Just stay still," he said.

Suddenly, more figures appeared around them. Amaline whirled her head around, trying to focus on them all but night was beginning to close in again, making it too dark to be able to see clearly. Slowly, the figures moved in toward them in a perfect circle.

"Wait, please. Please we mean no harm," Amaline said in a panic.

"Where have you come from?" a voice boomed, re-verberating all around them.

"Grustmiener," Omire said equally loud.

The man laughed. "And you say you are here for peace?"

"We are," Amaline said. "We are here with news from our land. News we have risked our lives to bring to you. News that goes against our kingdom."

All movement toward them stopped and a silence fell upon them. Amaline froze, silently wishing they would all believe her. The original figure stepped farther out from the circle toward them.

"What are your names?" the man said.

Amaline could almost make out his features.

"My name is Omire, and this is my partner Amaline. We are guards of the king and queen."

"And what made you risk your lives, risk the lives of your kingdom, to come here today?"

"We cannot allow war to come to our lands. To your lands. It will rip our lives and worlds apart," Amaline said.

"So there are preparations for war," the man said in a quieter voice.

Another figure walked toward the first man and the two began conversing.

"What shall we do with them?" the second man asked.

"They are no use to us."

"Understood."

"No!" A woman broke ranks and walked toward the two men. "We need to take them to camp."

"Impossible," the first man said.

"It is too dangerous to talk here in the clearing," the second man said.

"We need to bring them somewhere more secure,"

the woman demanded. "Then we can find out exactly what they know."

"What if it is a trap?"

"I do not think it is," she said. "There would be more of them. They would have waited until we were all baited out into the open like this then attack. At least that is what I would have done." The three looked at Omire and Amaline. "It is just the two of them. We can secure them and then see what information they may have."

"Fine," the first man said, turning to the woman. "Eir, they are your responsibility. All of this is on you. You must get all the information you can. If something bad comes of this, it will be entirely on your shoulders."

She nodded and motioned for Amaline and Omire to dismount and follow her. Amaline felt lightheaded and realized she had been holding her breath during the entire conversation. She felt relieved to be out of danger for the moment, but was worried about where they would take them, and what they would do to them once they got there.

They soon arrived at a large tent. Amaline heard numerous voices all around them, but was unable to see the other tents and structures she was sure were littering the area. Eir showed them where they could tether their horses then held the tent door open for them.

The canvas structure was surprisingly roomy, holding a small table, various chairs, charts, and graphs of the surrounding area. Even though the structure was flimsy, Amaline felt trapped. She began looking around to see if there was another exit and was disappointed to realize the only one that existed now resided behind where Eir sat.

"All right, I am listening," Eir said.

"What do you want to know?" Omire said with a touch of proud defiance.

"I think the time for such formalities is over, Mr. Omire. You walk into our camp, are lucky our forces did not kill you, and now want to play cat and mouse with me? I stuck my neck out for you. Do not force me to take yours because of it."

"Fine. The army of guards of Grustmiener is preparing an attack on your people," he said.

"Under what authority?"

He exchanged a look with Amaline, who took a deep breath and nodded. "It is a complicated story."

"I am an intelligent woman," Eir responded.

"They have the Missing Link."

The air stood still.

"Impossible," Eir gasped. "It is a myth."

"It is nothing of the sort," Omire said and proceeded to inform her of all they knew.

Eir was spellbound and shocked. It was several minutes before it sank into her brain as it did for every new person who had been told the information. "So this is all really going to happen?" she said.

"Unfortunately, yes," Omire said. "But with our help, possibly the casualties can be minimized. We know a wealth of what the army is planning on doing. We can help prepare. We can help—" He broke off.

"Why? Why would you help us?"

"What is happening is not right," Amaline said. "The boy, they have brainwashed him. They have forced him to do this."

"I am going to need you to talk to the head of our guards. He is the man you first spoke to, Kolas. He will know what to do." Eir rushed from the tent.

"Omire," Amaline said.

"I know. I know, but we have to do this," he said and she nodded. "There is nothing about this situation that is right, but we must make the best out of it that we can. We must salvage some piece of humanity where none exists."

The tent door opened and the man called Kolas and the other man in the clearing walked toward them.

"Eir informed me that your names are Omire and Amaline. I am Kolas, and this is Milskar." They all nodded at one another. "Is what you told her the truth? The absolute truth?"

"Every word of it, I am afraid," Omire said.

"All right then. We must come up with our plan of action. How much longer until your army will be arriving?"

"They were not supposed to leave until the day after tomorrow," Amaline said. "With bringing all the people, tools, and animals along, I expect it to be a two-day journey. Possibly with some scouts and light infantry arriving late tomorrow. We rode hard. It was just the two of us and it took a solid day."

"However," Omire added. "I expect some of that to be expedited. Once they discover we are missing, and once it is found that we spoke to the boy, it will soon be concluded what we have left to do. I expect first arrival will be late tomorrow evening with the entire army following late the next day."

"Kolas, we are not prepared to fight so quickly," Milskar said with fear flashing in his eyes.

"We must be prepared," Kolas said. "We will have better information and will be more ready just on that fact. Pack the army up and move them back to the castle. Leave several runners here who can inform us at the first signs of enemy forces. Upon our return, we must prepare the dragons and first line so they will be ready. We will have a little more time with the rest of the army and civilians. This is what we have been preparing for. We just have to implement our procedures as practiced. Now go. I would like to leave as soon as possible."

Preparations could be heard all around the site as Milskar ran out of the tent.

Chapter 26

Discovery

What do you mean you cannot account for them?" Lady Grustmiener boomed. "Where could they have possibly gone?"

"I—I do not know my Lady."

"That. Is. Not. Good. Enough!"

The man standing in front of her cowered as the others in the room tried to avoid all eye contact with each other. They had all been in a last minute meeting for final preparations when the man had burst into the room. He had clearly been running for some time and was covered in sweat and gasping for breath. It was obvious he did not want to share the news he held, but also knew obligation forced him.

Lady Grustmiener was furious. "Who would know? Who knew these people? Who would know where they went? Who was the last to see them?"

"I am not completely sure, though I know Sauture was tasked with retrieving them for you the other night."

"Then get him," she spat. "And the rest of you," she

said, waving her hand around the room. "Out. Now."

The room began clearing in complete silence. The occupants were afraid to even breathe loudly, in case it would cause some of the wrath to fall upon them. Winester was the last one in line and just about to exit when she called him back.

"My lady," he said respectfully to her.

"What are we going to do about this?"

"I am not sure."

"That is simply unacceptable. These people may jeopardize our entire operation here and all you can say is 'I am not sure.' I need something better than that."

"All right. I say we send a few ahead. They should leave as quickly as possible and try to track down Omire and Amaline's exact location. It is likely, depending on how long ago they actually left, that they have already arrived in Esotera."

"Esotera!" she yelled.

He took a step back from her. "My lady?"

"You think they went to Esotera?"

"Where else do you think they would have gone?" he asked, backing up a little farther. Winester had decided it would be safer for him to not mention his chance meeting with the two as they were fleeing, though he was not cursing himself for letting them go. It was not until hours after he'd heard of their disappearance that Winester put together who they were. "I assumed they just ran away. That they did not want to fight."

"Let us hope that is the case," she spat.

Of course, though, that was not the case, and a few hours later a search party was dispatched to find the traitors. The truth was confirmed when Sauture informed them about finding the two in a secret meeting in Omire's quarters a few nights before and the information pried out of Abaddon about their discussion with Levi.

"How could this have happened right under our noses?" she asked Winester.

"There has been so much going on, so many preparations for this battle, it is a small wonder you are on top of as much as you are," he said, hoping she would not press the matter much further with him.

"That is not good enough. I need everyone to be on top of everything. Things like this simply cannot occur. If it is something I am not able to keep my eye on, I need eyes I can trust on them. What is your role in all of this?" she asked, suddenly turning to him.

"I am here to do whatever you ask of me. I am a very thankful bystander in all of this."

"You are a little too involved to simply be a bystander. You are telling me that you did not hear a breath of any of this?"

"Of course not, my lady. If I knew any of this was happening, I would have stopped it myself. I have the most at stake here."

"Do not," she said curtly, "even try to take that road. I am the one with everything at stake here. I am putting my guards, no, the king's guards, and turning them into an army for *you*. I am doing all this for *you*. It is I with everything to lose and little to gain, actually."

"It is not about gaining," Winester said defensively. "It is about repaying old debts. What you gain is that you no longer owe me anything."

"That is correct. I will owe you *nothing*," she said scathingly. "I do not know of all the powers you possess but you better channel all of them into finding these two or it will be more than just your future at stake."

Winester stormed from the room moments later, too angry to stay still, and walked around the perimeter of the castle walls. Each time he felt like he was getting closer to his goals, some type of block would appear to thwart him. He was no longer a young man and, in the last few years, he felt some of the magic he possessed slowly drain out of him like sweat on a hot day. He tried desperately to hold on to it. To see if the process could be halted, he'd even seen a shaman, but there was nothing to be done. This made his power struggle even more important. If he was ever contested, he needed his position intact, for he feared if someone did try to take his rule away from him, they would succeed.

He watched as three guards, who were fully dressed and riding horses with large packs on them, galloped off the grounds. He sent what little energy he had left to follow them and guide them on their quest.

❧❧❧

Early the next morning there was still no word back from the three sent ahead, though there was little expectation that anything would be heard back from them. The chances of them finding Omire and Amaline, capturing them, and returning them back to the castle in mere hours were unlikely. Still, when Lady Grustmiener learned of their continued absence, she went into another rage.

"What do I have all of you here for if you cannot protect this kingdom? You have been charged to do this for me, to ensure I and all my people can live a safe existence. What am I supposed to do with this information?" she yelled at a guard named Belial.

"My lady, there are few options for us," he said softly, trying to keep his tone even to calm her.

"Well, you had better come up with an option."

"The troops are gathering now. We will be ready to leave in a few hours." But this apparently was not the answer she wanted to hear.

"Hours! Hours!" she shrieked. Those standing in the courtyard around the two all stopped what they were doing, scared into a stunned silence. "I need you to do better than that."

"There is no better we can do. We were not prepared to leave for several days. We cannot be rushed. There are supplies, preparations, things that take time. I will send out each group as they are ready, but the entirety of the guards will not be gone from this castle until late afternoon." He stood as defiantly as one could in the face of a fire-breathing dragon. "I can call for the king if you wish."

Again, this was the incorrect thing to say.

"You will do nothing of the sort!" she bellowed. "I am in charge of this operation. There is nothing here that I cannot do that the king has capabilities for. Now go," she said between her clenched teeth.

Belial, glad for an escape route, quickly fled the scene.

"Can you believe that man?" she said to Winester, her eyes still blazing red.

"There are a number of supplies and affairs to put in order, my lady. War is not something that can be thrown together quickly."

"It is a good thing that battle is not a common occurrence here, or I fear Grustmiener would not last to see much of it."

With that, she stormed back in the castle, her long robes billowing out behind her.

Chapter 27

Explanations

W hat is there left to do, Aura?" Theirra asked. She had stopped with the formalities several days prior.

"I need you to round up as many beasts in the kingdom as you can find. Obviously, all the dragons, but I want any large beasts. For that matter, I want any beast you can find that may seem useful. I do not care if it is simply a flying insect whose sole purpose will be a second of distraction for the enemy. We will need every advantage we can get."

Theirra exited the room with a solemn glance at Kolas, who nodded imperceptibly back at her. Standing in front of Aura was another bunch of vagabonds. If her father could only see her now with the rag-tag bunch she kept company with these days. A pardoned outlaw, an ex-stable hand, a large guard, a sorceress, and a girl from another world. Add to it these two. She smiled slightly to herself. "I thank you very much Omire and Amaline for your loyalty."

"It is our pleasure, Queen Aura," Omire said, bowing. "It is equally important to us to have a world we are proud to live in. While we are doing this partly for your kingdom, do not think we have abandoned all loyalty to ours. We just do not want to see the future destroyed by greed."

"I feel exactly the same way. When all this is over you will be welcomed back to Esotera with open arms anytime you would like to visit here."

"Thank you, Queen Aura," Amaline said.

Amaline felt uneasy around the ruler, sure that Aura would somehow recognize them as Levi's captors. Omire had said not to bring it up, though Amaline felt increasingly guilty as praise was heaped upon them. While they were trying to help, they also were the ones who were the catalyst for the mess Esotera was in. She decided that saying little was the best route to take.

Aura noted that the woman, who appeared around her own age, was obviously quick and smart, but tended to take a back seat to her elder, Omire. Aura felt a pang in her heart for the loss of her father, though she felt losing him had shown her strength she hadn't known she possessed—strength she would need in the days to come.

She showed Amaline and Omire to two chambers at the far end of the hall where the guards slept. She wanted them to feel as welcome as possible, especially because of the great risk they had partaken in coming here. The extent of the human will awed Aura and what people would do to help, not only themselves, but also those around them.

Hearing the information they relayed on army size, weaponry, and training, Aura was thankful beyond measure that these two had arrived. She would have been taken by great surprise if an army like the one described had shown up without warning. Now further preparations were being made by her own guards and she felt, for the first time, that they really had a chance to end this all. To save all of them.

Of course, it would not be easy. She could not fool herself into thinking that this would still not be a difficult endeavor, but she hoped that their losses would be greatly reduced with the new information they had. From what Emily had told her, it was a fact of war that some who fought would not return home. A new pain saddled up next to the hole in her heart for her father, keeping it company with a dull ache. She had to ignore it, though. If she thought about what losses she could incur—Theirra? Milskar?—the hole would threaten to eat her heart and kill her. Drifting thoughts were dangerous and she kept a tight lock on them.

It felt like hours later when someone came to inform her that Theirra had returned. Aura put on a long coat to protect against the early evening chill that was beginning to settle upon Esotera. It was entirely too early for this type of weather and she wondered if somehow the land and sky knew danger was upon them. That their mournful preparations were coinciding with Aura's.

She stepped into the crisp sunshine, her breath momentarily leaving her body before she remembered how to drag it back in. Hundreds of faces turned toward her. Some she recognized. Heza stood out in the middle, surrounded by the other royal dragons, but flanking them were several dozen more. It had been some time since Aura had seen her beloved dragon and she had to suck back tears at the sight of her. Heza appeared to feel the same way, pushing through to meet her.

Aura heard a loud gasp behind her and turned in time to see Emily stride out of the castle, mouth agape in horror. She looked like she wanted to yell a warning at Aura, to protect her from impending danger, but was unable to find her voice in all the shock.

"Emily," Aura called back. "I want you to meet my dear, dear friend Heza. My darling." Aura stuck out her arms and the dragon's head fell into them. "Thank you for coming. I am sorry it has been so very long since I have seen you. I shall make it up to you. I promise."

After a quick kiss on the nose, Heza returned to the group, obviously proud to be at the receiving end of so much love and attention.

There were all kinds of winged, horned, and scaled beasts standing before Aura. Some she did not even know the names of or what to call them. There were also smaller furred animals and, as requested, an assortment of flying insects.

"There will be more arriving in the next few hours," Theirra said, walking toward her. "I gathered all that would come with me immediately, leaving a few behind to round up some more."

"You did well." Aura beamed and addressed the massive crowd. "My friends, it is a great and honorable thing you are all doing today for me and this kingdom. Your actions will not soon be forgotten. Please, make these grounds your home, sleep, and eat without fear. No one here will bring harm upon you. As danger looms closer, I will address you all again and inform you of how and where you are needed. But, for now, rest."

She linked arms and pulled Theirra back into the castle, her mind lightened for the first time in weeks. They passed Emily who was still wide-eyed. Aura used her other arm to drag her into the castle as well.

It was not until they were back in Aura's chambers that Emily found the ability to speak again. "What—" She hesitated. "What was all of that?"

"Reinforcements," Aura said with a smile in Theirra's direction.

"Dragons?"

"Some of them, yes, though I am embarrassed to say I did not recognize all the species you brought with you."

"Some I was not sure even still existed," Theirra said. "I have only read about them or heard stories. Those small furry creatures? They are called adrasteia. They are fierce little beings. They use their size to their advantage and are often able to catch attackers off guard who do not see them as a threat. I figure the Grustmiener army will be so busy paying attention to all those dragons and mostlespries—those are the scaly ones," she said to Emily, "—they will not see the little guys coming. They may actually be our most dangerous weapons."

"I am grateful to each and every one of them. And am I assured that each and every person in the town knows to treat them with respect and not to hassle them?"

"I sent a guard door to door to ensure it."

"This is really happening," Aura said, a little bewildered.

"It is, my queen."

"Do you think we are going to win?" Aura said with the same look in her eyes as when she was ten, pools of liquid blue begging for the truth.

"I know we are. We have to."

Aura nodded.

Emily's brain was swirling and it was making her somewhat nauseated. Dragons? Mos…somethings? Bunny looking creatures that killed? She wished she had clicked her heels three times to go home when she'd had the chance.

She was not really sure what was expected of her when this great battle, or whatever it would be, broke out. Granted, these people had been very kind to her and she was slowly growing to love this exotic and beautiful land, but enough to fight for it? Plus, after seeing the dragons and knowing what kinds of magical powers some had, what would she be up against?

Emily had tried to broach the subject with Resbuca, though really found no easy opening to ask her. The woman had also been even more distant, if it were possible, since they had spoken.

Theirra and Aura seemed so busy and Emily did not want to trouble them with her own wandering thoughts. Making up her mind, she left the room, neither woman noticing her departure with how engrossed they were in conversation.

Emily was able to retrace her steps from days before and find Milskar's door relatively easy. She had not realized how much she had missed him in the days since he'd departed, but now faced with the prospect of getting to see him again, her heart raced. She knocked several times on the door and was disappointed to have it unanswered. He was probably busy as well, she told herself. There must have been hundreds, if not thousands of preparations all the guards were going through.

Emily was not sure when the battle was supposed to begin, but the increased pace that accompanied the arrival of the two strangers made her think it was closer than any of them had anticipated. She made her way to the great hall to gather her thoughts and had a small glimmer of hope that she would run into Milskar there. She was disappointed not to see him, but quickly brightened when she noticed one of the strangers, the female one, sitting alone at a table.

"May I join you?" Emily asked and the girl nodded. "My name is Emily."

"Amaline."

"You all have such beautiful and interesting names. What does it mean?"

"Mean?" Amaline looked confused. "It means my name."

"Oh," Emily said, feeling foolish.

"Emily is an interesting name as well," Amaline quipped. "Are you from Vertronum?"

"No, I am not from here, actually."

"Oh, Omaner then? I know Emily—" Amaline said it as though she were trying to get a feel for the letters and sound in her mouth. "—is not a name from where I am from." She said it with such authority Emily wondered how she could be so sure. There were so many names out there, so many variations. It seemed bold to make such a statement of guarantee.

"No, I mean I am not from *here*. I am from the other world."

"Really?" Amaline's eyes bulged slightly and she moved to sit on the same side of the table as Emily.

"Yes," Emily said uncomfortably.

"Tell me everything. How did you get here? Do you know Levi?"

It was Emily's turn to stare in wonder. "How do you know Levi?"

"So you do know him?"

"Of course, he is my cousin. We arrived here together, but then he was taken…" Emily trailed off.

"By my people, yes. Well, in fact, by me."

"You?" Emily said incredulously. "How dare you!"

"Well, to be fair I did not really know why we were taking him. I was told it was a mission of utmost importance to secure the future of my people. One does not take an order like that lightly. It was not until later that my partner and I discovered the truth about him. Are you an heir as well?"

"No." Emily was finding it difficult to stay angry as she was bombarded with information and questions. The woman before her seemed so genuine, though it was because of her Levi was gone. She decided to make up her mind on the matter later. "Actually, Levi and I are cousins, but not technically related. He was adopted."

Amaline looked suddenly less impressed with her. "So what is the other world like? I have only heard stories. I hear it is glorious."

"It's okay, I guess. This place, though, is amazing. I have never seen anything like it. All the trees and green, and the animals! Seriously, dragons?"

"Actually, dragons are not native to where I am from. These here are the first I have ever seen," Amaline said.

"Pretty intimidating, huh?"

"To put it lightly."

The two smiled at each other.

Amaline suddenly grabbed Emily's hand and stared deeply into her eyes. "I hear you know of war."

"Yes." *How strange what information travels around this place*, Emily thought.

"What is it like?"

"Terrible really. There is a lot of death and destruction. Entire villages, even people, can be wiped out."

"How?" Amaline asked, intrigued.

"Bombs," Emily said. Amaline looked confused so Emily rushed to explain. "I don't really understand how they work, actually. I mean, I know about the end result but not really what they are made of, or whatever. I just know they are dropped out of planes and when they hit the ground, they explode, killing everything in their wake."

"Why would you want to do something like that?"

"People in my world do all sorts of things like that," Emily said with a shrug.

"How can one be so careless with life?"

"I can't answer that either."

"I hope war is not like that here. I do not think we have these things you call bombs, but I am afraid of the killing. I left behind a lot of friends in Grustmiener, and while I think what my people are doing is wrong in attacking you all, I still hold the dearest amount of love for them," Amaline said somberly.

"War is a tricky thing."

"The trickiest."

"May I ask you something?" Emily said.

"Of course, though I do not know what I could possibly shed light on for you. You seem to know so much I know nothing of."

"Why do you all talk the way you talk?"

"Excuse me?" Amaline asked.

"You all talk in complete sentences. In my world, we drop words and use contractions all the time, things like that. But not here, why?"

"It is simply a lazy and improper way to talk," Amaline said in a very matter-of-fact tone.

"Oh, of course." Emily felt slightly foolish and made a silent promise to herself to work on that.

Soon after, Amaline excused herself when Omire appeared in the doorway to the hall. Emily bid her a good evening and turned to go back to her room as well, deciding, for the time being at least, to forgive Amaline.

Chapter 28

Searches

They had been wandering the forests for hours with still no sign of the missing pair. The three Grust-mieners had split up over various parts of the journey to try to cover more territory, but had now reconvened, as they got closer to the Esotera border. They slowed slightly to pay more attention to their surroundings. Each man was uncomfortable, being so close to enemy lines, and they were all waiting for some type of ambush.

"How far should we go?" Garson asked.

"I am not really sure," Achan responded in a whisper, searching the woods for any sign of movement.

"Me either," Lieal piped up quietly, "but we need to figure it out soon."

"I would prefer not splitting up."

"Agreed," Garson said.

Lieal walked forward slightly away from the group and dismounted. The other two followed and were soon standing beside him. The forest was silent. Actual silence, not just the type where no one was talking but the birds and insects. It was eerie how quiet it was and made their ears rush with the pulse of their blood.

"We are too exposed," Achan said. "We have to move. This way."

He turned his horse and began walking into some of the denser tree coverage around them. They paused every few steps to listen, but their breath was the only noise they heard. Suddenly, a tree branch snapped and they all froze, muscles tensed for battle.

Five men and four women stepped out and surrounded them in a loose circle. Achan immediately went up on the balls of his feet, ready for the impending attack. Garson took a half-step back, but stopped himself when he realized there were people behind him as well. Lieal stood still, reconsidering his life choices which had brought him to this very situation at this very moment.

"What are you here for?" one of the women asked.

"I think you know," Achan said through tightly clenched teeth, his hand hovering over his short knife.

"We are trying for hospitality here and benefit of the doubt. If you would prefer not to answer the question, then we can just proceed how we deem fit," one of the men behind them said.

Without a word, Achan pulled the knife from his hand and rushed toward the woman who'd spoken. She quickly kicked his wrist, punched his ear, and dropped her elbow hard on his shoulder. He fell to his knees in one quick motion, not even fully comprehending what had happened. She kicked him again in the face for good measure. Lieal and Garson moved to stand back to back and began slowly turning to view those around them.

"Again," the man said, "what are you here for?"

They stayed silent and continued moving around. Their horses, sensing some impending danger, pressed

into each other and began moving closer to an impercep-
tible hole in the outer group. One of the women reached
up to grab the reins and led the large black horse away,
the other two following dutifully behind it.

The man moved toward the two still standing with
his hands raised, the rest of the circle tightening behind
him. Garson and Lieal unsheathed their weapons and held
them at the ready. Lieal began sweating and he was afraid
the knife might slip from his grasp. His heart was racing.

When Lieal decided to enter the guard-ship and protect the kingdom, his parents were so proud. He'd left
home and moved to the inner castle grounds, ready to
make a name for himself, when Lady Grustmiener approached him for her personal protection. Lieal was
proud that he had been noticed and jumped at the chance
to really be a part of something. Now, though, he wished
he had stayed to carry on the family farm and longed for
the simple life he had been so terrified of living.

Garson made the first move. He rushed the man in
front of them, knife waving in the air. The man was fast,
but Garson was able to slash a deep cut into his forearm
before moving past him. The man fell to the ground,
clutching his blood-covered arm in his other hand and
trying not to cry out in pain.

Lieal made a silent plea before moving on the man
and woman coming toward him. With one swift upward
motion he stabbed her in the ribs and turned to do the
same to the man, but was suddenly overtaken by three of
them and pinned to the ground. A black bag was placed
over his face as the knife was ripped from his hand.

The struggle with Garson lasted a few moments
longer. He was able to cut the other man in the leg and
was about to turn on the last woman before the group
converged upon him. It took more time, but they were

able to disarm him as well and placed a similar bag over his head.

Achan, who was still on the ground in pain, was hog tied and placed in a horse-drawn cart. The injured man gingerly climbed in, as well, and sat keeping a wary eye on him.

Lieal's hands were bound and tied to something, a horse possibly, that dragged him slowly forward. He stumbled and fell several times but the march continued. He tried to get his bearings and figure out in what direction they were moving, exactly, but it was all so foreign to him. The birds and insects were back, but nothing sounded familiar. It seemed as though they had changed direction several times from the feel of the ground and hills, but again, he could not pinpoint a single thing.

It seemed like they had walked for close to an hour before finally coming to rest. Lieal blinked against the sunlight pouring into his pupils as his hood was ripped off. He looked around his surroundings, but again, he was not able to tell where he was. Garson was in the same position on his knees, trying to adjust to the brightness as well. Lieal tried to make eye contact, but Garson was in a bit more pain for putting up such a fight.

Another man came out of the clearing and addressed the woman traveling with them. The men left them staked to the ground and went to join the newcomer.

"I need a full report," Kolas said.

"Well." The woman shifted from foot to foot and looked at the men before answering. "There were some, complications."

"Explain."

"Resna was badly injured and we lost Zilpah."

His brows furrowed. "Lost?"

"The one man stabbed her. We did all we could," one of the men said somberly.

"And Resna was cut," the woman said, pointing to the man slumped in the cart. "He will be fine, but he will need to be seen by a skilled healer to close the wound and counter his loss of blood."

"All right, I will send for the queen's personal health aide." Kolas put a hand on her shoulder. "You did well today, the queen and the kingdom thank you for all you have done. Now please, return to your homes."

Several more guards followed him as he moved forward toward the two kneeling men. One of the guards climbed into the cart and kicked Achan out of it. He fell to the ground with a soft thud and lay still. The group of citizens gathered their things and moved on.

"Zilpah?" the woman said over her shoulder before disappearing into the dense brush.

"We will take care of everything."

She nodded and followed the rest out of the clearing.

"One dead already," Milskar said as he approached Kolas after the last villager had departed. "I hope this is not an indication of what is to come."

"Do you think it is?" one of the guards asked.

"Probably," Kolas answered solemnly. "Though it cannot hurt that we have captured three more of their soldiers. One can only hope that if the men they keep sending out continue not to return, it shall make them rethink their plans on attacking us."

"Or bring more with them," Milskar countered.

"An equal possibility," Kolas said.

"Where should we take them?"

"The dungeons. There we can question them and see if they will be any use to us."

"And what happens if they are of no use to us?" Milskar asked.

"The outcome of the war will determine their fate."

Kolas turned and walked away, leaving Milskar to ponder the severity of his words.

They blindfolded the group again and marched toward the castle, using a confusing route of switchbacks. The method was somewhat archaic, but if any of them escaped the chances of them being able to get their bearings and retrace their steps was minimal.

So that the prisoners could be taken directly underneath the castle into the holding cells, they were taken through a back gate. Crime was not a prominent feature in Esotera and there was only one large caged room to hold them all.

Kolas would have greatly preferred separating them, but attached to the cell was a smaller room where he could, at least, perform the interrogations.

After removing their blindfolds again and quickly assessing the three, he determined the taller, slim, blond one should go first. He looked no older than eighteen, and Kolas hoped he could use the obvious fear the boy held to his advantage.

"Sit, please." The boy did as he was told but found some difficulty with his hands still bound behind his back. "My name is Kolas. Yours?"

"Lieal."

"Very good, Lieal. The more you cooperate, the more you help us, and the more I am able to help you. If you are difficult with me, I will have no choice but to be the same way with you. All of this, this entire interview is dictated by what you say. Do you understand?" The boy sat motionless. "I will take that as a yes. Now, what are the three of you doing here?"

"Going for a walk," Lieal responded mechanically.

"A walk?" Kolas laughed, thoroughly entertained by the imagination of this person. "And what was the purpose of this walk?"

"What the purposes of most walks are. Fresh air, exercise for the horses, exploration."

"Ah, exploration. See, that is the part that I am most interested in. What were you exploring?"

"Trees, plants, animals. The forest as a whole." Lieal was sitting as straight as possible and looking directly in front of him while he spoke.

"Lieal, I need you to be truthful with me."

"A simple mid-day walk."

Kolas pounded on the table, making the boy jump, but he returned quickly to his motionless state. "Lieal, if you are not going to corporate with me, I am going to have to make you. You seem like a nice boy and I would rather your mother recognize you the next time she lays eyes on you."

That seemed to touch something. Lieal looked up briefly and locked eyes with Kolas before bringing his gaze back down to the table. A little of his erectness faded and he slumped almost imperceptibly in his chair.

"Now, let us try this again," Kolas said trying to grab on to the momentary defeat, "Why are you all here?"

"I told you," he whispered.

"I know what you told me. I know what your superior told you to tell me in case you were caught. I know all of this. But now I need you to skip all that and tell me the truth. Tell me what you are actually here for."

The silence began filling the room and Lieal was finding it difficult to find air that wasn't tainted with anticipation and fear. He could feel himself wanting to break and tell the truth, even though he was taught to answer such questions in an unassuming manner. Would it really be that bad if they knew why they were here? Would it really change anything, good or bad?

Kolas jerked him from his thoughts by grabbing him

around the neck and throwing him to the floor. The chair crashed beneath him. His brain was trying to quickly work out what hurt more, his constricted neck or throbbing hands.

Kolas lifted him to his feet and pressed him into the wall, a look of pure hatred in his eyes. "Tell me."

"I cannot."

Kolas slapped him, keeping one forearm pressing his chest against the wall. "Tell me," he repeated.

"No."

The boy began crying and Kolas punched him. "Tell me." He was about to hit Lieal again when the boy cried for him to wait.

"Please, please take mercy on me."

"Mercy is given to those who earn it. What can you give me that will earn it for you?"

"We are looking for two of our guards who disappeared a few days ago."

"Good boy." Kolas brought him back to the chair and righted it before sitting him back down. "Continue."

"All I know is we are looking for one man and one woman."

"Names."

"Amaline and O something. O…Omire." Lieal had hot tears streaming down his face. He hated himself, at this moment, but he was scared and he just wanted it all to stop. He just wanted to go home, see his parents, and forget everything he knew about fighting, war, and honor, and go back to being a small boy who others took care of.

"Good. What else about them."

"I do not know much about them. They are guards and they have gone missing. We were sent to find them and bring them back."

"And that is all you know."

"That is all I know," Lieal said quietly and Kolas

swiftly moved closer to him. "I swear!" he yelled in a panic. "I swear that is all I know. I just started. I have only been with the guards for a short time and they do not tell me much. They do not trust me. They tell me nothing. It is all I know."

Kolas could see past the pain of the current situation into the deeper rooted pain of not belonging that he saw in the depths of Lieal's eyes. Here was a boy who was trying to do good and finding it difficult to get a hold on his place in the world. Kolas had seen the look many times before and knew there was an innocence and sweetness to boys like Lieal—characters who had no place in an army. He knew the boy was telling the truth simply by the fact that he did not have it in him to lie any more. He had been broken, possibly beyond repair, and definitely beyond usefulness.

He made a bit of a show of it as he violently threw the boy back into the room to make it appear as if no information was obtained from him. Coupled with the bruises already appearing on his face, Kolas hoped it would add a little meat to the story if Lieal claimed he told Kolas nothing.

Next, he picked up the biggest of the group. A slightly shorter man who had about fifty pounds and twenty years on Lieal. Kolas knew this man would be trouble, but he also had a feeling that the he would garner the most information. Men who looked like that were often trusted to defend secrets. The other man in the cell looked useful as well and Kolas hoped he did not have to use him to gain any more bits of information.

"Your name."

"Achan."

"Achan, I will ask you the same questions I asked your friend here moments ago, and I better not get the same made up story about you all picking flowers in the woods. It is a clever and well-thought-out story, but I am a man of truths and I do not appreciate it when people lie to me. Do you understand?"

"Completely."

"So why are you here?"

"On a flower-picking trip," Achan said.

The punch Kolas threw launched the man out of his chair and on to the floor. Kolas's hand hurt slightly from the force but the added adrenaline from so much anger was helping to coat the pain. "I will ask you again," he said after sitting the man back upright. "What are you doing here?"

"Hunting."

"Hunting what?"

"You," he said with a sneer.

Kolas hit him again, this time feeling a small crack occur in his knuckles.

Achan spit blood on the floor before turning to Kolas and smiling with red teeth. Kolas wanted to kill him. The satisfying image was running through his brain, but he had to fight against it. Only a momentary relief would be gained before the reality would have set in. They needed this man, maybe for nothing else than a bargaining tool, but a tool all the same.

Kolas figured that if the queen had sent these three as a search party, she must hold some stock in their ability. They were probably not her best fighters, too much of a risk for that, but they all had to be capable men in case they ran into trouble. She needed to make sure they would return to her with the information she needed. She would not be very happy to find another part of her army under Esotera's control.

"You will not get anything out of me," Achan said.

"Then you shall get nothing out of us," Kolas turned

and exited the room, locking it behind him. "He is to get nothing. No food. No water. Nothing until I say otherwise," he said to the guards surrounding the holding cell. "If I hear that anyone showed this man mercy, I will kill that person myself."

Chapter 29

Final Preparations

Emily's heart was racing and she felt more exhila-
rated than she had in all her life. She clutched a
long stick and was trying not to think about her
hands being sweaty. She needed to hold it firmly, needed
to know it would not slip from her grasp. She was worried but tried desperately not to focus on it. She tried to
focus on the real danger in front of her.

A man was coming at her full speed. She lowered
herself into a crouch, prepared for the impact she knew
was coming. Emily was not a fast runner or fighter, but
she found she was skilled with the long bat and was often
able to get in the first shot. Moments before he reached
her, she threw the stick toward the ground and planted
herself into it with all her might. Immediately, the huge
figure crashed to the ground. She placed one foot on his
neck, dropped her stick, and quickly pulled out her knife,
putting it against his neck.

Milskar beamed. "Good job!"

Emily was panting with the effort and adrenaline. "I think I am finally getting it."

"Getting it? You are a natural!" He reached up a hand and she grasped it, pulling him to his feet. "You just have to make sure to stay calm and not react too early. That will give your attacker a heads up to what you are doing and give that person time to prepare for a counter attack."

Emily nodded. She'd felt renewed with purpose the last two days since approaching Milskar with a proposition of having him train her. She hated the feeling of just sitting around the castle while everyone else was preparing for battle. This war involved her. Involved her in some deeper and greater way than anyone else. This was not her home, but Levi was her family. All of it needed saving. They were heading back to the castle, laughing and talking in equal measures, when Milskar suddenly froze. Emily's heart stopped. She heard what had halted him. There was rustling to the left of them.

Milskar slowly put his arm back around Emily, forming a protective circle around the front of her. The hairs on her neck began to prickle.

Resbuca confidently walked out between two trees. Milskar immediately exhaled and returned to a more relaxed pose. Emily was trying to brush the fear off her, but was having trouble returning her heart to its normal pattern.

"Resbuca," Milskar said in an even tone. Emily could still barely breathe normally.

"Milskar." Resbuca nodded to him. "The time is coming soon."

"You are sure?"

"Positive. Twenty-four to thirty-six hours. War will soon be upon us."

"We must go inform Kolas. I thank you for your foresight."

"I have limited abilities to assist in this great battle. Any advantage I can give you all is my priority," Resbuca said.

The three turned and followed the path back up to the castle. Resbuca and Milskar talked quietly the entire way back, leaving Emily to stew in her own thoughts.

Was she really ready for all of this? With the battle preparation the two of them had done, Emily had known it was coming. Now, at the first sign of danger, her body completely failed her and fear took over. What would actually happen when the battle started and people were falling all around her? When Milskar would be nowhere around her and she would have to fight on her own? Fear began breeding in her stomach.

Emily found herself following the others into the queen's grand meeting room. There was a polished mahogany table in the middle of the large circular room. All over its surface were strewn maps, diagrams, and pictures. She tried to read some of them, but was unable to decipher their complicated meanings. Aura, Kolas, and several other members of the guards looked up as the three entered.

"Milskar, Emily, Resbuca," Aura said with a bit of apprehension. "Did you bring updated information with you?"

"We did, my queen," Milskar said before gently prodding Resbuca with his elbow.

"They will be here this time tomorrow at worst, early the next morning at best."

The information had clearly shaken Aura, but she nodded slowly. Resbuca looked her straight in the eyes, waiting for further questions she knew would soon be coming. Emily stood in the corner, dumb and mute, feeling very out of place but not knowing where else to go. Milskar took a step back to stand next to her and she was grateful for the company.

"What do we do first?" Aura asked Kolas.

Emily could tell Resbuca was a little offended that Aura was not paying more attention to her.

"We let all our forces know they must be prepared to fight within the next day," Kolas said.

"We also need to move all those who are not staying and fighting into the reinforced areas deep within the forest. There are some old underground bunkers," Milskar said.

"There are bunkers?" Kolas asked.

"There are hiding places all over the forests. Just because there has not been a war before, it does not mean no rulers have feared they would occur one day. Luckily, your father's father was one of these men. There should be enough room to hide the rest of the town for five or six days. If the battle goes on longer than that, we may need to have them enter the fight anyway. I've had some of our men and women stocking it the last few days, so it should be comfortable," Milskar said to him.

"Thank you all," Aura said suddenly, her eyes slightly moist. "Thank you for all your preparations, for all your sacrifices, for everything you have done for me and Esotera these last few weeks." She looked each person in the room in the eye and nodded her appreciation.

Emily couldn't help but look away when it was her turn.

All those around the table stood up and left the room, followed by Kolas and Milskar. He nodded to Emily and squeezed her shoulder before shutting the door behind him.

"I want to thank you both again personally for all of

your help," Aura said turning to the two women. "I understand that you owe no alliance to Esotera—"

"My queen," Resbuca cut her off. "There is no need. What you have done for me is thanks enough. Now, if it is all right with you, I would like to meet with Kolas before any battles begin."

"Of course. Emily, may I ask you to stay a moment longer?"

"Yes, yes, of course." Emily smiled slightly at Resbuca as she left the chamber.

"Emily, this is not your war," Aura said softly to her, almost as if she were a child.

"It is a war my family created. It is my war." Emily believed the words as she was saying them. She spoke them with such conviction it made her stand just a little taller.

"I need someone to inform those in hiding when it is safe to come out. I need someone who can run between our lines and those in the bunkers. That person must ensure they are never followed and be able to hide well. No one must find the hiding places. Can I entrust you with this task?"

"I have been training to fight," Emily said, somewhat dejected. Now that she really considered it, not fighting was no longer an option. She needed to do something, to contribute in some meaningful way.

"I need someone who is trained to fight to be able to ward off any who may want to compromise the rest of my people. I also need someone who is fast and stealthy. It will also help that you look unfamiliar enough that their army may think you are one of the peasants brought along to fight. They may mistake you as an ally and thus leave you alone. You are the only one I can truly trust with this job.

"Then it will be my honor to do it."

ᥱᢣᥱᢣ

Emily left the room with a pile of neutral looking clothes.

They were large enough that she would be able to wear her minimal armor under it and in a color that would, hopefully, allow her to just blend in. Aura also gave her a hat to contain her hair so nothing about her would stand out.

"I've just been working so hard," she complained later to Milskar.

"You will personally be in charge of the safety of hundreds of people. It is more than you can do as a fighter. You should be proud of the task."

"I am trying, I really am, but it just doesn't feel…I don't know." Emily's voice broke.

"Yes, you do. What does it not feel like?" he asked.

She was almost too embarrassed to say and lowered her eyes. "It does not feel important enough."

Milskar placed his fingers under her chin, lifting her face to meet his. "It is important. Why do you feel like you need to do more?"

"It is partly my fault," she choked out. "He is my family. I have to take some responsibility for that. I also—" She paused.

"What?"

"I was sleeping next to him. I didn't even wake up." She was trying desperately not to cry but a few tears were able to battle their way out against all her defenses

Milskar pulled her into a firm hug. "Oh, Emily."

His kindness took her by surprise and the sudden gesture pushed her over the edge. She was soon sobbing uncontrollably. He rubbed her back and softly spoke to her.

"I am just being silly," she said, pulling back from him and wiping her face.

"No you are not. It is a terrible burden that you are living with. You need not apologize for feeling the effect that comes along with that." He lifted her face again, "But you also do not have to put your own life in danger."

She nodded. "I know."

"It is imperative to the future of our kingdom that those in hiding are not found. If you ask me, I think the queen is placing too much upon your shoulders, but if you are really feeling like you need to repent for something you really had nothing to do with, there is no better opportunity than this. I just hope that all the training I have done with you will be enough to keep you safe."

Emily nodded again and took a deep breath to steady her emotions. She wished she had not cried in front of him. Milskar had so much on his mind, he did not need her emotions added to it. Almost as if reading her thoughts, he smiled reassuringly at her and she tried to match his enthusiasm.

"Plus, if nothing else, I will feel better that you are off the front line of fighting."

"Excuse me?" His words were moving through her brain as if they were made of Jell-O.

"If I knew you were in danger, if your life was in danger—" He broke off mid-sentence, slowly moving forward, and kissed her.

All the feelings that had been bottling up that he had tried to ignore these last few weeks poured out of him as he moved his lips against hers. Finally, what felt like a blessed eternity later, they broke apart, both slightly pink in the face and gasping for air.

She had to return to her room, to rest before the battle began. He kissed her one more time, softly, sweetly, before letting her go. Milskar watched her walk away and didn't turn to go to his room until Emily was completely out of sight.

He shut his door and leaned his forehead into it. He ached to pull the door open and run down the hall after her. Force her to stop and pull her into a tight embrace. Would he try to talk her out of the battle? Would he talk himself out of it as well, suggest they leave in the night and escape any danger that may face them? He quickly pushed the idea out of his brain.

What was wrong with him? He hadn't felt this way in…well, probably in forever, and the feelings caught him completely off guard. At first, Emily slightly annoyed him. Her incessant whining, holding them up on their journey, and her moping around the castle the first few days had made her quite difficult to be around. Lately though, she had been acting differently, or maybe he was just seeing her differently. At first, he just started meeting her for breakfast. They always sat in silence, each of them on the brink of saying something, but neither wanting to be the one to make the first move.

One day though, and he was not sure exactly what had caused it, she began talking. They covered all sorts of topics, but all very benign. Emily asked him some questions about his past, and he did the same to her. And slowly, over hot meals of some questionable foods, they began to get to know each other.

Milskar told Emily of how he ran away from home when he was fourteen, lied about his age, and joined the king's guards. He always had a feeling the king knew he was younger than he pretended to be, and Milskar wondered out loud for the first time if this was why the king took the young boy under his wing.

He came from a very large family of nine brothers

and three sisters and felt he was doing his parents a favor by leaving them with one less mouth to feed. They were farmers and, while they yielded enough crops to sell at the local market, they always went just hungry enough that their stomachs were constantly growling for more. Milskar sent them money whenever he could and visited them from time to time, but he really had little contact with them.

It broke Emily's heart to hear it, always having been so close to her own family. They were silent for a long time after he told her the story.

Emily talked about growing up with a slightly over-bearing father and a mother who stayed mostly silent. She spoke about growing up with Levi, her best friend and closest ally, but she soon broke off mid-sentence and avoided eye contact with him. Milskar had reached across the table to take her hands. She smiled weakly at him, her eyes just a little wet with unspent tears. After that, they talked little of their pasts.

Getting to spend extra time with her in training had been a complete joy for Milskar. Emily was a quick learner and seemed to revel in finally having a purpose. It had been fun for him as well and he really enjoyed getting to spend so many long afternoons with her. It wasn't until Emily spoke of being angry about being left out that it all really hit home with Milskar about what they were really training for.

Now the thought of her fighting, the possibility of her being hurt, or worse—

He shook his head to remove the troubling thoughts. He would keep her safe. He would do whatever it took.

Chapter 30

March

The first waves of guards were beginning to make their way from the castle. Lady Grustmiener watched them from her window, high in the castle tower. She was angered over how long it actually took them to organize and ready their things. They all knew this battle was coming and she did not understand their lack of preparation. Her temper was becoming shorter and shorter by the hour, to the point where people were starting to avoid her, if at all possible.

Even though she could tell he was slightly wary about it, she kept Winester close by. She needed the protection of his powers and the desire of a shared goal to make sure everything stayed on track. They'd had little physical contact since that first night and she felt an added level of tension because of it.

"How is this going to turn out?" she asked him, still staring out the window.

"We will conquer," he said matter-of-factly.

"Good."

She dismissed him to gather his belongings and to make sure the next wave of guards was preparing adequately to leave on time. She began moving around her room, deciding which of her own items she wanted to take. While she would have a place far from where the actual fighting was, she wanted to be close enough to make decisions and get regular updates.

As far as she knew, the king still had no idea what was occurring back in his kingdom. She needed to do everything in her power to keep it that way. It wasn't that he wouldn't have agreed with the decision to wage war, now that waging war was possible. It was whom it was for. Whom it was about. It was that Winester was involved.

When Lady Grustmiener first married the king, Winester was deeply involved with the inner workings of his court. His position as a counselor to the previous king was passed along to his son. The king held an air of resentment toward him, though. He felt unable to get out of the shadow of his father while his aides still had old alliances. He pawned Winester off on his new wife, happy to have the sorcerer away from him and keeping an eye on her.

The affair started almost immediately. Lady Grustmiener thought Winester really loved her and, to his credit he thought he did too, but soon realized he was more in love with her position of power than with her. He was also smart enough not to let her know this. It continued for years until one day when an aide caught them.

Lady Grustmiener was terrified of what would happen to her if the king found out. While she loved Winester, she knew he would not be able to provide the same level of lifestyle she was now accustomed to living. Winester erased the memory of the aide and they both decided to end what they were doing. She told Winester that she would be forever in his debt for saving her from the king's wrath. She promised that when the day came where he needed something from her, she would do everything in her power to make it come true. Now he was cashing in. While it was a much larger endeavor than she ever imagined the promise would entail, she was bound to the promise and had to stay true to her word.

She just hoped they could get everything completed and with as few casualties as possible. If the king returned to find half his kingdom destroyed, she would have to confess her sins to him and just hope that time would help erase the edges off what she had done.

Her country was so much stronger than Esotera. This she knew. They also had always kept a stronger army-like guard-ship and would be better prepared for the events that would be occurring. It did worry her, though, that none of her guards had returned from their missions. Though she knew deep down they had been captured, she still hoped they had just gotten lost in the woods.

It was something she was not able to deal with mentally at the time. When all this was over she would need to tie up all the loose ends. She would deal with those responsible and punish them when the battle was done and they were victorious.

A soft knock came to her door and a small woman entered tentatively.

"My lady," she said, bowing deeply. "Your horses are prepared and ready for you whenever you wish to depart."

"I shall be out in just a few moments."

The woman nodded and rushed out of the room as quickly as possible. Lady Grustmiener finished gathering her things and placed them in several bags that her servants would bring to her location. The moment was finally here and she felt a few beats of apprehension in her heart, but quickly dismissed them. This was it. This was all she would have to do and the sins of her past would be able to remain there. Winester would disappear from her life forever and she would be able to focus on her future without fear of him coming back to haunt her.

She informed her servants where her bags were and left it to them to find out where to bring them. She mounted her great white mare and followed several members of her court out of the castle walls and into the forest to begin their day-and-a-half-long journey.

They would be setting up camp a few miles away from the battlegrounds. She had been assured she would be able to hear what was going on and runners would keep her informed, but she would be far enough away to stay out of trouble and be moved quickly if need be. She turned and took one last look at her beloved castle. It had been a much smaller structure when the king first occupied it and, even though most of it was still buried underground, she considered it her crowning glory in making it into the impressive building it was now.

She now needed to focus on the impeding battle. She needed her army to prevail with minimal losses. When the king returned, she would be able to tell him about Levi, about the war that was breaking out so fast she could not spare a single guard to fetch him. He would be relieved that it was over and would be proud of her for handling the stressful situation gracefully. Their victory would be the icing on the cake. His joy at the defeat of Esotera would prevent him from looking any farther in the matter and just enjoy the riches she would bring him.

The noise they made moving through the forest drowned out all other sound. It made her feel slightly vulnerable, not being able to hear any danger if it came close. She tried to feel safer in the company of so many armed people, but really, it did little to quell her fears. She wondered how great armies in the other world moved forward with their swelling masses while still being conscience of their surroundings. There were a number of things which confused her about war and how it was a constant entity in some parts of the other world. How did people function in a place where battle, death, and destruction were normal backdrops to their lives? She would be glad when this was all over and she could live in her peaceful expanded kingdom.

It was decided, after hours of marching, that they were in a safe enough place to make camp for the night. Lady Grustmiener didn't see how this area of the forest was any different than any of the others they had passed through, but she trusted her guards and dismounted from her horse. While those around her set up the site, she took a seat and rested. She was mesmerized by their clockwork efficiency. She wasn't often able to witness the execution of her orders and it intrigued her to see it.

She eventually settled into her spacious tent and lay on the plush cot. She could see the outline of two guards standing in front of her tent door, shifting their weight from foot to foot. There was faint rustling all around her as horses and people settled for the night. Hushed whispers whirled around the thin fabric of her shelter, like ghosts haunting the night. It made her shiver and pull the blanket tighter around herself. She wondered how the king lived in the forest like this for months at a time when he traveled. It was not something she thought she would ever be able to get used to.

Soon she was able to fall into a deep sleep, though one wrought with terribly dark dreams. They skimmed the surface of her mind and caused her to breathe in quick, shallow pants.

Lady Grustmiener was being chased though the woods and, no matter how hard she spurred her horse forward, she went no faster. She looked down and noticed there was no longer any horse under her, just her feet moving as fast as they could. The forest floor felt damp under her naked feet and they made soft noises on the leaves they crushed.

She couldn't see anyone anymore, but she could hear their voices breathing all around her. She didn't know if she was even running in the correct direction and, with the fear that she would unexpectedly run into them, she stopped in her tracks.

The noises came from all around her. She was panicking. Where should she run? Suddenly, a huge black horse came out into the clearing. It stared straight at her and walked forward with purpose. She began walking to meet it, a single hand outstretched, reaching for its face. Just before they met, the horse's head shot straight up and it burst into flames, disappearing in an instant. Screams resounded around her and she bolted upright, ripped from her dream by a firm hand.

It took her a second to separate the dream from reality and to realize the hand on her actually existed. She followed it up and came face to face with Winester.

"I just had the most terrible dream," she breathed out heavily.

"What happened?" he asked with a worried expression on his face.

"There was a horse and he burst into flames right in front of me."

A moment of concern seemed to sweep across Winester's face, but he quickly removed it and composed himself. "Interesting. Would you like me to help you fall back asleep?"

"What time is it?"

"A few hours before dawn."

"I could use a few more hours," she admitted.

Suddenly, she felt deeply relaxed and was having trouble keeping her eyes open. She faintly heard the tent flap shut before she drifted into a dreamless slumber.

Chapter 31

Places

The sleep seemed to last for a single blink of an eye and soon the noises of the camp breaking down around her woke Lady Grustmiener. She quickly changed and stepped out of the tent amid a flurry of activity. There were people moving all around her, packing up bags, tacking up horses, and putting out fires. It seemed like only seconds since she had left her tent, yet now she noted that it was completely disassembled and moved into a trunk filled with the other enclosures.

"My lady, please, come and eat something," a timid woman said without making eye contact. She gestured at an area where a fire was still going and people were standing around eating steaming plates of food.

Someone prepared a plate for Lady Grustmiener and she was guided to a small table and chair. Movement was happening all around her and it made her suddenly out of breath. She pushed herself out of the chair and walked toward where her tent had just been.

"How much longer until camp is completely broken down?" she asked one of her aides.

"Should only be another few moments. We will be ready to leave soon. May I get anything else for you, my lady?"

"No, thank you. I would just like to leave as soon as possible."

Staying in one place was starting to make the inside of her skin itch in a place too deep to scratch. She felt like leaving here would be the only remedy for it. She remembered her dream suddenly and shivered a little. This place was holding too much darkness even with the light streaming through. She made a mental note to avoid this clearing on their way back from the battle, hopefully in a few days' time.

To her right, a rider suddenly burst through the forest and spoke hurriedly to a guard standing there before spurring his horse back where he came from. It happened so fast Lady Grustmiener wasn't completely sure she even saw it. The guard started walking toward her with a quickened pace.

"The first wave of guards has arrived at the edge of Esotera. They are awaiting our arrival before proceeding."

"Good. Have they seen any movement from their army?"

"Nothing as of yet, but someone will be sent to us the moment that changes," the guard said.

"When shall the rest of the forces join up with them?"

"Two more groups should be there within the next few hours. The other sections will be scattered throughout the surrounding area to be spread out better for the march into Esotera."

"Good. Let us not delay any longer and join up as quickly as possible," Lady Grustmiener said.

"Yes, of course."

The guard sprinted off as aides gathered any straggling items that needed packing. Soon they were all mounted again and moving off in the direction of Esotera.

Lady Grustmiener was not very familiar with this part of the woods and she was feeling a little more uncomfortable with each step they took away from her castle. She had played in the forest growing up and considered herself somewhat of an expert on the Grustmiener woods, but these areas were uncharted territory.

For a flash she felt like she were ten years old again, careening around the trees playing hide and seek with her friends. They were having so much fun they lost complete track of time and it was soon very dark out. The only light pushing its way through the treetops was that of the stars. The girls were terribly lost and scared. She and the three other girls spent the entire night out in the woods until a search party stumbled upon them right before dawn. After that, she did not venture too far away from her house, resigning herself to the few miles surrounding the castle grounds.

Now she felt that familiar pang of panic in her chest. If somehow she got separated from her group she did not think she would be able to find her way home. Subconsciously she urged her horse forward a little quicker and moved into the middle of the group. She felt safer being completely surrounded and stayed in that placement the entire rest of the journey to their base for the battle.

It took longer than anticipated for them to reach the predetermined spot on the edge of the forest and tempers were running short. The light was beginning to fade. The sun fought against being pushed below the horizon and had turned the color of burning blood. Winester seemed to sense the bad mood Lady Grustmiener was in and gave her a wide berth while camp was being set up and food prepared. He would wait to approach her until she had eaten and settled in.

There were small globes of fire all throughout the clearing, shedding small pockets of light dancing all along the forest floor. Winester slowly made his way to the royal tent, nodding to each guard as he passed through the thin door.

She was sitting at a makeshift desk looking at maps by candlelight. She was so beautiful, it was almost as if all the years behind them had been erased. He remembered suddenly why he had loved her so.

"My lady," he said, bowing respectfully.

"Winester. Please come in. I was hoping to see you this evening."

"I figured I would wait until you were settled before bothering you."

"You are never a bother."

Winester was unsure what was causing this behavior. She had been in a foul mood for days leading up to their departure. It had only gotten worse on their journey these last two days.

He'd basically avoided her all morning, especially after she snapped viciously at a groom who was trying to get her horse ready.

Now, though, she seemed perfectly happy, almost ignoring the situation around her.

"Are you feeling all right?" he had to ask her.

"Perfectly fine. It feels nice to be settled in a new place for a few days. Traveling is not one of my favorite things to do."

"I agree with that," he said.

She smiled at him. "What did you want to talk to me

about? I do enjoy the visit, but I have a sneaking suspicion it was not just to drop by and say hello."

"Unfortunately not, my lady." He hesitated. "I—I wanted to talk to you about after this war is over."

"After?"

"Yes, what will happen to me, to us, when all this is said and done?"

"I shall return to Grustmiener, a hero to my people and king."

"And I?" Winester asked.

"I assumed that you would stay here, rule this land you have coveted for so many years."

"I am greatly pleased by your answer. That is what I want to happen as well." He turned to leave, not wanting to press his luck or take anymore of her time.

"Though, of course you cannot rule exactly as you wish," she added.

He stopped in his tracks and turned back to face her. "My lady?"

"With the help I have provided you, I am expecting that Grustmiener can now count on Esotera as one of its most important allies. Am I wrong in that assumption?"

Winester dropped his head. "Of course not, my lady."

He should have known that he would not be able to walk away with everything he wanted. Everything that she owed to him, without owing a little back. He resented her so much right now, his hands were shaking in anger. She must have noticed this and got up, moving closer to him. He took a step back, unable to trust himself not to lash out at her. She grabbed his hand and pulled him back into the space he had just occupied. He tried to move backward once again, but she held him there, planting a kiss on his pursed lips.

Suddenly, through all his anger, he realized he was

kissing her back. He was transported to a time many years and miles away as the familiar feelings came flooding back to him. He was not sure how much time had passed, but slowly reality came back to him. He was shocked to find his hand woven through her hair and their bodies pressed tightly against each other. He pulled back and smiled at her.

"I will do what you ask of me, my lady."

And with that, he turned and left the tent, leaving Lady Grustmiener trying to catch her breath behind him.

Chapter 32

The Approaching Hour

Aura was finding it hard to breathe. She was doing laps around her chambers so quickly it was making her dizzy. She felt like a hummingbird. If she stayed still for an instant she would die. So she paced.

Theirra watched her and bit her tongue, wanting to tell the queen to stop and sit down, but knowing she was in no place to tell her what to do.

Her own worries were mounting, as well, and it was taking everything she had in her to not join Aura in her pacing.

Emily and Milskar entered the room soon after, but stood silently off to the side. Emily wrung her hands together, but no other movement came from the pair.

Aura was making them all anxious and it was a relief when Kolas came in and broke the silence.

"Everything is in place, my queen."

She stopped in her tracks, eyes wide. "Already?"

"We knew they would be here soon."

"But already?" Her breathing quickened even more.

"Yes. They are setting up camp. Our scouts have found where Lady Grustmiener is staying and it appears that more troops are moving in as well, though where their exact placement will be is unknown. We know where the main army is stationed. They have been there for almost a whole day, but we knew that they would not concentrate all their troops in just one area. Once the other placements are known I will give you an update. Then we can move our forces in to counter them."

"Thank you for the report, and please inform me the second any information changes or gets updated," Aura said.

"Yes, my queen." He turned to leave.

"Kolas?" she called.

He turned back. "Yes?"

"Amaline and Omire."

"Yes?" he asked again.

"Please give them the option to join the townspeople in the bunker. I do not want them to have to fight their own people, or risk being found if they are hiding out in the open," Aura said.

"Of course, my queen." He bowed to her and left the room.

For a moment Emily considered telling her that Amaline and Omire were the ones who had attacked them and taken Levi. Part of her wanted no mercy shown to the two, but Amaline's confession seemed remorseful and sincere. Emily decided it wasn't her place to tell the woman's secret. It would only further complicate matters.

The silence returned, as did Aura's pacing.

Finally, Emily couldn't take it anymore. "Please stop."

Aura felt as if she had been slapped in the face. "Excuse me?" she said, annoyed.

Theirra tried to grab Emily's hand but she shook her off. "We are prepared. The army is ready. The villagers have boarded up their houses, packed their belongings, and are making their way toward the bunkers. We are prepared," she repeated because she felt it needed repeating.

"Emily is right," Theirra chimed in. "All we need is the word from you to proceed. There is no added preparation that needs to be done."

"All right," Aura said, snapping out of her daze. "Emily, you begin moving them all and tell Kolas I want him to start positioning the troops at the known locations. When more are known, we will be able to move those to the new locations easier. Theirra, please make sure all the animals are ready and positioned with their assigned handlers for the battle. I want them to start moving into position as well."

They all began moving out of the door. Aura called Theirra back briefly once the rest had left.

"My queen?" Theirra asked, confused.

"If you happen to make noise while positioning them, or if those from the other side happen to catch a glimpse of them, I understand this might be an unavoidable condition of their movement through the forests."

"Yes, my queen."

"Make sure they look as menacing as possible when these glances are seen." Aura winked and dismissed her.

ᘓᘓ

Emily and Milskar met up again, momentarily, at the castle entrance, each tasked to go an opposite direction from the other. They stood without speaking for several moments while groups of people moved around them.

"Milskar…" Emily trailed off.

"I know. You, too."

She tried to smile up at him, but was only able to manage a weak grimace. "I just need you to be careful."

"I will be. And I need you to keep everyone safe," Milskar said.

"I will."

They embraced tightly and he had to push Emily away when the risk of them staying like that forever was too great for either of them to ignore. He kissed her lightly on the lips and forehead and was gone by the time she opened her eyes. She wiped the tears off her cheek and turned to go toward the village.

She walked slowly, constantly getting blocked by groups of people and horses, all walking in the opposite direction. Several times, she turned around and looked longingly in the direction they were traveling before turning back around. She had lost sight of Milskar long before, but still tried to make him out in all the faces of the crowd as it swelled behind her. Soon she turned a corner and was only able to see those before her. Luckily, Kolas was in the castle grounds and she was able to relay the queen's information to him.

They quickly parted and she found another villager she had struck up a mild friendship with over the last few days of preparation. He would be her go-to person in all the movement. The majority of villagers who were going into hiding were children and their mothers, though a few older or infirmed men had stayed behind, Cyden being one of them.

"Emily," he said to her with a worried look on his already wrinkled face.

"Cyden, how is the move coming along?"

"Not particularly well."

"Why is that?" She knew they did not have a lot of

time to move everyone and she was already a little edgy at the prospect of being rushed.

"A lot of the older people do not want to move," Cyden said.

"But we have been telling them for days that they have to, but they will be able to return as soon as the battle is over."

"I have tried telling them that, but they do not want to leave their homes."

"All right, you continue helping those who are willing to move. Make sure no one gets lost on the way. I will work on those who wish to stay behind."

He grasped her hands and shook them minutely before turning to help a woman and her three small children place their belongings in a wagon.

Emily knocked on the first door she passed and an elderly woman answered. Arthritis and years of probable fieldwork had bent her into an upside down J shape. She looked up at Emily and smiled broadly, pulling the door open wider and revealing a man behind her sitting in a chair by a window.

"Ma'am, my name is Emily, I was asked by Queen Aura to help those villagers staying behind to get to the safe zone."

"Oh, I know who you are, sweetie," the woman said. She turned away from her and sat down next to the man.

"We are going to need you to leave here today and move to the bunker," Emily continued firmly. "That is what I am here for, to help you gather some things to take with you, and help you move. It is not terribly far away and we have several carts to help those who may not be able to walk the entire way."

"We know. Cyden told us all this yesterday," the woman said sweetly.

"Well, good, then let me know what you would like me to carry and I will get you on your way."

The woman smiled up at her. "Oh no, we are not leaving."

"You cannot stay here," Emily explained. "It will not be safe here, but you will be able to return as soon as it is."

"We have been told all this, sweetie. We would prefer to stay."

"What I am trying to tell you, though," Emily said, trying not to raise her voice in frustration, "is that I cannot allow you to stay. I do not want to scare you, but your chances of being hurt or killed are too great. The queen cares about each and every one of her people. Please do it for her, please. It will just be a few days and then you can return."

A soft knock at the door revealed Cyden. Emily shook her head somberly at him. He nodded and gestured for her to leave with him. The process was repeated over and over, with just as much success as disappointment. There was one woman with a very small child in her arms who did not want to leave her home. She was terrified at never returning.

"Her husband and eldest son died suddenly last year," Cyden whispered to Emily.

Emily was shocked and saddened. "Ma'am. I am so sorry for all the loss you have recently had in your life, but you must think of yourself and this child here. For this child's life you must come with us." This seemed to snap the woman out of her trance and she wordlessly followed them into the streets with the other villagers.

After several more hours, they had done all they could. They would have to pray that whoever was left behind would stay safe and be there upon their return.

Emily and Cyden, each with their own few belongings, followed the straggling pack of people into the forest. It became increasingly dark as they got closer to the underground dwellings and Cyden produced a lamp to light their way. Emily could hear hushed voices all around them and the people moving through the trees alongside them. It was an eerie feeling and put her a little on edge.

She was relieved when they reached the entrance of the bunker a few moments later. There were two large guards stationed in front, ensuring the correct people entered the dwellings. They had been having some problems the last two days with people perfectly capable of fighting, trying to enter—to the point that now these guards were needed at all times to turn those away and back to the lines.

Emily felt bad for them, usually they were at each end of the age requirements, quite young or almost too old, yet still slated to fight. She wished that their desires could be taken into account and they could have been spared, but there were not enough people to fight all those from Grustmiener. Emily knew this was unavoidable if Esotera ever hoped to have a chance at victory.

She said her farewells to Cyden and watched him enter—the last to do so. She had previously debated spending the night in hiding and coming out first thing in the morning, but she feared that she would be unable to leave the guaranteed safety and had decided against it. After Cyden entered the guards promptly shut and locked the door behind him, placing foliage all around the opening. Resbuca emerged from the clearing and spoke soft incantations to the plants. In the time it took Emily to blink, the entrance disappeared and, as hard as she tried, she was unable to find even a hint of the place it once occupied "How will they get out when it is all over?" Emily asked.

"They are able to leave whenever they wish, though

they have been advised not to," Resbuca answered. "This just makes it extremely difficult for others to find the place, especially if they do not know it exists."

"But when everything is all over, how will we tell them? I cannot even see where it was."

"Oh, I can fix that," she said a few more words to Emily, who then felt a slight shiver go through her body. Now when she looked to her right, she noticed a faint rectangular glow around where the door once was.

"Neat," Emily said and Resbuca smiled.

The guards nodded at the two women and headed to their designated stations. While Kolas assured them the town would be safe, Aura said she would feel better if a few stayed behind to protect the place. The two men split up and disappeared into the forest.

"Now what?"

"Now we wait," Resbuca said and sat upon a fallen tree trunk.

Chapter 33

Waiting

It was as if the stars had decided to remove themselves from the sky, not wanting to be a part of what was about to happen below them. The night became crisp without their presence and the breath of every living creature began fogging up the air.

The rest of the Grustmiener army had arrived and were setting up their positions along the lines between the two kingdoms. The scouts had informed Aura of this fact and she had responded by sending the rest of her forces into countering positions. Now it was just a matter of waiting. She had forbidden her army from using any fires to avoid letting the other side know of their exact positions and now she was regretting it with how cold it was becoming. They could see hundreds of fires burning off in the distance, almost as if Lady Grustmiener was teasing them with their nonchalance about the impending war.

"Our people will freeze soon," Kolas said through clenched teeth.

"I know," Aura replied.

"I have an idea."

"I am listening."

"We light as many fires as we can," Kolas said. She cocked her head and glared at him. "Hear me out," he said raising a steady hand. "We light more fires than are necessary. It will make them think our army is larger than it actually is. It is a scare tactic. Plus we can place fires in spots where there actually are not any guards. This will confuse them even more."

"Gather all the help you need. Thank you, Kolas. For everything."

He smiled at her and turned into the darkness. Moments later, Theirra materialized next to her with a slight blush on her cheeks. They stood there in silence, watching small pockets of light start appearing all over the horizon. Kolas was right, it did make their side look more impressive. It looked almost as if all of Esotera were on fire, the light almost daring their enemies to come closer.

"It is beautiful," Theirra said.

Aura nodded. "How are the animals settling?" she asked.

"Good, the narstles are a little grumpy from being kept up all day, but now they seem be to be getting along all right. It is certainly tough working with nocturnal creatures, but it seems to be working out. I keep promising them this all will not take too long. I just hope I am telling the truth. They do not particularly appreciate lies."

"I hope so, as well."

Aura sighed deeply. Theirra moved closer to her and held her hand. The two stood there, taking comfort from each other while the soft breath of those around them filled the air. Milskar walked toward them and stood on the other side of Aura, staring out at the fires, as well.

"We are all ready," he finally said, his breath traveling up above them.

"Good. And everyone knows what is expected of them?"

"Yes. At first light we will begin."

They fell into silence once more.

༄༅༄

A few hundred yards away, another army was staring back into the same space. Lights were popping up all over the horizon making it look like the ground was completely on fire. The Grustmiener army sat in silence, staring at the developments happening all around them. Winester stood outside Lady Grustmiener's tent and soon she came out to join him.

"Wow," she said in awe.

"I would not worry. I bet it is a trick."

"A trick?"

"To make you think their army is bigger than it actually is, to make you worry," Winester said.

"It has worked."

"I would not fall for it," he said.

"That is why you are not the head of an army."

Her words stung him.

She turned to an aide and bid him to find one of her top guards with the instruction to spread out the army a little better to counter this new development.

Movement was again happening all around the campsites. Soon it was almost possible to see, despite the lack of stars in the sky, as more fires were being lit on their side.

It was during all this confusion that Levi was able to slip out of his tent. Abaddon, who had been charged with watching the boy in the lady's safe zone, had long since fallen asleep. His old body was unable to stay awake any longer after the difficult and exhausting journey.

Levi stole the knife off Abaddon's belt, before creeping quietly out of camp. He was not sure where he was going, exactly, but his feet moved him forward all the same. He slipped past numerous men and women—some sharpening tools, others deep in quiet conversation, and still others slumped against trees in stolen bits of slumber. He barely noticed any of them. It was almost as if an invisible string was dragging him to some unknown destination. He decided not to fight against the pull. It would be many hours before they noticed he was missing. And, by then, it would be entirely too late to do anything about it.

The branches slapped against his face, bare feet, and legs. His shoes had gone missing at some point, but he could not remember exactly where. Had he not brought them with him when he first entered this world? Or had they been missing only for moments? Time had been bending and folding around him for the last few days—at least he thought it was days—and now he had lost all sense of it. It was like those Las Vegas casinos he'd heard stories about. No clocks, artificial lighting—you sat down for what felt like one second and came out hours later, shielding your eyes against the sun, even though it had been pitch black out the last you remembered.

Still, he walked on. His brain barely registered the slight downhill slope he was on. The splashing sound his feet made registered to his ears first before he really realized he was wading through a shallow stream.

There were fires all around him and, for a moment, fear started wrapping its long fingers around his heart, but he batted the hand away and continued on up the next hill.

In the distance, he saw two women sitting on a fallen tree trunk. One was very old and one much younger, her dark hair looked like it was on fire with all the dancing lights around her.

He sat directly on the ground and kept all his focus on them. His only movement was the rise and fall of his chest as he breathed.

Chapter 34

It Begins

It is time," the aide said softly to Lady Grustmiener.

"Yes."

"It is advised that you stay here. You will be informed throughout the day."

"Yes, I shall."

The woman left and Lady Grustmiener was again alone. She could hear movement around the camp, but most of the noise was coming from farther down the valley where her army resided.

She exited the tent and wrapped her robe a little tighter around herself against the briskness of the morning air. There was a faint blanket of fog cutting the little bit of visibility there was and letting her hear more than she could see. Winester came up noiselessly behind her and startled her slightly when he started talking.

"This is it."

"It is," she said, recovering quickly.

"Is it difficult being this far away?"

"I was debating on if it was far enough away. You?"

"I am mixed. Part of me wants to be right down there in the thick of it all, but I am an old man," he said wistfully.

"That you are."

He let the comment slide. "This is a young person's game."

"For the benefit of the old," she replied curtly.

"It will ultimately benefit them as well."

"You should tell that to the ones who do not make it out."

"I shall." He walked away from her, the steam coming off his body helping to burn off some of the fog surrounding him.

Her eyes narrowed as he left. She was tired of him trying to make it seem as if this was his war, that the only thing put at risk was his people. She was risking everything.

The thought of being ruler of Esotera floated like the fog around her head. How wonderful it would be, the king ruling over Grustmiener and her having all this land at her mercy. They would be a supreme force. It was a tantalizing idea, something she would mull over during the impending battle.

ᥱᠵᥱᠵ

On the other side of the small river, Aura awoke with a start. She had been dreaming about a large serpent slithering toward her in the forest. She had fallen asleep on the ground and, while she knew there should be hundreds of people all around her, she could not see a single soul.

The closer the snake got to her, the more erect it became so that, when it reached her, the two were face to face with each other. Aura tried desperately not to breathe. She remembered hearing somewhere that while snakes cannot see particularly well, they are able to hunt on scent. She sat motionless, yet somehow she knew the creature sensed exactly where she was.

It turned its head and looked at her sideways. She knew in the pit of her being that it was going to kill and eat her.

She took a slow inhale of breath and again desperately fought against releasing it. Suddenly, the serpent displayed the most glorious set of shimmering wings. Aura had to duck her head and shield herself against the intense brightness of the light coming toward her. There was a bright flash and, the next time she looked up, the creature was gone.

She sat straight up, ripped from the dream, and tried to catch her breath. Each noise around her was making her jumpy and entering her brain at almost half speed, as if she were still sleeping. Aura stretched and exited her tent. The crisp air from the night before was still enveloping the forest.

Kolas was standing on the edge of a group of soldiers who were packing up their tiny campsite and extinguishing their fires. Aura stood perfectly straight next to him. She did not speak to him at first, just staring out at all the movement.

"Are we ready?" she finally asked, her breath cutting through the air between them.

"Yes," he said firmly without looking at her.

"Good." She touched his arm lightly before turning back around. "Thank you for everything, Kolas. I will forever be indebted to you for all you have done."

He smiled out of the corner of his mouth. "You are very welcome, my queen."

"Take care of yourself and all these people. They are

my charges and I am putting you as guardian over them," she said over her shoulder.

"I will take care of them as if they are my own," he called back, a smile still on his face.

She walked past the place her tent had just occupied and its sudden absence startled her. Only a slightly indented place in the leaves indicated that something had once been there. It amazed her how quickly the remembrance of things could be removed from the earth. How, if you did not look very closely, you could miss your entire past as it broke down around you.

Aura gave up a silent prayer to her father, asking him to look down upon his people and to protect them. Irrational or not, she felt that he'd had a small part in her dream. She took it as a sign that victory would be theirs.

"I think it is time for you to move back, away from the majority of the fighting," Milskar said, a moment before actually appearing out of the trees.

"No. I am not going anywhere." Aura had been debating the last few days on where she would stay during the fight. Originally, she was going to stay close to the castle, high up enough where she would be able to see everything, but far enough away to be out of any danger. Now, though, she wanted to be right where the action was. She did not want a second's delay between what was happening and her ability to respond to it. She felt more sure of herself and more powerful than she ever had in her whole life.

"My queen," Milskar said in a concerned tone. "I really think it would be advisable if—"

She cut him off. "I have made my decision."

"If you stay here, I will need to waste several guards who could be fighting to stay and protect you directly," he said, trying to persuade her.

"Nonsense. You will not spare a single person. I will

stay enough out of the way, but I am not going to run to the castle with my tail between my legs and just cross my fingers that it all works out. My people need to see that I am with them. That I am so sure of our victory, I have no fear of standing here during the whole battle."

The determination in her eyes told him the discussion was over. There was no sense in arguing. He nodded at her and made a mental note to make sure he tightened the forces around this area without her knowing. He would be damned, if he'd let something happened to the ruler of their kingdom on his watch.

"Where will the fighting begin?" she asked, looking back out at the horizon.

"Well," he said, turning to look in the same direction, "I do not think that it will be as simple as starting in one concentrated area. I have a feeling it will all break out all over all at once."

"And when will that be?"

"Soon, I would imagine, though, honestly none of us really knows. It seems like the other side is waiting for us to make the first move as well. None of us has ever been in battle. We are not really sure how it is supposed to go," he said, somewhat sheepishly.

"We should make the first move then."

"My queen?"

"We are not weak and will not allow them to think that we are. We are brave and we are good fighters. There is no reason to delay showing the residents of Grustmiener that fact. Once everyone is awake and camps are properly broken down, send the word along the line that fighting is to begin as soon as possible."

"Yes, my queen," Milskar said with slightly widened eyes.

He could not help but feel affected by her assurance

of their victory. He stood a little taller and saluted her. She made the same gesture back, patted him lightly on the shoulder, and turned to walk farther down the line.

Milskar went the opposite direction, telling all those in his path to prepare for the battle that would be starting momentarily.

Chapter 35

Battle

Far off in the distance, a large boom was heard cracking through the silence like a bolt of lightning. Emily jumped and almost slipped off the tree trunk. Her whole body ached from sitting up all night. She looked around but was unable to find Resbuca.

"Hmm," she said out loud to herself. "Guess she left."

Another loud bang and her gaze flicked around at her surroundings. The noises came more quickly and from all directions. The wind carried several screams and yells to where she was standing. It felt as if the battle was breaking out all around her. She desperately wanted to run but, unsure of which direction, she found herself frozen.

Emily shut her eyes and tried taking a deep breath. She knew that she was far away from where anything was actually happening. Plus, she was now trained for battle. It was just hours ago that she'd been begging to be on the front lines. Maybe it was a good idea that Aura had decided to keep her away from it all.

A few more deep breaths and she was able to get her heart rate back down. She opened her eyes and screamed when she saw the figure standing in front of her.

∾∾∾

Kolas was poised on Gilbert next to a few hundred villagers on top of a hill. The first line of dragons and other creatures were already moving up the other side, bombarding the Grustmiener soldiers who stood there. The booms from their tails and fireballs shook the trees and ground all around them. The men and women, standing on either side of Kolas, appeared entranced by the overwhelming clatter. He could hear similar noises coming from various places along the line. The battle had officially begun.

"I want you to all be ready," he hollered over the noise. "The line will only hold for so long. Soon their army will break through and start charging up this hill. You must stand your ground. We are higher up than they are. Just wait and let them come to you. We have the advantage here."

He looked up and down the line. There was a mixture of anxious and scared faces, and a few where Kolas found it hard to put a name to the emotion. They almost looked eager. He hoped that these people would not be the ones he would have to worry about. He knew the key to their kingdom's success would be keeping the upper hand. Their placement on top of the hill was just a small part of that.

The men and women, from the guards and the villagers, had been training for weeks, so he knew they were physically prepared for the impending fight. But the mental aspect of the battle still worried him. It was impossible to know how a person would react when placed in a life-

or-death situation. None of them had ever experienced war before, and it would be more terrifying than they could have ever imagined.

The first few Grustmienerian soldiers had broken through the first wave of creatures and were making their way up the hill. Kolas had about half the army visible and the rest hiding behind trees and shrubs. He wanted it to look like there were just a few of them so the enemy soldiers would be confident in confronting them. He also hoped the decision the night before to light all the fires had actually clued the other side in to the fact that they were bluffing about their number of people.

Kolas hoped these few dozen rag-tag-looking guards standing beside him would solidify this fact. He just hoped those in hiding would be able to bide their time until the perfect moment and really catch the enemy off guard. Too soon, and the other army would be on to their plan and possibly retreat or change their own plan of action. Too late, and they risked losing some of their people before they could regroup and start fighting back.

He held his breath and prayed. "Hold it," he said through his teeth. He saw slight movements, more like twitches, coming from the trees and shrubs. "Hold it," he said again, more loudly.

Gilbert danced under him. Kolas squeezed a handful of mane under his fist to steady the nervous creature.

The people standing next to Kolas started shifting their weight from one foot to the other. They looked at one another, trying to find some level of reassurance that they should be standing their ground, fighting desperately against the instinct to either run forward and meet the other side head on, or turn and flee.

The sound of the two armies colliding registered in Kolas's ears before his brain actually realized what was occurring. Suddenly, his body took over and he found himself wielding his sword against two large men.

He swiftly cut back and forth and the two disappeared from in front of him. There wasn't even a moment to process that before another person had pulled him from Gilbert and was on top of him.

Human cries were now coming from all around him and Kolas knew the army was surrounding them and fighting all their people. His mind quickly fluttered to Theirra and Aura. He hoped both would be safe.

ᑯᓍᑫ

"D—dragons," the woman stuttered.

"Dragons?" Lady Grustmiener yelled back.

"Y—yes. And some other creatures that I did not recognize," the woman said with terror in her eyes.

"How many?" Winester and a few more of her aides walked forward as the conversation continued.

"A lot. Almost a hundred?" the woman said nervously.

"What is going on?" one of Lady Grustmiener's aides asked.

"Their front line is composed of dragons." Lady Grustmiener turned on Winester. "How did we not know this? How did we have zero information that they would be fighting with these filthy beasts?"

"We did not think they would go that route," a guard said. "There were no indications."

"No indications?" She laughed. "Gather up every creature you can get your hands on. Now."

The man turned and ran the other direction.

Winester was not sure exactly what the guard could come up with to meet the queen's demands. Grustmiener was not known for its animals. The extreme conditions kept many creatures farther south, save for a few birds and small animals that could burrow underground for protection.

Lady Grustmiener buried her head in her hands. "What kind of losses have we suffered?" she asked the aide.

"I am not sure of the exact number," the woman said.

"An idea," Lady Grustmiener demanded, exasperated.

"A few dozen. I do not think it is much more than that."

"For your sake, it had better not be. Come back when you have good news for me."

The woman flinched and scurried away.

"This cannot happen this way," Lady Grustmiener told Winester.

"It will not," he said with conviction.

She looked at him and Winester could see the fear brimming in her eyes. "If this gets out of hand…"

"It will not," he assured her again.

"For both our sakes, you better ensure that is the truth."

Moments later, she sent the majority of her aides out to check on the various lines, too impatient to wait for the runners to get back to her.

Winester could see her calm demeanor breaking under the pressure and stress of the situation. He was struck dumbfounded as well.

None of them had expected the Esoterans to be so well prepared. They had all assumed that the battle would only take a few hours at the most. However, now it was shaping up to be much more of an endeavor than any of them had imagined.

Winester just hoped, as he figured Lady Grustmiener was doing as well, that this would all be over long before the king returned.

Chapter 36

Trust

The hand was rough against Emily's mouth and she could feel the knife pressed to her neck. She scanned the clearing, desperately hoping to see someone who could help her. But she found—as she'd known she would—that she was completely defenseless.

He pressed her back against the front of him. She was trying desperately not to cry, but tears still escaped out of her eyes, wetting his hand slightly. Her mouth moved as she tried to reason with him, but it all came out muffled. Each time she tried to move or struggle, he pressed even harder. The knife cut her skin and a small trickle of blood ran down her neck.

For a few seconds he relaxed his hold on her and she took the opportunity to throw her head back with as much force as she could muster, hearing a loud crack behind her.

He dropped his hold completely and she ran several steps ahead before—terribly conflicted—she turned back to him.

"Levi?" Emily said with the most terrible pain in her

voice—pain that went much deeper than her throbbing head and hurt neck.

His eyes bore only hatred as he glared back at her. He was unrecognizable. Emily took another few steps backward, confused. Who was this person standing in front of her? She had longed to see him for so many weeks and now she felt like she couldn't get away fast enough. Still, something was keeping her rooted in place, though. She didn't want to believe that he was capable of hurting anyone, much less her.

"Levi," she tried again, more softly, and took several hesitant steps toward him.

She removed her hat, freeing her hair, hoping he would recognize her. He raised his knife again and brushed away the trickle of blood coming from his nose with his other hand.

"Levi, it's me, Emily. Levi, please."

His eyes narrowed. It was as if he was even angrier with the knowledge of who she was. Levi held the knife out at heart level with a steady hand. She kept walking forward, anyway. Part of her hoped the guards stationed around the area had heard her scream, but she was equally scared of what they would do to him if they found the two of them in their current positions. There was so much noise all around them, though, that she doubted anyone would come running.

"What happened to you?"

"I was shown the truth," he said in a flat, unrecognizable voice.

It startled her and she took a moment to recover before speaking again. "The truth? Levi what does that mean?"

"The truth of what King Aldric did to Winester and the Grustmiener people."

"Levi, what does that have to do with anything?"

"It has to do with everything!" he bellowed at her. "All of this," he said, spreading his arms and gesturing all around them. "He did not deserve this land."

"What?" Emily was so confused and resumed searching the trees for movement, for help.

"These lands should never have gone to him."

"To Aura's father? I don't understand."

"Her father." He laughed. "Her father's father's father. Years ago. Many years ago. This land should have been Winester's. It never should have gone to anyone else. Today, though, it will find its way back into rightful hands. Anyone who stands in the way of that must be eliminated," he said and brought the knife a little farther forward.

Fear froze Emily in place. All around the forest, the fighting was continuing. Members of each army were falling in great numbers and there was chaos everywhere.

∽∾∽

The Grustmiener army had added some strange animals to their ranks and they were currently doing battle with the dragons and the little mostlespries. Theirra was becoming concerned as the new beasts were unfamiliar to her.

The dragons had an advantage with their ability to fly and breathe fire, and their tough skin, but these new creatures were unbelievably quick and had long, dagger-like tails. It did not take long for them to take one of the dragons down. Theirra didn't see which one, but desperately hoped that it wasn't Heza. But her attention was suddenly focused on several men running toward her with large axes, and she was unable to give the animals, which she had devoted so much of her life to caring for, any more thought. It would be several days before she discovered it was one of the older males that had fallen and not Heza, after all.

She was momentarily mesmerized by the men who ran toward her. It wasn't until she felt a push from her side and an arm wrap around her waist that her brain finally clicked in to what was happening. She raised the sword Kolas had given her and brought it down heavily on one of the men. The man's yell mixed with hers, rose above, and swirled with the cries all around them.

☙❧☙❧

Aura's mind reflected the horror of the carnage happening all around her. She was terrified yet unable to look away. Perched a little higher than most of those fighting, she was able to view a large radius around her. It was difficult, from this high up, to tell what side the fighters were on. When the battle had first started, it had been easy. Her army was on the top of the hill and seemed to have the upper hand all over. Now that they were all mingled, after the first several waves of fighters, she was barely able to tell where each side ended and the other started.

She originally had runners keeping her updated, but realizing these precious few were needed in the fight, she waved them off to join the battle permanently. However, now desperate for some piece of updated news, she was beginning to regret that decision and moved closer to the battle to better see what was happening.

She paced along the edge of the hill. There were a few guards around her, which were there were under the pretense of wanting to have a birds-eye view of the battle, but she knew in reality they were really guarding her. At first it had bothered her, but seeing war in its truest form made her glad these men were surrounding her, providing a last barrier between her and all the terrible destruction.

Men, women, and beasts continued to fall as the night started creeping down the sky. Soon it became apparent that each army had started to retreat to its own side as fires began burning all around them. Those who were wounded were gathered and brought to the healers, who worked late into the night and into the next morning, trying to mend and patch the damage that had been inflicted.

Those who did not survive were placed with the others who perished in battle on the far side of the forest. Aura knew she would have to go over there at some point and take note of those who had died for her kingdom, but she was unable to muster the courage to do it that evening. One more day. Hopefully, in one more day this would all be over and she would be able to give the proper burial due to all those brave souls.

"My queen."

"Kolas!" Aura spun and flung her arms around him.

He seemed slightly startled as she pulled away but was kind enough to give her a small smile in return. She hadn't realized how worried she'd been until she actually laid eyes on him.

"The fighting has broken up for the evening. We are going to retreat a little farther back and leave a few at the front line to awaken us at the enemy's first movement, but I think we will have a few hours to rest before the battle starts up again in the morning."

"Yes, thank you. I am glad you will all have an opportunity to rest. Please make sure you rotate those on the line so each can get a little sleep."

"Of course," he said.

Out of the clearing walked Milskar and Theirra. Both had numerous cuts and Theirra walked with a slight limp.

Kolas made a move toward her but stopped himself as Aura embraced them just as strongly as she had Kolas. Theirra gently wiped a tear from her face and hugged her once again.

"I am so glad you are all safe," Aura looked around expectantly. "What about Resbuca and Emily?"

"I have not seen them since last night when they were gathering the town's people," Milskar said, looking more than a little worried.

"I am sure they are fine. Possibly they assumed, as I think we all did, the fighting would be over today. Maybe once they realized that would not happen, they kept a little more in hiding so the fighting would not move to them."

"I hope," Theirra said quietly.

"We must all get some rest," Kolas announced.

The others nodded and started to walk away.

"Theirra, will you stay up here this evening?" Aura asked. "I have some things I would like to discuss with you before tomorrow."

"Of course," Theirra said.

Kolas squeezed her upper arm as he passed her and they exchanged a pained look between the two of them. She nodded to Milskar and turned back to Aura.

"Please, sit," Aura said.

Theirra obeyed. "What is on your mind?"

"How did everything go today?" Aura asked, moving forward in her cross-legged position. "I only had minimal visibility of everything, and only of what was directly under me."

"It was very difficult. A lot of people fell—died, I guess," Theirra said, dropping her gaze to the ground. "We lost three dragons and a handful of other creatures. I think it will be quite difficult to get them all back to fight in the morning. Most fled once the serious fighting started and the creatures the Grustmiener's brought showed up. I really thought we had the upper hand. Everything seemed to be going our way, but then these…things showed up. I do not even know what type of animals they are, but suddenly the dragons started falling and running away and then their people moved in and we seemed to get pushed back toward our lines. It all seemed to fall apart after that."

Aura placed a hand on her arm. "Shh. It is okay. Calm down"

Theirra had not realized how worked up she had gotten but she suddenly realized tears were running down her face and she was shaking. "I just do not know how it will go tomorrow."

"It will all go fine. We will be well rested. Those who were injured are being healed as we speak, and we will be back to fighting in full force tomorrow. I am sure that the majority of the dragons will come back. I know Heza will."

Aura smiled down at her and Theirra tried to return it, still unsure if Heza was alive or not. They talked for another hour before Theirra's yawning forced Aura to send her away to sleep.

There were muffled noises all around the forest but, other than the cracking of fires, it was relatively quiet. This was partially due to the exhaustion of most of her army. She hoped they had enough time to get the sleep they needed to fight in just a few hours. She drifted off a few moments later, her sleep riddled with dreams.

Chapter 37

Fallen

Emily was still frozen in the same place she'd been for hours as the sun was starting to set. Levi stood just as still in front of her, his knife still held out. She had stopped pleading with him and was just hoping if she stood her ground long enough, he would break down and return to his former self. Her body was aching with the effort of remaining motionless and she didn't know how much longer she would be able to keep it up.

"Please." The exhaustion in her voice made it crack.

Emily felt her knees slowly buckling beneath her and she crumpled to the ground. Her head fell forward and her hair covered her eyes. She could barely make Levi out her through her long bangs, but she no longer cared what would happen to her. She just wanted to sleep. She heard him take a step forward and, with all the effort she could muster, lifted her head.

The fire in his eyes appeared slightly dimmed, but Emily could not tell if it was just her brain playing tricks on her. He cocked his head to one side, almost as if the sight of her confused him, as if she had just materialized in front of him and had not been standing there for hours.

"Levi?" She tried again, her voice small and husky. "This isn't you. I love you and you love me." He squinted at her and turned his head again. "Remember?" she pleaded. "Remember when we used to play at your parents' house? Running through the sprinklers, and your mom got so mad because we stepped on her roses?"

He took another small step toward her, lowering the knife a little.

She laughed weakly. "And that time, we decided to build that fort and used all the wood my dad bought for his fence? We ruined a whole load of it. I thought we would never be able to hang out together again."

Emily used every ounce of strength she had left and lifted herself off the ground. Levi was close enough now that she could have reached out and touched him, the knife only inches from her waist. She took a hesitant step forward.

She lifted her hand and placed it on top of his, lowering them both. "Levi."

He looked down at what she was doing and then quickly back up at her.

"Please remember," she begged. "I don't know what they did to you, but this person isn't you. You are kind and decent, and you think with your heart. Think. Remember me."

She reached up and touched his chin, turning his face to meet hers. His eyes appeared to clear slightly. Hope flickered in her heart.

"Come back, Levi. Come back."

"Emily?"

She threw her arms around him, flying back out of his embrace when she felt the knife slice her side.

e⁄ɔe⁄ɔ

The next morning started with a literal bang. Lady Grustmiener was sleeping soundly when a large commotion awoke her with a start. The yelling barely registered in her brain before her tent door was ripped open, momentarily blinding her with light. Slowly, her eyes focused on the man standing in the doorway.

"What in the hell is all of this?" the king boomed at her.

She flinched a little, but quickly recovered. "My king," she said, bowing her head. "I was worried you would not be able to get here in time. I trust the messengers found you quickly."

"Messengers?" he shouted, his eyes blazing.

"Oh, yes, we sent some a few days ago to find you and tell you of the impending battle. Did they not arrive?"

He looked confused, as did the several aides standing behind him. "I did not hear from a single messenger."

"I am sorry that they were not able to find you in time," she said sweetly. "This all happened so suddenly I thought you would want me to act and you would meet me when you had the time. So it has worked out in the end. You have only missed the first day of battle."

"Only the first day?" His temper began to rise again. "You have been fighting. What is going on here? I need an explanation!"

He walked the rest of the way into her tent, dropping the flap behind him and plunging them back into darkness. It took several moments for her eyes to adjust enough for her to see the lamp by the side of her bed and light it. The soft glow of light helped take the edge off his appearance, but she could tell he was still just as angry.

She began explaining the events over the last few

days, leaving out some key parts and embellishing others. By the time she was done, he was under the impression that Winester showed up at her door with this powerful heir of Lord Vertrous. She was left with little time to gather an army to fight against the Esoterans who, she informed him, had first declared war before Winester was able to pull Levi away from their clutches and convince him to fight on Grustmiener's side.

Winester came into her tent, obviously he'd heard the loud voices inside, but it was clear he was not prepared for the sight before him. He bowed deeply. "My lord."

"I should have known you would be the one to bring this to my door step," the king said.

"It was good he came to us," Lady Grustmiener retorted. "If he went to another kingdom, they would be the one poised to benefit greatly from this discovery."

"And what will the other kingdoms say when they discover what you have done here?" the king demanded.

She was speechless. Winester took his opportunity. He'd been saving this particular piece of information until it was utterly necessary. "They will be grateful," he said.

"Grateful?"

"That you not only secured our future, but helped eliminate a great enemy of Omaner."

The other two occupants of the tent turned to him with quizzical expressions. Winester hurried on without prompting. "They are harboring a fugitive in Esotera, a very desirable one."

"A fugitive?" the king asked.

"Kolas." Winester's words hung in the air.

"The murderer of the heir of Omaner?" Lady Grustmiener asked.

It was clear she was happily surprised by this turn of events.

"Yes. He has been traveling with Queen Aura. She is protecting him. I am not sure what exactly her plans are, but it is clear she is up to something sinister. It is a good thing we are fighting her. She does not deserve to be a ruler of this great land."

The king's posture shifted imperceptibly. He still did not seem happy with either person standing in front of him, but he seemed to be on board for the day's fight.

Most of the camp had awoken once word spread the king had arrived. Soon their troops were ready for another and, hopefully, the last, day of battle.

Lady Grustmiener was slowly walking along the lines of troops when she saw the king in the distance. Concerned, she walked swiftly toward him. He was pulling a large plate of armor over his head and two aides were helping him fasten the sides of it.

"What are you doing?" she asked him.

"Preparing."

"I can see that. Preparing for what?"

"These are my people," he said, lifting his face to her. "I must fight alongside of them. How can I ask them to fight for me if I am not willing to do the same?"

"Because you are their king. You tell them what to do and they do it because they are your people and you rule them."

The aides on either side of him gave her a quick glance before putting their attention back on the work at hand.

"My lady, everything will be fine." He leaned down and kissed her gently on the forehead. "I will see you when all of this is over. You have led them all this far, let me lead them the rest of the way."

She nodded reluctantly at him. All the men and

woman took their places along the front, leaving her alone again. She could no longer see them but heard the renewed sense of fervor that the king's presence brought them all. Maybe it was a good thing, after all, that he had shown up. She doubted her ability to gather the troops like her husband had just done. She truly felt this would be the last day of battle, and that they would be victorious over their enemies.

☙❧☙

"Today," Aura said on the other side of the forest, addressing thousands of pairs of eyes, "will be the day we recapture our future. Those people, standing on the other side, are trying to take that away from all of you. They are trying to claim what we have for themselves. We have all worked too hard, our fathers and mothers have all worked too hard, to let it slip away to them. I want you to hold your heads up and fight harder than you ever have before. I want you to fight for your children's future and their children's. We will look back on this day and be proud of what we have done here. We have lost some along the way, and we must not forget the sacrifices they have made, but we must not let them leave this world in vain. We will fight for their memory. We will fight with their fire inside of us."

She looked around the group and noticed everyone pulling him or herself up just a little taller. "I have never been more proud to be your queen. Now go—go and fight for what is rightfully ours. I pray that each and every one of you will come back safe and can enjoy what your bravery and strength will give us all."

A cheer went up through the crowd and she couldn't help but feel the electricity buzzing all around her. She was not sure, at first, if she should address them all, but once she awoke in the morning and saw their scared faces, she knew she had to do something to reassure them. Part of her wanted to join the fight as well, but she resigned herself to watching from her perch of the day before. She held Theirra, Kolas, and Milskar fiercely before letting them go fight. The pinch in her heart rang through her whole body and she had a terrible, sickening feeling that they would not all return to her.

Aura knew this day of fighting would result in more casualties than the day before. This war could not continue for another day. This would be it. Whoever was the victor today would rule over this land. She just hoped it would be Esotera.

Suddenly, Resbuca came out of the forest and stood beside her. Aura whirled to face her, eyes wide in disbelief. "Resbuca, I was terribly worried something had happened to you."

Resbuca looked incredibly tired. "I have been doing what I could to heal those injured."

"I appreciate that greatly." Aura hesitated for a moment. "Were you able to save most?"

"Oh, yes, of the dozens injured, we only lost two."

The number still stung Aura, but she was deeply grateful that Resbuca and the healers had been able to save so many.

"How is Emily?"

"Fine, I believe," Resbuca said. "I have not seen her since yesterday morning. I got a feeling that I was needed elsewhere and left her. Probably a good thing, as I soon stumbled upon the healing tents."

"Would you like to watch the battle with me?" Aura asked hesitantly. "I am not sure if I will be able to stand it alone."

"Of course, my queen."

The two women exchanged a glance and moved closer to one another, sides pressed firmly against each other.

The armies wasted no formalities, did not worry about front lines or first attacks. The battle just suddenly began, almost as if it had formalized out of thin air. Each side seemed to have a renewed ferocity. Aura gasped and found it difficult to look sometimes, but then was uplifted by moments of sheer bravery from her people. They felled several of Grustmiener's soldiers but suffered losses of their own. They were all too far away for her to be able to make out who they were.

Down in the forest, Milskar, Kolas, and Theirra were spread out, too far away from each other to keep tabs on one another. Theirra was able to gather a few of the dragons and other creatures, but several did not return from the day before, as she had feared. However, some of the creatures from the Grustmiener side also had not returned, so both sides appeared somewhat evenly matched.

A woman ran out of the woods toward Milskar. She was incredibly beautiful, her blonde hair swirling around her face as if caught by some imaginary wind. He was momentarily rendered frozen by the sight. She looked about fifty, but unbelievably strong and graceful. She moved toward him slowly, eyes locked on his. Milskar heard the fighting all around him, but he felt like she held him in some sort of spell. His arm started to lower when he suddenly sensed another person standing close to him.

He wielded his sword at the last possible second, bringing it down on the man's shoulder, crumpling him to the ground. By the time Milskar looked back up, the woman was gone, a dozen or so guards taking her place. He searched for her all around him, but it was as if she had vanished just as mysteriously as she had arrived. His thoughts soon focused back on the battle and on the others around him, fighting for their lives, each wanting to win but only one in each pair successful at their goal.

ↄↄ

The king stood as powerfully as he could, adrenaline plunging through his veins. He zeroed in on a man in the distance, one who had taken out about a dozen or so of his soldiers. The king had been watching him for some time. The man was a skilled fighter, always one step ahead of his opponent. He even took down several, who were not directly fighting him, moments before they took down one of his comrades. He looked vaguely familiar and the king moved slowly forward.

Suddenly, Kolas was aware of being watched. He turned and came face to face with the King of Grustmiener. Immediately, both their swords went up and began clashing against one another, sparks flying in all directions. Kolas could not help but be impressed by his opponent's skills.

"You," the king said, turning Kolas's blood to ice.

"I will not allow you to take this kingdom," Kolas replied through clenched teeth.

"I do not believe you have the power to stop me," the king said, his voice cold.

The two began circling each other, alternately taking turns at throwing failed strikes at the other. Those fighting close by abandoned their battle to take a step back and watch. Both sides appeared mesmerized. For each step Kolas would take forward, King Grustmiener would take a step back. The dance continued until each decided they would rather finish the fight than continue this spectacle.

Kolas made the first move, going in close and holding his ground as the king raised his sword. Kolas brought his sword down in several forceful swipes, yet each one seemed to skim off the king's armor. The king seemed to be biding his time, waiting for Kolas to get tired before he made his move. Finally, the king thought he saw his opportunity.

Kolas brought his sword straight up into the air and the king met it with his own. The sound boomed around the forest, making most watchers pause. Kolas and the king each took turns clashing with the other's sword, sparks, again, falling all around them, giving them a glowing, almost angelic, haze. The king seemed to be weakening quickly and soon Kolas was pushing him backward. Finally, he was able to lock his sword with the king's, bringing them both to the ground and pinning the king's sword beneath his. The look of triumph on Kolas's face excited those Esoterans watching, and they turned back to their fighting with renewed fervor.

Kolas leaned forward to whisper something in the king's ear, still having the man pinned in place, but suddenly the look of fear on his face hardened. Kolas released the grip on his sword and it fell to the forest floor with barely a sound. He looked down, confused at the gilded hilt in the middle of his chest. He tried to pull the small dagger out, but found he hadn't the strength to do it.

Kolas looked up at the king, a wash of relief filling him. After all these years, after running for more than a decade, he knew it was finally all going to be over. Even when Aura had granted him sanctuary within Esotera, he'd had a feeling his past would eventually catch up with him, anyway. He'd made peace with the fact that he would be leaving this world soon. He was just terribly sad that he would be leaving Theirra behind.

They had known each other mere months, but the possibility of what his future could have been glowed all around him. Kolas's life was slipping out of his grasp after he'd spent the last ten years trying to grab back onto it again.

This was it. He had to let go.

His lifted his head slightly and his eyes got their last glimpse of the forest canopy and sky above, before finally closing in eternal slumber, a relaxed, almost peaceful expression on his face.

Chapter 38

News

The battle raged on and—as word spread about the demise of Kolas—the Esoterans began to panic. Milskar momentarily forgot how to breathe when the news got to his ears. But he knew what he had to do and sprinted into action.

He ran from where the battle was currently being waged and began climbing the steep face of the hill where the queen was safely atop. He hoped no one would notice his absence, no one from either side, and that he could travel to her alone, without creating a trail. Milskar peeked behind his shoulder once and was relieved to see that he was alone in his ascent. Moments later, and out of breath, he reached the peak where she was standing next to Resbuca. He hadn't even taken a single step before a knife was at his throat.

"Do not move," the voice growled.

"My name is Milskar. I am a guard for Esotera. I am here to deliver a message to my queen."

The guard suddenly recognized him and removed the

pressure from his neck. He nodded and gestured for Milskar to continue.

Aura whirled at the noise of the intruder, eyes wide in panic. She was holding Resbuca's hand and they both seemed to take a single, large breath once they realized it was Milskar.

"Milskar, you gave me quite a fright. Why did you not come up through the main road where we could have seen you?" she asked, her voice still a little shakier than she would have wished it to be.

"I was afraid if I came up the main route, someone would be able to follow me."

"You could have gotten yourself killed," she scolded. "What did you come up here for?"

"My queen, I have some terrible news."

Her face blanched, and he noticed how she gripped Resbuca even tighter.

"Tell me. Who?"

"Kolas."

Aura's hand flew to her chest and she stumbled. Her head shook from side to side as she quickly paced back and forth, her mind speeding even faster than her legs. Kolas? Not Kolas. Not the one person they really needed to win this. He was the strength that gave her army structure. The foundation on which it was all built rested upon him. Without him, she was unsure if they would be able to win. Without him, she was unsure of all their futures.

"My queen, the soldiers are starting to become increasingly concerned. Word of his death is spreading through the ranks."

"Theirra, does Theirra know yet?"

"I do not believe so."

"We must make sure it stays that way until the fighting is over," Aura said and called over one of the guards. "I need you to find her and tell her she is needed with the healers, tell her that an animal is hurt and she is needed. Do not allow her to talk to anyone who may tell her of his fate. She is not to be told by anyone but myself. Make sure to inform anyone you may come across of that. Do you understand?"

The guard nodded and ran to find the queen's friend.

"We must do something to control this matter, my queen," Milskar lamented. "We are at a crucial part in the fighting and cannot lose focus. We cannot afford even a second of distraction."

Aura nodded, head again spinning with options. What should she do? What would her father have done? What would he expect her to do? Suddenly, the knowledge came to her. The only option that would work, that had to work.

"I will go."

"What?" Milskar and Resbuca—who had been silent up to this point—said in unison.

"I will go down there and fight. My people need to see I am on their side. They need to see I am so confident in a victory, I would put myself in danger. I must take the focus off of him. It will snap them out of it and give their courage back."

"I am terribly against the idea," Milskar said.

"I am your queen. I am the one who makes the rules."

Anger over Kolas's death burned like a fire in Aura's heart. She could not stand by while this army tried to take what was hers. She would fight back. No one else's life needed to be lost.

"I am terribly against the idea," he started again. "But it is the only thing I can see working. I will fight alongside you, I will protect you in any way I can."

"No, I need you elsewhere. If you fight next to me,

you will end up trying to fight for me. I cannot allow that nor have you wasting your energy on my protection. You need to fight for all of us. You were next in command after Kolas. You are now in charge. I need you to go through the ranks, encourage them, and help where you can. I need you totally focused on that task. Do you understand me? I do not want to see you trying to save my life."

He nodded reluctantly.

Fetching a sword from the stack of reserves and sheathing a small knife in her belt, Aura marched down the hill into the battle she had been watching from afar for two days now. All the preparation, all that went into this moment, yet here she was, a lamb walking into the den of a hungry lion. She hoped, in this case, that the prey would become the victor.

Aura thought back to her childhood, and all the years between this moment and her youth seemed to vanish. She felt her father whispering in her ear, telling her about holding the sword firmly but lightly, feeling the weight of it in her hand, almost as an extension to her own body.

Her father had been a very busy man, often waking well before the sun rose and finishing his day long after it had set. During the work day, she was often left to her own devices. Typically, she spent her time wandering the castle, stables, or once Theirra had arrived, stealing her away to play at any opportunity. His days off though, both blessed days, belonged to the two of them. Unless there was some kind of highly urgent matter, like a great flood or fire, he never missed a single one with her.

At first, Aura and her father just walked the woods for hours. Sometimes, they would ride Alcippe and Serenity out along the mountain ridges miles from the castle. Other times, they went by foot and would stay quite close to home.

Once she got a little older, their outings took on quite a different purpose. The king brought a few members of his guard with them on their trips and even some of their weapons. It was great fun for her, but she didn't understand the importance of sword fighting, tracking, or hunting game. However, her father felt it very necessary for her to learn these skills.

She had put an end to the hunting portion of it quickly, though. They had spent the better part of a day tracking a group of erons, small long-legged creatures with spots and long necks. They were extremely fast and intelligent and it had proved quite difficult for the small hunting party to stay on their path. Suddenly, they came to a small stream where the animals had stopped to drink, their long tongues pulling the water into their mouths. Aura's father nodded at her and she placed an arrow into her bow.

The animal fell quickly. It was a good, clean shot. The silence that followed was broken almost instantly. The pained shrieks and cries from the surviving erons tore straight through Aura's chest and nestled deep into her heart. She was too busy trying to blink back tears to hear the congratulations from her father. He quickly caught on to her emotions and moved to comfort her.

"Oh, shh, my dear Aura. There is no need to shed tears," he said and knelt down to place a large hand under her chin.

"But—they—sound—so—sad." The words came out in gasping sobs.

"I know it is upsetting, Aura, but we must thank this creature for giving up its life so we can live."

She nodded, but really didn't understand. The group of animals had moved on farther into the woods and, while she could no longer see them, their cries lived in her brain for months. She brushed off any future attempts to get her to go hunting, and soon their outings stopped all together.

It made her sad to think of all the time she'd missed with her father. How he was just trying to show her a life outside of her own privileged one. The king could not have known how important all that training would truly be for her. How it would hold the key, not only to her survival, but also to the kingdom's.

The cries of the erons, creatures she never saw in Esotera again, mixed with the sadness of Kolas's loss in her chest. Instead of dwelling on being sad and letting that overtake her, she took that pain, that deep burning anguish, and marched into battle.

Chapter 39

Redemption

Milskar did as the queen told him. After watching Aura descend the hill, he ran the opposite direction and began overseeing the fighting. He gave supportive help where needed, but tried to keep moving as much as possible. He wanted each of the soldiers to see his presence, to know that, while Kolas was dead, there was still someone in power, someone watching over them, reassuring them. He had reached a far outcropping of fighting when he heard movement behind him. He pulled his sword around but, almost immediately, it fell out of his hand to the ground. Panic flooded him as, out of the clearing, walked one of the worst things Milskar had ever seen in his life.

Emily clutched her side. Blood stained the front of her shirt and found its way around her arm and down the rest of her body. She looked pale and a little shocked, but her eyes were focused solely on Milskar. He ran to her, dropping to his knees, and begging the air around them not to take her away from him. To not let her die. Not her and Kolas, not both. One would have been hard enough, but both—both would have been unbearable. If he lost her, he thought he would stop living, the pain of it killing him instantly.

"I'm fine," she croaked out. "I am fine. See?" She lifted her arm and, while there was a considerable amount of blood on her, he could see it was just a superficial cut. It was quite large—the reason for all the blood—but it did not appear deep, almost like a paper cut covering her entire midsection.

"What happened to you?" he asked, looking up at her, his hands clutching hers.

"Levi."

"What?"

At that moment, Levi walked out of the forest, looking a little bewildered and confused. He had some blood on him, as well, but it did not appear to be his. His eyes held a deep pain, but Milskar was unable to notice that at first. The rage filled him so ferociously, he simply leaped to his feet and began running toward the terrified boy.

"No!" Emily yelled, seconds before Milskar was on him. While it hurt terribly, she ignored the pain and ran toward the two men, separating them with bloody hands. "Stop! It was an accident!"

Milskar paused with his sword raised in the air, moments before bringing it down on Levi.

She breathed a sigh of relief. "He had a knife and, when I went to hug him, it cut me. It was an accident."

"An accident," Levi repeated, out of breath, fear still lacing his voice.

"I am fine," she assured Milskar. "It was an accident."

The sword Milskar held clattered to the ground and he stepped forward to embrace her. The relief that washed over them both brought tears to their eyes. Emily let a few escape while Milskar successfully fought against them.

They finally pulled apart and looked at Levi who had respectfully averted his eyes at the show of affection, even though it visibly confused him.

"Milskar," Levi said. "How do we end this? What can I do to stop this all?"

"I do not think there is anything that can be done," Milskar said solemnly, his arm still around Emily's shoulders.

"That can't be true. I am the one who started all of this. I should be able to end it."

"Too much has happened. This just is not something you can simply take back."

"Fine," Levi said curtly. "Then I want to fight. I want to help. I need to do something to help counteract this terrible thing I allowed to happen."

"You did not do this," Emily protested. "They made you. They brainwashed you and forced you to help them, Levi. When I first saw you, you were, you were—" She paused, not wanting to say the words out loud. "—terrifying. That wasn't you. They did that to you."

"What do you remember after you were taken?" Milskar asked.

"Not much." Levi shrugged. "I vaguely remember being brought into a room and there were lots of loud noises. And, honestly, the next thing I remember was Emily's face and somehow I was in the woods, holding a knife, with her bleeding."

He hung his head in shame and Emily walked to him, wrapping her arms around him for comfort. She spoke softly to him and, finally, they separated, each a little more composed.

"I knew it," Milskar said, pacing. "I thought I saw

Abaddon on the other side. It was briefly, but this sounds exactly like one of his experiments."

"Experiments?" Emily asked.

"We used to have more communication, the Four Corners, but differences arose, since each ruler did not agree with certain aspects of another. Finally, they went their separate ways, but I remember Abaddon. He was crazy, even back then, talking about experiments he wanted to try out on people—mind control, things like that. I do not know all of the details, but it really shook up King Aldric and it was one of the contributing factors to communication ending between us. Seems like Abaddon has continued doing them, even after all of these years…"

Milskar's voice and mind drifted. He sounded a thousand miles away, instead of directly in front of them.

Emily reached out a hand and touched his arm, bringing him back to them. "I left another guard in charge of the bunkers. The people are well protected. It is my turn to fight now. Milskar, take us to the line, let us contribute." He shook his head. "Yes," she said softly. "You trained me yourself. You know what I am capable of. Let's go."

She turned and Levi followed her. Several seconds, later Milskar fell in line behind the two, his mind trying to figure out an alternate plan.

His reaction to seeing her covered in blood shocked him, and he did not want to know what he would do if she faced mortal peril while he was present. He hoped he would not have to find out.

The entire time they marched, Levi willed with every step that Aura and Esotera would be victorious. He did not know how large a thing his influence could be, but he hoped he could help protect them all. He pictured the victory in his head and replayed it over and over again, hoping that, if he thought about it strongly enough, it would happen.

Chapter 40

Thwarted

Aura's heart was pounding so violently in her chest it almost hurt. She could feel every part of her almost down to the cellular level. She felt her skin prickle, the blood flow through her veins, and she could hear herself breathing. Slowly, she moved through the fighters, eyes locked on one person in particular. Something in her told her that this would end it. That this would be how it would have to end.

It seemed as though everyone parted in front of her as she walked. Those, who appeared to be standing in her path one second, simply seemed to vanish the next as soon as her feet thought to place themselves in the space the person had occupied. She was aware of the fighting all around her, how could she not be? The noise of it all was deafening, but it was almost as if a separate compartment of her brain was processing it. She was aware but, at the same time, tuned out those clashing, falling, and possibly dying all around her. She focused her eyes in front of her.

He was fighting three people at once, but somehow still sensed her walking toward him. He felled one of the guards, a boy who looked only about sixteen, before the other two slowly started backing away. Looking up, he locked eyes with her. She nodded, sure that he was aware of how this would end as well. He bowed his head to her and took a firm stance, sword in front of him.

Aura approached the king with slow but authoritative steps. Those around her, once realizing what was happening, stood in awed silence. Both sides ceased fighting. It was as if they knew this would be the end of it and they were no longer required to shed any more blood. Neither army really wanted to be involved in all of this combat, but they also could not stand idly by as one side tried to overtake the other. They seemed relieved to be done with their duty of fighting.

The two leaders began circling each other. Aura's heart was no longer pounding in her chest. It was now beating just as if she were just on a pleasant walk around her kingdom. The king, however, looked nervous at the confrontation.

Not only did he not want to fell another leader but also, with her being a woman, he did not want her blood on his hands. He wondered what it would to do his image if he killed a young girl, but quickly dismissed the notion. She was not just some young woman. She had harbored a fugitive and was the ruler of a kingdom he wanted to have control over. And she was the heir to a man, whom King Grustmiener vehemently hated, as he'd always felt the lands of Esotera should have belonged to him. He wanted to destroy her.

Filled with this rage, he suddenly moved forward in attack. His sword came crashing down on hers and, for a moment, he thought this battle would last only seconds.

Her arm shook under the strain of fighting against all his strength, but she was quick and was soon able to move out from under his hold.

The king was large and had sheer brute strength on his side, but Aura's upbringing of playing for hours in the woods and play sword fighting were proving to be an advantage. She was nimble and moved quickly out of the way of his advances. After that initial confrontation, his sword barely came close enough to move a hair on her head.

They danced like this for what seemed like hours, though really only several seconds had gone by. Upon hearing of this duel, fighters from all over the lines began converging on this small clearing, forming a circle around the two. Those who had engaged in an intense battle only moments before now stood side by side, mesmerized at the fight before them.

"You will not take my kingdom away from me," she said between clenched teeth after barely avoiding another crash of his sword.

"Not only will I take it away," he said, the exertion of their fight heavy in his voice, "but I will burn it to the ground. I will destroy every inch of it."

He suddenly turned on her, slashing his sword through the air, and catching her cheek with the tip of his blade. The instantaneous pain shocked her and she almost dropped her weapon as her hand went to her face. It was just a superficial wound, bleeding but not terribly deep.

Still, it angered her greatly. Made her mad that she'd allowed him to get close enough to touch her.

A low, guttural, animal-like sound came out of Aura and she attacked. With her sword level with her waist, as her father had taught her many years ago, she swung sideways at him. The clash of her sword meeting his armor rang off the trees around them and the ground trembled. The pure fury in her eyes went straight to his core and shook something in there. He suddenly wanted very badly to just walk back to his wife and take her home. To return to the safety of his castle and rule as he had for many decades.

A few hundred yards away, Winester was slowly making his way through the woods toward the commotion. He could feel his age in his bones, the last few decades seeping the majority of his strength away. These last few days had invigorated him and he felt some of his power coming back to him. Suddenly a cry behind him caused him to whirl around.

"Busu?" he said, confused.

He hadn't seen the bird in weeks and wondered why he now flew overhead. Winester was about to call the bird again—Busu was now slowly circling to land—when Winester heard another sound close to him.

Resbuca stood before him, looking about a hundred years older than she actually was. The intent on her face was clear and he began thinking up an escape route. He would not allow her to thwart him. She would not be the one who would stand in his way.

"You have done enough here," she said to him in her sweet voice. "You will not contribute anymore."

"I do not believe that you will be the one to stop me," he said in a laughing voice. He turned to continue walking, but suddenly found his legs immobile.

"Leave now."

"So now you are giving me options?" Winester said, finally able to turn back around once her hold on him weakened.

"I do not want to hurt you, but I will if that is what it takes." Resbuca stepped closer to him and raised her wand. She knew she was an old woman and was not as powerful as she had been years before, but she also knew Winester was not the sorcerer he had been in his strongest days either. She believed they were on a level playing field. She just hoped she would come out on top this time.

She felt a grip on the back of her knees and slowly fell to the ground. Winester's stare was intent on her and it took all her strength to break the curse he had placed upon her. In retaliation, she threw her full force at him, knocking him backward.

"Leave."

"Never, now that I am this close," he said, his own wand clutched tightly in his hand.

"What ever happened to us?" she asked somberly.

Winester was still on the ground, panting, but Resbuca knew not to let her guard down. She worked on keeping up her defenses, as she felt his powers pressing in around her.

"I wanted a bigger life," he said harshly. "And you were only going to stand in my way."

He jumped up in anger, breaking her concentration. Suddenly, she fell to her knees, sharp pains running through her body.

"I will never allow you to stand between me and what I want again."

"Again?" she gasped, the pain Winester had inflicted on her slowly receding. "I never stood in your way. Together we could have been great. Together we would have ruled this world with perfect power. You are the one who held us back. You."

She stood, her eyes burning through the middle of him. Resbuca felt him try to fight against her, struggling to push her out of his head, but she was stronger than he was. She had more fury, more years of vested hatred toward him than he could have ever imagined.

He writhed in pain as she walked closer, intent still fully on him and her wand pointed directly at his chest. His eyes pleaded with her as he realized that she was the more powerful one. He had wasted so many years of his power and energy for evil. He'd wasted so much of himself for obsolete causes.

She had honed her powers, had been saving them. If this were the last thing she did before moving on to whatever was waiting for her in the next life, she would die a fulfilled woman.

"Resbuca," he said weakly.

She shook her head, raised her wand, and whispered several words. A large ball of yellow fire began to burn in between her hands. Winester had just enough time for fear to register on his face before the ball raced toward him. He tried ducking, but it came too fast, consuming him instantly. The trees and leaves whirled at the force as a large swirl of ash took his place, falling softly on the forest floor like fresh snow.

A part of her heart broke off and joined the pieces of him. She collapsed and fell to the ground. She had finally defeated him—after all these years.

Chapter 41

Victory

I can help, I want to help," Levi pleaded with both of them.

"It is too dangerous," Milskar said flatly. "I am bringing you both straight back to the castle. I will not risk either of your lives." He looked pointedly at Emily.

"Maybe we can help," Emily said softly, taking his hands. "All of my training…" She trailed off.

"I've been trained too," Levi said without emotion, causing Milskar and Emily to glance his way.

"Hey." She took a step toward him and put her hands on his face. His eyes glazed over. "Hey, come back to me."

Levi's head snapped up and he looked around, trying to get his bearings. He reached up and took hold of one of her hands, nodding his head. She smiled weakly back at him and let her other hand drop.

"What do you mean you have been trained?" Milskar asked, pulling Emily protectively back against him.

"My, umm, powers, or whatever? They figured out a

way to harness them. Figured out a way to teach me how to harness them."

Emily stared, shocked. "Levi?"

"Can you use your power against them?" Milskar asked, moving a bit closer in.

"No! It is too dangerous," Emily said, fear lacing her voice. "You were right. We should just go back to the castle."

"We will not look for trouble," Milskar said firmly, "but if it happens to find us, we will be ready."

They made their way slowly through the woods, pausing often to listen for others. They heard a commotion ahead and peered through the trees to find two men in intense battle.

"The one in the blue is from Esotera," Milskar whispered. The man dressed in brown was clearly gaining the upper hand. "I must go help him."

"Wait," Emily said, grabbing his arm, "Levi, can you help?"

"I'll try," he said, his voice shaking along with his hands. He felt weak and terrified, but worked at clearing his mind and concentrating, just like Abaddon had taught him.

There was a sudden loud crack and a large tree branch fell, killing the Grustmiener fighter instantly, but also partly crushing the man in blue as well. The three rushed to his aid and lifted the heavy branch off of him. His leg was clearly broken, but at least he was still alive.

"Is the fighting almost over?"

It wasn't until he spoke that Emily realized how young he really was, maybe in his teens. He had looked so much older fighting, but now lying on the ground in considerable pain, he seemed just a young boy. Part of her wanted to stay and hold his hand until help, or maybe his mother, arrived. She wondered for a split second if his mother was even alive or if she had perished in the fighting. She quickly dismissed the idea.

"I am so sorry," Levi said, pain on his face as well as in his voice.

"Lord Vertrous must have been looking out for me today." The boy smiled up at them. "He must have made that tree fall to take out the man who surely would have killed me."

"Yes, I believe he did," Levi answered. "I believe he did."

They moved the boy under some low-lying trees and bushes and promised to send someone to help him as soon as they could. He thanked them again for all their help as Milskar, Emily, and Levi—who was still shaken up—moved back through the woods.

They walked for another few yards when everything around them went silent, freezing Milskar, Emily, and Levi in place. They all looked at one another and shrugged. Milskar held up a finger, telling them to wait quietly for a moment.

"Where did everyone go?" Emily finally whispered.

"I do not know," Milskar hissed back.

"Shouldn't we be seeing more people?" " Levi asked anxiously.

"This is where I left my group," Milskar said, looking around and trying to get his bearings to make sure that they were in the correct spot.

"Shh," Emily said suddenly. "Do you hear that?"

Slowly a rumble started through the trees. In an instant, the three began sprinting toward the sound. Branches caught Emily's hair and cut her face and arms, but she didn't care. Her lungs were screaming for her to stop and she felt fresh blood ooze from her wounds, but she pressed herself on faster. She didn't know what the noise was or what they would stumble upon, but something in all of them said they should be in that place. They crashed through a small clearing and into a large group of soldiers from both sides. Gasping for breath, they pushed through to the inner part of the circle. What was left of Emily's breath rushed out of her lungs when she saw what was in the center.

Aura's face was damp with sweat and concentration as she wielded her sword back and forth, clashing it against King Grustmiener's. Milskar's hand searched and found Emily's. The two stared into each other's eyes, one's fears reflecting in the other's. She looked back at Levi, but his eyes were locked on the battle in front of him. His lips were moving silently and Emily hoped he was using all his power to will Aura to win the battle.

"I do not need outside help from anyone," Aura yelled breathlessly, and it was clear that she was feeling whatever Levi was trying to do to her. "There will be no assistance from either side."

Blood was clotting and oozing from various spots on her face and she had a deep cut on her arm. The king was bleeding freely from a wound on his thigh, though he seemed not to notice the pain.

Her sword clashed down again and it was clear the king was tiring more dramatically than Aura was. He stumbled backward and tried to regain his feet before she moved upon him again.

Sensing him weakening, Aura strengthened her attack. She found a new place of power somewhere inside her and used all of it on the king. It was not long until the battle was over.

She drew her sword up with both hands and was just about to bring it down on the king when he lowered his sword and placed an arm in front of his face. She stopped inches away from his heart, panting with the effort finally catching up with her.

"Do you surrender?" she asked him in a tired, hollow voice.

The sword was trembling as her muscles began to realize their fatigue. The look on his face said he would have rather she killed him, but he was debating his options. He was a powerful man and did not want to have to willingly give up his kingdom to this girl. After a split second of weighing all his options, he shook his head. Her eyes shut as she plunged the sword straight down.

A deafening cheer broke out through the crowd and, soon, Aura felt herself being lifted by dozens of hands. Her eyes remained closed as she was carried off. She wished the events of the last few days could be erased from her memory but, behind her eyelids, all she saw was the defeated yet defiant face of the once-powerful ruler of Grustmiener.

♥⁓♥⁓

An aide burst out of the woods and was sprinting toward her. His face was almost translucent, it was so white. He looked terrified. Lady Grustmiener, having heard the cheers weave their way from the distance to her ears, didn't really need to hear what the out-of-breath man had to say. She already knew.

"The king," the man stammered. "There—was Queen—Aura—" He was gasping and stopping between broken words. He finally took a deep breath and straightened. "Queen Aura just felled the king."

The aide pressed his eyes shut, waiting whatever pain or wrath would come his way, though the only thing presented to him was silence.

A small gust of wind brushed his hair back off his

face. When he opened his eyes, no one was in front of him. The tent was empty and his former lady was gone.

∽∾∽

The Grustmiener army was disbanding all around them as Aura and her people made their way back up to the castle. She had sent a jubilant Emily, Milskar, and Levi to gather the town's people who had been in hiding so they could join the celebration. Levi had pulled Aura aside to apologize for everything that had happened. His eyes were so genuine, she could tell how much pain the knowledge of what he had done had caused him. Aura was not sure of all the specifics of what had happened to him. There would be time for that but, for now, she hugged him tightly and sent him off.

There were several members of the opposing army injured in the last day of battle and left without care, having been abandoned by their lady. Aura instructed her already overwhelmed healers to help all they could. The fighting was over and their worlds had to go back to being one again. The Four Corners had been separated for too many years, not only by distance, but also by prejudice against each other. She hoped this coming together today would help spur a resurgence of unity in her world.

Aura made her way to the same clearing she had stood in only hours before, addressing her troops, to speak to them once more. "I am so proud today to be your ruler, more than anyone has ever been of their people." A deafening yell went through the crowd and she had to wait several moments to continue. "The bravery and courage you all showed, not to mention the love of your kingdom, has humbled me."

She was fighting her own emotions now, and she

hoped she would be able to get through these next few sentences while still keeping her composure. The sheer weight of the last few days was pulling all emotions out of her and she was finding it difficult to hold them in.

"The people of Grustmiener—" she started again. Several boo's and jeers came out of the crowd. She held up her hand against them. "The people of Grustmiener fought bravely for their own homes as well. They too are proud and love their kingdom. And we should respect not only what they did but the losses they suffered."

The crowd somberly nodded their heads and became silent once more.

"I offer to them, each and every one, a home here in Esotera if they wish it. Those who do not wish to stay, I will grant safe passage back to Grustmiener. No one from this army will stop you but, remember, a repeat of the events of today will not be tolerated. It will take many years to fix what has been broken today, but we are on that road and, if we work together, we will be successful. Now, I want each of you to celebrate. Celebrate your lives and celebrate what you accomplished today. Remember those who bravely gave their lives so you can have what you hold in your hands and see around you. We have much work ahead of us, but let us not forget what it took to get us here." Her face brightened in a smile. "Now, go, all of you. I best not hear that a single one of you shut your eyes in sleep before the sun rises again."

A happy cheer again erupted from the group. To ensure that peace was kept throughout the celebration, Aura turned to one of the guards, standing beside her, and informed the young man what she expected. She would not tolerate any continued violence and any offending parties were to be taken immediately to her chambers.

"Your chambers?" the man asked.

"Do not tell, but I am going to break my rule and try to get a little sleep in." She winked at him and turned to leave. It took her some time to make her way through the crowd. It seemed everyone wanted to touch, thank, and simply look at her.

Eventually, running on sheer will itself, she was able to make it all the way up to her room. She knew, though, that there was one final act she would have to perform before she would be able to rest. She asked the aide who had been traveling with her to find Theirra and bring her back. She instructed the woman not to allow Theirra to speak to anyone and bring her directly to her.

Aura slowly paced her room as she waited. Several times, she peered out her large windows and could see several hundred fires burning, but this time those around them danced instead of fretted for what would come the following day. She shook her head in disbelief. Aura wasn't sure how long it would take to really hit her with all that had happened these last few months.

From the first moment she'd found out about the curse, her father's death, the journey to recover Levi, and the heartbreaking loss, then the terrifying truth of what was needed to secure their future, she'd felt like she had lived about twenty lives. She only wished her father could have been there, not to take over—no she was confident enough now in her ability as a ruler that she no longer felt like she needed his input—but to just see her and his people. He would have been so proud.

Theirra finally walked through her door and a lump rose in Aura's chest. She knew this information had to come from her, but she also wished someone else could have broken the news to her friend. She knew this would crush Theirra. Aura just hoped that somehow they would be able to pick up the pieces and move on.

"Aura," Theirra said, running forward to embrace her. Dirt covered her face and she had several twigs twisted in her hair. Her face beamed with the joy of the victory, but quickly fell as she noticed the somber look on Aura's face.

"Theirra—"

"No," Theirra pulled away from Aura, backing slowly toward the door.

"Theirra, Kolas—"

"No!" Theirra screamed and ran toward the heavy wooden door, grasping at it with ragged fingernails, but the tears streaming down her face blurred her vision too much for her to see where the handle was.

Aura held her from behind, softly cooing to her. Theirra's screams sounded as if they were coming from all over the kingdom, her cries reverberating around them.

Aura felt something fragile shatter inside her heart, leaving painful little shards behind. More than anything, she wanted to take this pain away from her friend, wrap it in something, and throw it out her bedroom window. They would watch it fall a hundred feet to the ground below, no longer a concern for them.

Theirra pulled every drop of liquid she held in her body and forced it out of her eyes. Aura was not sure how long they stood there, clinging to each other as if some gust of wind was threatening to blow them away. Slowly, Aura was able to pull Theirra toward her bed, softly laying her down, as her sobs got more and more quiet. Aura combed the debris out of Theirra's hair as she finally fell into a deep, yet tumultuous sleep.

Chapter 42

Pieces

Staying up all night stroking Theirra's hair had left Aura exhausted. Several times, Theirra yelled out in her sleep, but did not waken. Aura had shut her eyes for just a moment when she felt Theirra stir. Theirra's eyes were almost sealed shut, they were so puffy.

Aura rose from the bed and got Theirra a glass of water and a warm washcloth. "I have to leave you for a little bit," she said hoarsely. "Stay here, I will be back a little later."

Theirra nodded and lay back down. Aura felt like she was a hundred years old. Her bones and joints creaked with the strain of the previous day's fighting. All she wanted to do was go to bed and sleep all this pain away, but she knew it would really only take the edge off. She was weary all the way through to her bones and out the other side. It felt as if it was unrecoverable.

She met several of her aides and servants as she walked, each shaking her hand and, in one case, embracing her. She could not help but be slightly rejuvenated by their joy. It was as though a blanket of sadness had been lifted off the kingdom. All the anxiety from the last few weeks had melted away, run into the river that cut through the kingdom, and been taken out to the sea.

A healer walked up to her, patched the ragged cut on her arm, and put medicine on her face. The cool gel brought instant relief to the throbbing of her skin.

Aura left the castle and made her way through the crowd. There were people everywhere. Some were still sleeping, the late night celebration exhausting them all. Others huddled around one another in quiet conversation. They nodded at her and she smiled back at them.

Through the crowds, she eventually found what she was looking for. "Good morning," she said to Emily and Levi, who were sitting on the ground, backs against the wall surrounding the yard.

"Aura," Levi said, standing and taking her hands in his. "I know we spoke last night, but again, I'm so sorry for all the trouble I brought you."

"Please." She waved him off. "You were under powerful spells. Plus, it all ended up fine in the end."

Milskar had informed her of the state Levi was in when he found him and, while she was sickened to learn of what the boy had done, she could hardly blame him for falling under the influence of such powerful people.

"How is Theirra?" Emily asked, concerned.

Aura shook her head. "She will be fine with time, but a piece of that pain will probably be carried with her forever."

Levi looked away and toed the dirt with the tip of his shoe. Emily stood beside him and took one of his hands in hers. It was clear they had been up most the night, as well, probably talking, Aura assumed.

She could see the remorse all over Levi's face and wished she was able to take some of it away from him, but deep down she also wanted him to carry some of that pain with him.

While he could not be faulted for everything that had happened, he did have a hand in it. And, as much as she wanted to, she would not be able to forgive him completely. Her kingdom had been ripped apart and lives were lost. It was not something that she could easily forget.

"We have an important matter to discuss," Aura said.

"Matter?" Emily said with a quizzical look on her face.

"Getting you both home."

Levi instantly brightened, finally looking her in the eyes. Emily, though, she noticed, quickly glanced over to the place where Milskar was making rounds, talking to several soldiers.

"When can we leave?" Levi asked, beaming. "I know you must be busy, trying to get everything in order, so we don't have to leave right now, but I am ready whenever you are. I am glad that I was able to help secure your kingdom, though I am sorry at the way it had to happen, but I think I have done enough for you all. I think it is time we went back home now." He wrapped an arm around Emily's shoulder, and she attempted a weak smile back up at him.

"Tomorrow, I believe," Aura said. "While there is an awful lot that we need to do around here, I think it will be several days before we need to make any major decisions. Honestly, before those issues are addressed, I would like to wait for things to return to normal. We will follow the same route as before, but with a few more guards for protection." She looked over at Levi and he reddened.

She apologized for having to leave so quickly but told them she had some other affairs to put in order. Aura turned to leave them, imploring them to eat in the hall and enjoy the day.

For a second, she was sure Emily was about to ask her something, but then she quickly closed her mouth and turned to walk away with Levi in tow, a happy spring to his step.

Outside of the holding cell where the three Grustmienerian spies were being held, Aura ran into Milskar and Eir. This was the first time she had visited the three prisoners and it surprised her how different they all looked.

One man seemed defiant, though it was clear he had been beaten quite severely. The other man, somewhat smaller than the first, appeared almost bored and annoyed about being held, but he did not look particularly dangerous. The youngest of the three looked terrified, eyes bloodshot from fatigue and, possibly, tears.

After some protest by Milskar, she entered the cell with the three to address them. "The war is over, as I am sure you have heard. The three of you are free to go." Aura heard a grumble of protest behind her, but ignored it. "As I have told everyone else from your kingdom, you are welcome to stay in Esotera, but I would especially implore the three of you to return to your lands. However, the decision is ultimately yours and I will honor whichever one you choose."

The largest man laughed. "Stay here?"

"Show some respect, Achan," Milskar warned.

"I am committed to peace between our two lands," Aura continued. "So, yes, if you wish to stay here you will be welcome to, but again, as your actions these last few days have proven, I believe you will be better off returning to Grustmiener."

"And we shall. Thank you," the second man said.

"What is your name?" Aura asked the youngest.

"Lieal," the boy said to the ground.

"Lieal." She smiled at him. "Will you be returning back home?"

"My parents—" he started as the rims of his eyes brimmed with tears.

"I am sure they will be very happy to see you," she said and could see the pure relief wash over his body.

Aura turned to leave when Achan called her back. "And how is the lovely Kolas doing? Not man enough to let us go himself?" he said with a smirk.

Aura whirled and punched him square in the face. Eir's soft hand was quickly on her shoulder, pulling her back out of the room. Achan sat on the floor, hand rubbing his sore jaw, a purplish bruise already starting to form. Milskar suppressed a laugh as he ushered the three out of the cell, freeing them to return to their homes.

～～～

It was several more hours before Aura finally returned to her room. Resbuca had kindly come to get Theirra a few hours prior, making up some excuse that the animals needed her. Aura had asked where Resbuca had gone during the battle, but the sorceress waved her off

She would fill in all the gaps with her in the morning.

Aura was thankful to have a moment of quiet for the first time in several days, yet a knock at her door quickly erased any ideas of her climbing into bed and succumbing to sleep at last.

Emily stood on the threshold with silent tears running down her face. Aura's maternal instincts took over and she forgot how exhausted she was.

"Emily." Aura embraced her as she blubbered into her shoulder. "Shh, I cannot understand you. What is wrong?" Aura pulled away and looked her in the eyes.

"I—" Emily choked. "I don't think I can leave."

"What?" Aura asked, confused.

"I—" Emily started again then paused and took a deep breath. "I know when I first got here all I wanted to do was leave, but now. Now, I don't think I can."

"Would Milskar have anything to do with this?"

Emily nodded sheepishly.

"I would be extremely happy to welcome you to my kingdom to live, Emily."

"Oh, Aura!" Emily exclaimed.

"But—" Aura held up a hand. "But you have a family back home. A family that I am sure is worried about you. Time does work a little differently here than it does in your world."

"Differently?"

"You have been gone for several months here, but in your world it has only been weeks. You will be able to come up with a story to explain your missing for that period of time, but how will Levi explain it when he returns without you?"

"I—I don't know. I will come up with something. I have to. Aura, I have nothing back there. Yes, I do have my family, but I have no direction, no future. Here—I could see myself making a life here."

Aura smiled and quickly embraced Emily once more. She turned back to her bed and sat upon it, gesturing for Emily to sit in the chair beside her.

"You will need to discuss this with Levi."

Emily nodded.

"And, more importantly, I think you should speak to Milskar."

"Milskar?"

"I do not want to sound insensitive, but I would also talk with him and see if this is something he would want, as well."

"Oh." Emily's whole demeanor changed, and she got very small and quiet.

"Emily." Aura reached out her hand. "I just want you to be sure that you are making the correct decision. I just do not want you to go through with this and regret it. I cannot just let you go back and forth once you are tired of living in one world or the other. Excessive travel is frowned upon. It would not look right if I allowed you to break rules that I force others to follow. Do you understand?"

Emily nodded. "Yes."

"I must get some rest, Emily. You will travel with us tomorrow and can give me your final decision then, but please promise me that you will think logically about this," Aura said as she climbed into her bed.

"I will. Thank you." Emily turned and quietly walked out of the room.

Aura was instantly asleep and didn't even hear the door shut behind her.

Chapter 43

Home

Aura woke up with just the edges of her exhaustion
dissipated. She'd heard the continuing celebration outside her window until late in the night.
The cries and shouts of joy from the courtyard below
wove their way into her dreams. She would give her people until her return from the journey with Levi and Emily.
After that, some semblance of order would have to be
reinstated so life could get back to normal.

She made her way slowly through the castle. It was
still early and there was not much activity going on. She
found several of her guards in the main hall and asked
them to join her on the journey to the portal later that day.

"We shall be gone for a few days, but I would prefer
it if you did not disclose the nature of our travels to anyone. As far as the people are concerned, we are taking a
trip to secure the rest of the perimeter around Esotera and
make sure there are not any residual problems from the
battle."

"Yes, my queen," one of the men responded in a husky voice.

Next, she went to the stables and informed the hands there that she would need several horses that could withstand the journey. In the battle, a number of them had been injured, including Serenity. It pained Aura's heart to see her beloved mare with cuts and scrapes all along her body, but she would heal quickly—her wounds were not that bad.

"Thank you for being so very brave." Aura stroked the horse's neck and gave her several treats before leaving.

They would be several horses short and some people would have to trade off walking, but Aura figured it would be a slow-paced journey, anyway. She was not concerned. With the danger of attack averted, they would not have to worry so much about their surroundings and could enjoy a leisurely remaining few days together. She was taking several more guards along with her, but they were really just for show. She was certain they were unnecessary but, at the same, she time did not want to chance it.

Leaving the stables, she ran into Gustado. He had done a wonderful job, just as Theirra predicted. While young, he was very capable and she was glad she had found a worthy replacement. She knew the other, older stable hands felt a little jaded that he was suddenly in charge, but if these last few months had taught her anything, it was that age did not necessarily dictate skill level and ability.

"Queen?" he called to her as she passed.

"Yes, Gustado?"

"What should I do about him?" he asked, pointing back over his shoulder. Aura followed his gesture and smiled when her eyes rested on where he was pointing.

"Where did he come from?" she asked, slowly walking in that direction.

Gustado shrugged. "The north, I assume."

"No, I didn't mean direction. Did he just walk into the stables?"

"Yes, gave the horses quite a fright." The look on his face said it gave him a fright as well.

"Oh, Gilbert." Aura patted the griffin's strong shoulder. "I am sure you know of Kolas's fate." Gilbert bowed his head. "You may stay here, for now, but I will arrange for you to return to your homeland. Gustado," she said, turning to the boy. "Please get in touch with a sanctuary there, inform them we have found a lost griffin, and ask them to take him."

"Yes, my queen."

She thanked him and gave Gilbert one more pat before walking away. After being so terrified of the creature when they'd first met, she now saw how truly beautiful he was. His golden wings shimmered in the sun as he butted Gustado lightly in the chest, begging for more attention.

She walked farther around the castle perimeter and soon came across Resbuca. The sorceress was sitting on a bench on the edge of a large courtyard, a large bird sitting behind her. They had not had a chance to speak and catch up from when they'd parted on the hill, and Aura was eager to get Resbuca's side of the story on what had happened. Resbuca had returned from the battle, looking exhausted but triumphant, and Aura wanted to find out why.

"Resbuca," she said, nodding respectfully at her.

The sorceress patted the space next to her, bidding Aura to sit down.

"I was wondering when you would come looking for me," Resbuca said, smiling at the queen.

"I appreciate you taking Theirra this morning. How is she doing?" Aura asked.

"Terrible, but she will live," Resbuca said, her smile fading. "It will take time, but she will recover."

They sat together, looking out at the courtyard for some time. There were several birds and a few small animals picking through the dew-laced grass, looking for food.

"So tell me what happened."

Resbuca looked confused. "Last night?"

"No, not last night. After I left you on the hill. After I went down to fight. What happened?"

"Winester."

Aura sat up, her rapt attention upon Resbuca. "Winester?"

"He was coming to help the enemy, or something of that nature. He was not about to get so close to his goal and let you take it away from him. I can feel him you know—well, at least I could."

"Feel him?" Aura asked.

"Oh, yes, those that have power can always feel when someone who shares in it is close. However, I have found that, as I get older, the person needs to be closer for me to sense them. That is how I knew he was approaching the battle. I could suddenly tell he was around. We spent so many years together, I recognized that it was him immediately—" Resbuca broke off and stared into nothing, her eyes looking out on a past that no longer existed. "But—" She suddenly came back. "—I met up with him in the woods. There was a bit of a fight, pathetic really, each of us have gotten so old. But in the end, I was able to defeat him, to kill him. He was not able to make it to you."

Aura leaned in to embrace her. The women held each

other for a long time before Resbuca broke away. They each wiped their eyes and Aura smiled at her. "Is that his?" she asked, pointing at the bird.

Resbuca smiled and nodded, a sly expression on her face. "After the fight, he has taken to following me around. I must say I enjoy the company."

"So, I need to ask you, is the spell broken now? With Winester dead, is that the end of it?" The question had been bubbling in Aura's throat.

"Spells and magic are powerful things. They can live on even after the one who cast them is dead. No, I do not believe the simple act of his death will end it."

"Oh," Aura said in a breathless whisper. "I see."

"But I do believe there is still someone here that is powerful enough to overturn it. You see, Lord Vertrous held supreme power over this land and all its inhabitants, including its people. Including Winester. Winester was a powerful sorcerer, but Lord Vertrous was even more powerful." Resbuca paused.

"I do not think I understand."

"That boy, Levi, he holds that blood in him. That same power he had to declare war he has to break spells. That is what makes him such an important and powerful tool. I think having Winester dead helps weaken the spell, but all the same, I believe that Levi can reverse it."

Her words swarmed in Aura's brain, fighting for position in her memory. "So this battle, all of this, could have been prevented, if we had just asked the boy when we first met him? All of this could have been avoided?" There was anger and pain in Aura's voice. All these months, all these lives lost, and there was no reason for it?

"The boy needed to come here. He has limited power in the other world. His words would have meant nothing. He was taken so fast and everything else happened so quickly, I did not know if we would have had time to even get to him. I am a foolish and spiteful woman. I selfishly thought we would be able to get Levi back and that I would have a chance to enact my revenge on Winester, but everything escalated so quickly." Resbuca fell quiet.

"It is done and I do not believe regretting our past actions will do anything to ensure our future," Aura said slowly and deliberately. "You did all you could for me and my people with the powers of which you are capable. You will have a home here for as long as you want it."

"Thank you, but I could not possibly stay, knowing what I know, living with the choices I have made," Resbuca said in a tired voice.

"I understand, though I wish you would not leave us. We do not live perfect lives without fault or regret—not even powerful sorceresses, I suppose," Aura said, smiling weakly. "Though, it is what we do with that regret, how we pick up our lives, and try not to repeat our mistakes, which truly makes this life worth living."

"You are a very wise ruler, my queen," Resbuca said. "Your father would be incredibly proud of you. Esotera is lucky to have you."

They sat for a little while longer and, then realizing the time, Aura regretfully excused herself. While the knowledge saddened her, deep down she knew she would never see the sorceress again. She hoped Resbuca would be able to find peace with the choices she had made, finding comfort in the help she had given Aura and Esotera.

With one final look back, Aura continued her walk, gathering people and supplies for the journey as she went.

~·~·~

Several hours later, Aura, Levi, Emily, and Milskar,

plus several of the guards, met at the stables. Theirra
came out briefly to embrace Emily and shake Levi's
hands. Tears started up again, and she had to excuse herself, apologizing profusely to Emily and telling her how
much she would miss her.

After some protesting, both Emily and Milskar opted
to take the first shift of walking, allowing the others to
mount up on their horses. Aura tried making eye contact
with Emily several times, but the girl avoided all glances.
She and Milskar held hands and were deep in conversation the entire time.

They camped along the side of the road when it
started getting dark. Sitting around the campfire, the
group traded stories and laughed well into the night. The
guards asked Emily and Levi questions about the other
world and were enthralled with their answers. Emily gig-
gled and laughed at their amazement of airplanes, televi-
sions, and, especially, cameras.

"So it captures you inside of it?"

"No, no," she said lightly. "It's just an image of you.
You are still there."

They shook their heads, unable to comprehend what
she was trying to explain. Emily and Levi put their heads
together and laughed, sending the group into giggles as
well. Suddenly, Emily grew quiet and Aura noticed how
she seemed to go inside herself for a second. Just as
quickly, her eyes adjusted and she rejoined the conversation.

It was well into the night before Milskar suggested
they get some sleep. They all lay directly on the ground.
The night air was just a little crisp, but the fire helped
make them all comfortable.

Soon they all drifted off to a much-needed slumber
and quickly soft snores were heard all around the
campsite.

Chapter 44

Finale

A pull in his gut wakened Levi. There were bodies scattered around him on the forest floor just like there had been only days before. He watched, momentarily frightened that they might be dead, until he realized they were all breathing deep, sleeping breaths.

He quietly pulled his legs under him and began walking. The pull kept getting stronger, and he knew he was going in the right direction. The same electric feeling from his encounter with the Grustmiener army tingled through his body. If he was afraid, that fear was too deep in the recesses of his brain for him to detect.

He was sure—more sure of this path he was on than anything else he had felt in his life.

Suddenly, there she was.

A short distance away in the clearing, a soft mound lay on the earth. It rose and fell with her breaths, as well, yet unlike his group, she was completely alone. She must have sensed his presence. Maybe she felt the same pull as he did, because she was quickly on her feet.

"Mr. Roberts."

"Lady Grustmiener," Levi said. The electricity kept building.

"It appears Abaddon has failed me, after all," she said.

"Not his failure, my success." He tried to ignore the crawling feeling. It was not time yet. "There is good in me," he continued, "good that your evil couldn't touch."

"Oh, I can touch it," she hissed and moved toward him, her hands reaching.

In a flash, Levi exploded. He felt his power reach all around him. Images popped into his head of Emily's face, then Aura's, and the hundreds of Esoterans he had seen. He felt it deep within him, mixing with the electricity, making it stronger. They needed his power, his protection from any force that intended to hurt them. He relinquished himself to it and let it flow from him, until it exhausted itself and every drop left him.

The figure was back on the ground again, much like when he arrived, though this time there he didn't notice any rise and fall of breath.

"You will never touch these people again." Levi's declaration reverberated around the woods as he turned and walked back the way he'd come.

It took him much longer to return to camp. It seemed as if it had taken only steps to get to the clearing where Lady Grustmiener was but, in truth, he had walked probably three miles. However, he felt as if he could have walked for days. The electric feeling was dissipating, but still palpable. After all this time, after all these years, he was finally able to use his powers for good. He'd never understood them and, in fact, had feared them and wished they did not exist. But now, he knew how to harness them. He understood them and himself in a way he'd never imagined. The peace that knowledge gave him was incredible. The story he told his parents was no longer a lie. He'd found out where he came from, and it taught him everything he ever needed to know about himself.

For the first time, Levi didn't feel worthless. Didn't feel lost in the world. He had a purpose, a purpose he was able to fulfill to help all these people. It had taken him on an incredibly long journey, but he had finally found what he was searching for.

Returning to camp, he woke Aura and told her what happened. Shock washed over her face and, when he was finished, she gathered him in a crushing embrace.

"Oh, Levi," she exclaimed. "You have no idea what kind of peace this gives me."

He smiled. "Or me."

She sent two of the guards to retrieve the body as they began slowly walking again. They were unable to find her, though Levi was sure he had pointed them in the right direction.

"Her body was probably recovered," Milskar said. "We are close enough to the Grustmiener line that I am sure one of her people found her."

Disappointment was clear on the guards' faces, but Aura would not let them wallow. They all soon caught her festive mood. Most dismounted from their horses and chose to walk on foot, instead. It was the last day of their march and their pace had slowed even more. No one seemed to want to get there first, to be the one who would end it all.

Though, eventually, they did make it to the portal with several minutes to spare. It glowed softly in the distance while they all stood there, looking at one another.

"It is time," Aura finally said.

Levi nodded and began shaking hands with those in the group. When he got to Aura, he paused for several seconds before embracing her. "I'm so sorry for everything."

"Sorry? No, Levi, you saved us. You secured the future of my kingdom. I can never thank you enough."

"No." He shook his head. "If it weren't for me, the war would have never happened. You never would have lost any of your people."

"Levi." Aura took his face in both of her hands. "Yes, things did not go exactly the way we would have wanted them to, but if it were not for you, my kingdom would have died with me. You changed that. You gave us hope for the future. There is one more thing that I need you to do for me, though, before you leave."

"Anything," he said.

She hesitated, picking her words carefully. "I need you to allow whoever is ruler of Esotera to name their successor. With or without blood relation. Can you do that for me?" Aura asked.

"I am not sure I know how," Levi said.

"Please."

For the first time Levi saw her as she was, so young, yet strong and determined. He closed his eyes and began to let his thoughts wander. He felt the blood pumping through Aura's veins and the same throbbing beat at his feet and through the air around him.

He could feel the blood of her father, and her father's father, running through this land. It covered every inch of it. Levi found that he had to concentrate harder than he had in his entire life to feel it all the way to the edges of the kingdom. Slowly, like pulling a blanket, he brought the pulsing closer to himself. Finally, when it reached him, his mind grabbed and held on to it.

He felt like he was going to vomit from the sheer size and magnitude of the power he now held within him, but it slowly ebbed and disappeared. Now when he let his mind relax, he felt no pull from Aura into the surrounding world. There was an empty feeling around him now and, upon opening his eyes; he could tell Aura had felt the shift as well.

"Your land is now free."

They looked at one another and, for a moment, he thought he had seen a wash of regret form on her face. He hoped the act he had just preformed would, in fact, save these lands and her.

"Thank you." She smiled and embraced him once more, though a little unsteady. "Good luck on your journey and safe travels home."

"I think I am a little more worried about what I will tell my parents than my journey to get there. Are you sure we cannot delay this any longer?"

They shared a quiet laugh. She looked as if she was returning to normal. Maybe his eyes had been playing tricks on him.

"Emily, are you ready to go?" Levi asked.

The group turned and looked at her. Panic was all over her face. She gripped Milskar's hand tightly and looked him nervously in the eye. He smiled down at her.

"Um…um…I can't go," she said with a shaky voice.

Levi held his hand out toward her. "Can't go? Emily, come on, the portal is going to close soon."

"No, Levi, I can't. I—I am going to stay here."

Again Milskar and her exchanged a glance and smiled.

Levi looked from Emily to Aura, who nodded back at him. Confusion washed over his brain as he tried to make sense of the situation. "What do you mean, you're going to stay here?"

"I am staying here with Milskar. I talked to Aura and she said I was welcome."

"She is," Aura chimed in, a smile tugging at the corners of her lips.

"But—but what am I going to tell everyone?" Levi asked, looking back and forth between her and the portal.

"Tell them the truth. We went on a journey to figure out where you came from, and I met someone. I met someone and I decided to stick it out and see what would happen."

She dropped Milskar's hand and walked toward Levi. The confusion was still fresh on his face, but she could tell he would do this for her. They had been through so much together in their lives. This would just be one more thing, and one more secret they would share.

"I need you to do this for me. Can you?"

He nodded and she threw her arms around him, tears splashing over his shoulder and down his back.

"Emily, please come with me," Levi pleaded quietly.

"No, Levi, your journey here is ending, but mine is just beginning."

They separated and she went back to stand with the group. Levi looked from Aura to Milskar then his gaze came to rest on Emily. She had been there for him for as long as he could remember. She had stood up for him and come on this journey, no questions asked, just to protect him.

He would do this one thing for her. He would give her this chance. He would take whatever their parent's threw at him, but he would do it, holding in his heart the knowledge that she had found happiness. He figured, even if he told his parents the truth, he doubted they would believe him.

A feeling crept into his chest and it took him a moment to realize what it was—pride. Pride in himself, in these friends standing before him, and in the countless others that helped him get to this place.

Levi would never forget what happened in these woods, or in this world. He would carry it with him and share it with others. He knew now this was his purpose. To ensure they were all kept safe, he would tell the world what happened here, though, he knew no one would believe him. If what he witnessed had been true, he wondered how many other countless tales existed in the world that seemed so fantastic, so unbelievable, yet were true, as well.

He'd entered this place scared—and while some of that fear still rested in him, coiled around his heart, his powers were stronger. He could defeat anything that came across his path. He left stronger than he had ever been in his life.

Levi turned, ready to go back and, wondering if he would ever see them all again, stepped through the portal.

Epilogue

She crouched behind a bush, leaves covering part of her face and body. She saw the small animal a few feet away from her and, in her head, she quickly calculated how fast she would have to run to catch it. She had gotten quite good, these last few months, in fending for herself.

At first, the notion of being alone had scared her immensely, but she became stronger by the day—by the minute, it felt like sometimes. She was able to hide from her enemies and prey on those she could take down. Somewhat wild now in nature, her want for revenge fueled her.

Vengeance ran through her body alongside her blood, pumping through her appendages. She knew she would have to bide her time. It was too soon now. What had happened was too fresh in the memories of the participants but, one day soon, she would be able to come out of hiding and fight again.

A plan was already forming in her mind. She would gather a larger army, possibly the largest ever in any world. She would march them—their numbers so great the trees would shake for hundreds of miles whenever they moved. Those they would fight would know their demise was coming, would feel it in their bones but be unable to do anything about it.

She would have her time. She would get her revenge. Those who had made her suffer would suffer.

Suddenly, the small creature, sensing something amiss, began running. Down a slope its legs propelled it, eyes focused on the entrance of its home, on the space that would provide it safety.

Just behind it, legs pumping even faster, gaining with every step, Lady Grustmiener followed.

About the Author

Kristin Durfee grew up outside of Philadelphia where an initial struggle with reading blossomed into a love and passion for the written word.

She has also been a writer since a very young age, writing short stories and poems, though now is focusing on longer works. She is currently working on her next novel for Young Adults.

Durfee currently resides in Orlando, FL, and when not enjoying the theme parks or Florida sun, she spends most of her time with her husband and their quirky dog. She is a member of the Florida Writers Association.

CPSIA information can be obtained at www.ICGtesting.com
Printed in the USA
LVOW01s0822170915

454068LV00002B/7/P